Now I Know
Everything

Now I Know
Everything

Andrew Postman

CROWN PUBLISHERS, INC.

NEW YORK

For Mom and Dad: for everything

Copyright © 1995 by Andrew Postman

Published by Crown Publishers, Inc., 201 East 50th Street, New York, New York, 10022. Member of the Crown Publishing Group.

Random House, Inc. New York, Toronto, London, Sydney, Auckland

CROWN is a trademark of Crown Publishers, Inc.

Manufactured in the United States of America

Library of Congress Cataloging-in-Publication Data
Postman, Andrew.
    Now I know everything : a novel / by Andrew Postman. — 1st ed.
    I. Title.
    PS3566.0685N68   1995
813'.54—dc20   94-5410
                                                               CIP

ISBN 0-517-59940-6

10   9   8   7   6   5   4   3   2   1

First Edition

Contents

Those who would prolong intercourse can only do so by substituting for the more intense sensations milder ones spread over a longer period. You cannot have it both ways. You have to choose.

—Eustace Chesser, M.D.,
Love Without Fear

Which of us is writing this page I don't know.

—Jorge Luis Borges

Now I Know
Everything

1/The End

HOURS before I'd hoped to be anointed the next Vince of the "Vince: A Man's View" column in a famous women's magazine whose name I prefer not to give here, I found myself not making love inside the Unisphere, the huge sad globe skeleton left over from the '64–'65 Flushing World's Fair.

This is hardly the way to kick off your career as Vince, I thought. Vince needs to be making love for reasons beyond the obvious. Vince needs to be making love for *material.*

With me in the Unisphere was Julie, my partner for the past year on citywide lovemaking safaris, from the Wonder Wheel at Coney Island to the more downtown of the Forty-second Street Library lions, from the Staten Island Ferry (upper deck, bow) to the U.N., just beyond the Chagall stained-glass window with the swirling centaurs and angels; from the Cloisters to a boy's personal favorite, the left-centerfield monument garden at Yankee Stadium. After we'd finished there, I remember, I tilted my head back in the chill prickly grass and read upside down a plaque with the raised accomplishments of Lawrence Peter "Yogi" Berra on it.

The night I found myself not making love inside the Unisphere, most of New York's touristy clichés still remained for Julie and me to sanctify and sully: the Rockefeller Center tree vicinity some Christmas, the Empire State Building observation deck (the open-aired 86th, not the cramped 102nd), F.A.O. Schwarz. Julie had once made noise about slipping backstage at *The Fantasticks* during the show-stopping "Follow, Follow, Follow" number. Though we could be clean and astonishingly quick about it when need be, the Pool Room at the Four Seasons would be a bitch. Julie expressed optimism; I said in your dreams. We'd yet to brave St. Patrick's or Temple Emanu-El, though we'd given each the once-over, casing unattended entrances and sepulchral alcoves. The confession booth, it was agreed, would be truly inspired, right beneath the scowl of God: Julie impaled on my lap, her tea-colored hair fanned out against the grill, the chrism of sex amid all those Bless me Fathers. Where else had we considered? Junior's on Flatbush Avenue, home of the world's greatest cheesecake (if you've never, try the Black Forest); Grant's Tomb; International Arrivals at JFK; a box at the Met.

Fun City.

I must point out here and now, without false humility, that these escapades did not reflect any prodigious sexual appetite on my part, nor—if you'll believe it—bravado. I never set out for this to happen. A few of Julie's investment banker pals knew about our peculiar brand of sight-seeing; I'd told two friends. Indeed, my history of intercourse and its sister-crimes is a fairly humble one. I came to sex late—late if we're to believe those polls always being done by CBS/*The New York Times* and ABC/*The Washington Post,* by Roper and Gallup, about how shockingly young American boys and girls get started. So maybe they do; maybe you did. The first time I saw teens necking—fused and rocking they were in the dreamy shade of a huge willow tree in Flushing's Kissena Park, where I was riding my bike—I immediately wanted to ask him two questions: Why are you doing that when you could be riding your bike? And, just for the record, How'd you get her to do that? Unable to answer either, from then on I cultivated the talent of *appearing* to know things others my age were only guessing at. When my eighth-grade bio teacher, who doubled as dean, was asked during Human Reproduction Week to sacrifice a student to the principal's office for emergency monitor duties (heart attack, secretary's husband), she tapped me—not because I was so responsible, I believe, but because she figured I already knew about fallopians and fertilization and, more to the point, foams and other preventive measures, not to mention all the hot jokes ("We have a name for people who use the rhythm method of contraception. They're called *parents*"). No, Mrs. Nedball, getting the notes from someone else was *not* sufficient. Who knows the damage wrought by this particular lacuna in my knowledge?

I stayed pure through that five- or six-year boner called adolescence, and like most boys in that predicament, I convinced myself that for all my admirable restraint some bonus would actually accrue to me, like the microwave a bank gives you for opening an account. And when I finally did come to sex, I didn't go mental, either. Don't get me wrong, I loved sex: the jigsaws, the punctuated grazing, the wet sweet, the snug expanse. I just didn't think that's how I would distinguish myself.

Then again, I didn't know I might become Vince.

Inside the Unisphere on this spring night it was almost black. Greasy light from the park lamps below stretched along the longitudes that spined the globe and splashed color across the Rorschachs of inside-out continents. Julie and I removed our shoes. Through my socks I felt the rough cold of the banked metal floor. I spread out a blanket and we lay down in one of the narrow steel wedges. Julie called out her name. It surfed up the side of the bowl and seemed to die somewhere near North Africa. She then began telling me, I seem to recall, more about her phenomenal recent success at work, in the endlessly inspirational field of investment banking. She put up her hand in that absentminded way of hers—swaying it above her head as if she were not so much having a conversation as conducting one; she might have been drying her nails to some inaudible music. Almost as absentmindedly, I reached up and abducted her hand, kneading its small, oily pad as I brought it to my mouth.

I hadn't seen her in weeks. The humidity was punishing. Julie was on the verge of getting the two things an investment banker desires most: a raise, and a bonus that makes the raise seem pointless by comparison. I was on the verge of becoming Vince, America's most eligible pseudonym. We were down to our underwear and slapping thighs when things suddenly just stopped.

It was an irresponsible cousin—a *second* cousin, my mother would want me to point out, a former shoplifter and street-sign stealer—who inadvertently got Julie and me started. Somehow Stanley had wangled a position at Yankee Stadium that defied job description. "Maintenance-related" was all he'd tell anyone in the family. For this maintenance-related job, Stanley was armed at all times with a jingling lump of keys that opened everything. Once, with the team on the road, I took Julie to the stadium to show off. I wanted her to see Monument Park, the memorial to great old Yankees. As we stood in the shady, penned-off area beyond the 399-foot mark, we could hear whipping around the stadium a patois of noise, as if through a tube: the keen scrape of the El, various breeds of electrical activity, wind, the squall of children, one of the salsa stations at the end of the dial. That afternoon Julie wore a coral pink gingham skirt of a diaphanous cotton and a plain white T with shoulder pads; modest ones, not the kickass epaulets she wore to investment bank in. She had dark shiny hair to just below her shoulders, wide-set eyes the unnerving color of toasted almond, and the hard, high cheekbones of a Slav, which gave her a look of antiquity. The premature creases around her tidy mouth accentuated this quality. All afternoon my fly was stirring like Jiffy Pop popcorn cooking in its crinkly foil pouch.

When the wind came up again, I interrupted my narration of the decline of the Yankees to hold Julie's hair away from her neck and kiss her there. I nibbled doughy earlobe and now she turned. Behind the most meticulously manicured green in the Bronx, there was much yes I said yes I will yes in the air imploring us to do it, so we did it. We left an imprint in the grass.

It really wasn't particularly Don Juan and Lady Godiva of us. When we met up afterward with my cousin Stanley, who was cradling three cans of Lemon Crush, he narrowed his eyes and began what I can only describe as *sniffing*, suspiciously, sensing we'd just done something unholy, or at least something that could get him fired. Stanley launched an icy can at each of us. Julie and I tipped back our Lemon Crushes simultaneously, like those twins in the gum commercial who do everything together. The soda tasted ambrosial, brassy. Julie held her Lemon Crush high and brashly away from her so that you could see yellow soda braid out of its teardrop opening and briefly into the spring chill, then into her small, strangely commodious mouth, which moments earlier had tasted so oaty and warm. I drank too fast and my head began hurting; lemon ice crystals pinched my brain. A moment later Julie put her hand to her temples and winced and we both started laughing. Only then did I realize that Cousin Stanley had been watching all this and now knew for certain what we'd done. He leered at Julie, then me, as if *I* were the one in the family, not he, with the legacy of truancy and deceit.

On the drive back to Manhattan, Julie smiled, the expressive lines around her mouth arching back deliberately, like curtain-opening at a Broadway show . . . then relaxing again. She folded her hands primly in her pink gingham lap. It may have been the last time I ever saw her shy.

"Yes?" I asked in the haughty tone of a movie butler.

"No, I was just going to say how I couldn't imagine that in my wildest dreams," Julie said. "But I have some wild dreams."

We joked about how—now that we'd chalked up Yankee Stadium— wouldn't it be cool to carve our own unique place in Gotham history by making love, never indecorously, in all the splashy spots. We spent the next weekend testing out several of our fair city's more memorable waterside locales (Ellis Island, the Ferry, the boat basin at Seventy-ninth), cinches all, really, and an unwritten charter was born. We hit bronzed monuments, commercial venues, transient hot spots *New York* magazine always ruins by raving about them. One by one the sites and edifices of a great metropolis grew more anecdotal to me, more comical, and at the same time, somehow, more sacrosanct now that I (without fail) and my safari partner (usually; at least I *think*) had climaxed inside them.

The sex we had was the best, most urgent I'd ever enjoyed, yet Julie and I realized early on—maybe that first afternoon at Yankee Stadium—that it was pretty much all we shared. My professional focus since college had been standard-issue English major: I hoisted furniture, hawked magazine subscriptions by phone (seven weeks, $0 in sales), interned in Washington for my congressman, analyzed for Wall Street's Evil Empire, Drexel Burnham Lambert. I taught Sunday school piano and copy-edited computer manuals. I wrote unpublishable stories, while working on a longer, more ambitious unpublishable novel. I hate dogs but I once walked nine of them simultaneously, twice a day. Obviously I gave blood. I landed a four-night-a-week piano gig (no singing) at an Upper East Side fern bar called Scrabbles: okay money, but I'd need a real job to go with it. When I heard about an entry-level opening at a women's magazine, the *éminence grise* of "The Seven Sisters," I applied. I got an interview, then a second, but no offer. ———'s called me in for a third interview. I wasn't sure what the problem was.

"There's just one gnawing thing," said Suzanne, the senior editor, briefly looking for support to the managing editor across the sofa. "Please level with us."

I raised my eyebrows.

"Are you absolutely sure," Suzanne asked me, "you'd feel comfortable working in an all-female environment? All kidding aside, we have two dozen editorial assistants and assistant editors your age, and you'd be the only male of that rank. We're frankly a little worried about that. Can you honestly see yourself getting along in such conditions?"

"I honestly can see myself, yes," I said after waiting the requisite thoughtful couple of seconds.

"You realize why we're being so cautious," the managing editor barked at me. "We're not about to upset the balance of what we've got here, you understand . . ."

"Under*stand?*" I said. "Abso*lutely* I understand. Even if I don't get the job, I feel good just knowing there are still some institutions that . . ."—easy, easy, don't go overboard, they'll hear the Sousa march stirring faintly in the background—"that still care."

Surrounded all day by women, I started thinking like them. More and more I watched my weight, the way I dressed. I dreaded the onset of love handles. For lunch it was salads and only salads. Leafy greens, dark whole breads: five grains, seven grains, nine. In conversation I divulged more, said what I felt more, told the truth more, lied more. My ratio of self-effacing to self-celebrating comments shot up. I wasn't afraid to touch. Psychologically, I got my period around the twenty-fourth of the month, in synch with most of my colleagues. It lasted three to five days.

My first writing assignment for ———'s, two paragraphs about a new treatment for endometriosis, was a disaster. The health editor chewed up my lead, which panted after cleverness ("Healthy uterine linings are all alike. Unhealthy uterine linings are diseased each in their own way . . ."). One morning the food editor marched into my tiny work space and sat on the corner of my desk. I pushed aside my slush pile of unsolicited manuscripts and my egg-white omelette and Nutra-Sweeted Diet Pepsi to make room. "If you were asked to say something about pasta," ventured the food editor, cupping her chin, "then what could you say that hasn't been said a thousand times before?" The dilemma's locution hurtled me back to Philo. 110a, freshman year. "*If Socrates is a man and all men are mortal, then . . .*" I studied the photo-spread-with-recipe she lay before me. "The octopus-ink vermicelli, buried beneath a scribble of clams and shiitake, writes its name indelibly in your stomach," I said.

She slapped on my desk a folder bursting with recipes and photos of culinary wonders. "You may just have that rare quality to be a food writer," said Food Editor.

I'd give her bang-up copy, by God, none of that "medallions of milk-fed veal" and "dollops of creamy butter" crap. By the following week I handed in such melodrama as "pesto-drizzled angel hair, pine nuts honeyed by the strong Tuscan sun" and "Try these summer veggies only a grill could love" and "Salmon, salmon everywhere and not a bone to pick" (a mousse recipe). I became a regular fourteen-thousand-dollar-a-year apprentice *Uebermensch*, lending my ear to everything micro: food copy, cover lines ("Gifts of the Rich and Famous: Ronald Reagan, Jimmy Stewart, Angela Lansbury celebrate birthdays and anniversaries"; "His Intimate Illness: It's *Your* Business, Too"), short-story blurbs ("Laurence did not know what he would do without Alexandra, nor did he want to"), and, most dreaded of all, tags for reader-written, one-page personal essays ("My daughter Tiffany sent her letter to The Great Pumpkin, fully expecting an answer. I prepared her not to be disappointed—but it was *I* who would be surprised").

The job at the magazine had its perks; at fourteen thousand dollars a year, I thought, it had better. There were always tickets to movie screenings, which meant that nights I wasn't playing piano at Scrabbles there were always dates with bright, socially aware, more or less unattached colleagues from Articles or Production or Home Furnishings. Would I recommend this job to any liberal artsy-fartsy guy not long out of college? In a New York minute.

By the following year I thought to myself, Yes, what *can* you say about pasta that hasn't been said a thousand times before? And, more to the point, who *gives* a shit? My heart went out to victims of osteoporosis and infertility and the often-deadening quotidian existence of the American housewife who was our demographically median reader—honest, it did—but I started feeling like a Venutian forced to write about Martians. I loved my soul sisters at ———'s but I was not of their kind. I'd been circumcised, I could write my name in snow, they couldn't. They could give birth and milk, I couldn't. Nine out of ten screenings were for movies that stunk, and because my movie partners and I worked together, our dates never attained the status of *date* dates; besides, now there was Julie to explore the city with. In my spare time I wrote short stories, my Early Smartass Period. Legend around the magazine had it that Joseph Heller had written *Catch-22* while working in the ———'s Advertising Department years before, and I hoped the good vibes might rub off on me. Mostly I just concocted clever openings that clearly had nowhere to go.

He started writing this story in the third person but before the opening sentence was even finished I'd changed my mind.

Where does one begin to talk about August Möbius?

Mother lied today. Or maybe it was yesterday.

I actually might have benefited from writer's block. There was "The Blot on Hermann Rorschach's Life." There was "A Coupla Leos," imagining a meeting between Leo Tolstoy and Leo Durocher. Real Pulitzer stuff.

I was riding the ———'s elevator back from lunch when I first heard his name mentioned.

"Brell says they're looking for a new Vince," one woman says to another.

"What happened to this one?" says the second.

"He's tired," shrugs the first woman. "She says the new one has to be young and active. A closet tomcatter, but *sensitive.*"

"Good luck," says the second woman. "Who's Vince now?"

"State secret. Brell won't even tell *me.*"

That afternoon I tapped on my boss's door. "Suzanne," I asked, "what do you know about Vince?"

In 1956, she told me, the "Vince: A Man's View" column first appeared in ———r, the famous women's magazine whose name, as I've already told you, I will not say here. Vince Gordon was the full pseudonym but everyone simply says Vince now. The column was a forum to present the "man's view" on women (or "girls," as they were known in 1956), relationships ("courtships" back then), marriage, occasionally sex. According to Suzanne, the column flourished because women love nothing more than finding out what a man is really thinking and why. Vince had been written by anonymous men for stints of one or two years, sometimes three. Some very accomplished men, ones whose names you probably know but I am legally not at liberty to share, had written Vince over the years. The column had caught on immediately after it first appeared and by the mid-sixties had become one of the most famous features in any magazine, eventually rivaled for name recognition only by "Can This Marriage Be Saved?," "They Said It," "I Am Joe's/Jane's Blank (Pancreas; Vena Cava; etc.)," maybe a couple others.

"They're hunting for a new Vince," I told Suzanne.

She looked at me a long moment. "I need you," she said. "You realize you can't work for them *and* us."

"Yes, I know," I said darkly as I handed her my sidebar on chlamydia treatment clinics. If I had to remain in women's magazines while working on my unpublishable stories and novel, I thought, then it might as well be at one of the cooler, smelly ones, where the real glamour girls worked and wrote about secrets to love and beauty, fashion and health, glass ceilings and cottage cheese–free thighs.

I unearthed back copies of ———r, I asked around. No one knew if the guard was changing because the current Vince had told the magazine he was leaving or because they'd canned him; anyway, it's irrelevant. He was around forty, I could tell, and had been writing columns about what scoundreling he and his college buddies had done back in the mid-seventies. It was boring stuff (sorry—you know who you are—but it's true) and outdated; a bit preachy and avuncular. If that wasn't enough (and it was), I found out he was getting married.

There's an unspoken rule that Vince must be unmarried; in the original column in the February 1956 issue (page 46; check it out if you don't believe me), Vince is introduced as "the most attractive, genial, and worldly bachelor we know." Obviously, no gay men need apply for the job, either.

I called Brell Maclaine, editor of "Vince: A Man's View," and told her I'd like to be considered for the job. In a scratchy voice, she thanked me and said the position had just been filled. "That can't be," I said.

"I'm afraid it is," she said.

"Just for the record," I asked, "what *were* you looking for?"

The new Vince, Brell obliged, was going to keep it very personal, describing what romantic and sexual adventures he and his friends were currently enjoying, what small epiphanies he was having in otherwise private moments.

"Oh, you mean, like, someone young and active," I said. "A closet tomcatter, but *sensitive.*"

Silence on her end.

"Listen," Brell said, "if you wanted to write a column by Monday—on spec, of course—I'd certainly look at it . . ."

With the money I made playing piano and being Vince, I could write my novel during the day and the world would open up to me like a great scallop shell, set amid fresh garni and drenched in dollops of creamy butter. I saw, oblivious to my own triteness, foreign sales, three-pic deals, an Aston Martin parked in the driveway of the mock-Tudor getaway in upper Rye, maple leaves floating curled up like hands in the swimming pool that's never used because I'm never home. I faxed Brell a column about bachelor parties and, certain of my impending Vincehood, quit my job at ————'s. The end of my last day there, after a sweet, spectacularly distaff send-off, I walked out of the office building and looked uptown at the city stardust. It was near twilight, that amethyst pause between day and night, the instant in the coin flip after the coin stops going up but before it starts heading back down.

What the hell is a sensitive closet tomcatter? I asked myself.

❀   ❀   ❀

The night of the Unisphere I surprised Julie at her office in a mean-looking building on Pearl Street. She wore a checkered Ann Taylor suit; I suddenly wished I had on something other than jeans, high-tops, and a threadbare tennis shirt. "Come," she said, taking my hand. "I want to show you something."

She led her boy-toy back through the office, past honeycombs of cubicles, most occupied by men and women staring at their flat amber monitors. It had been a good day on Wall Street, advancing issues outnumbering declinings five to two, and the start of an exceptionally hale month; most of Julie's colleagues slumped at their desks, exhausted, trying to will a brief bear market. We continued walking past cubicles, past Julie's usual place in this vast colony of worker bees, until we stood in a large, mostly bare office. I saw 1 Broadway across the street.

On a chair beside a desk and some unopened cardboard boxes, a giant Raggedy Ann doll sat promiscuously, arms and legs flaccid, as if she too might just sit up once this bull market frenzy subsided. Julie reached to close the door and her hand brushed me, awakening the hair on my arm as if it were some excitable variety of sea grass. But then she crossed her arms ceremoniously in front of her chest, Yul Brynner's King, awaiting approbation.

"One Broadway," I said, gesturing out the window with my chin. "Not Two Broadway, *One* Broadway."

"What do you think?" she said. Apparently I needed to bone up on blunter congratulations.

"Very impressive," I said. "It looks like you're really moving up. You didn't tell me anything about an office."

"It just happened. *This morning*, F.Y.I.," said Julie, clicking a bright pink fingernail on top of an exceedingly expensive-looking desk. "Check this out."

From the windowsill she picked up the classic Wall Street knick-knack, a block of Lucite, this one the size of a sandwich half. Inside it, a tombstone announced a recent transaction, co-sponsored by Julie's

Now I Know Everything

firm, for eighty million dollars. In a growing recession, at a time of downsizing and layoffs on Wall Street, when many yuppies were finally getting theirs, Julie had just gotten an office and the promise of much, much more. At that precise moment I felt closer to Raggedy Ann than to Julie. I apologized for showing up without warning and moved to open the office door, but Julie touched my elbow and all of a sudden my will dissipated. She picked Raggedy Ann off the chair, bopped me on the head with its arm, and insisted on dinner. "I have to celebrate, don't I?" she said, closing in. "Hemingway," she purred in my ear.

"J. Paul Getty," I mumbled.

Julie trailed her fingernail along the back of my neck, again stirring hairs in its wake. "Hi, F. Scott Fitzgerald."

"Howdy, John D. Rockefeller," I said. "Greetings, Secretary of the Treasury."

She exhaled in my right ear with a force usually reserved for fogging cold windows. "Hello, my little John Steinbeck, my William Faulkner, my Thomas Wolfe, you."

"Enough," I said. Outside, the sun had begun its swoon over Jersey and the haze had turned the early-evening horizon the unappealing color of chinos. At the market we bought salads, roast beef, cheese, bread, wine, bottled water, and a bag of Famous Amos's with the pecans. We walked to Bank Street to fetch my '79 VW Bug (235,000 miles, great shocks, nothing in car, nothing in trunk, nothing left to steal) and put the top down, stopped at her place so she could change clothes, and headed out toward Flushing, where I'd grown up. Despite her job promotion, something was disturbing Julie, I was sure, but then she put her head in my lap as we sped along the Brooklyn-Queens Expressway, and she named all the famous people she could make out in the sketchy constellations visible above us (Milken the Archer, Greenspan the Bear). We parked in a lot in Flushing Meadows, a sprawl that was past or present home to two World's Fairs, the United Nations, tennis's U.S. Open, the Hall of Science, a zoo, an aviary, a theater, a museum, the New York Mets, the New York Jets, a monstrous swimming pool, a huge lake, one police precinct, an ice-skating and roller-skating rink both, several homicides a year, my first kiss, and Esther Williams's early synchronized swimming career, as ingenue in the Billy Rose Aquacades. Our picnic, the conversation, along with the frank authority of the evening swelter, seemed to both animate and soften Julie. I drank too much wine for the heat. Finally, Julie asked about the Vince thing. She was more than familiar with the column and the magazine; when she was younger she'd been a faithful subscriber and reader. "They want a man who's expert at being a man," I said. "I wonder if they realize that that means being an expert on women. Ipso facto."

"You're an expert," Julie said.

"How am I an expert?" I said.

Julie considered this briefly. "You don't abuse women," she said. "You're good to your mother. You know what it is to have women friends. Sure, you're an expert," she decided.

I lay back and put a blade of grass in my mouth to help me think. "If I can be an expert deal-maker," Julie said, tugging at the pink sash holding in her ponytail and shaking her head with cliché sexy-librarian vigor, "then you can be an expert on women."

She leaned over me and her loose hair swung down like a sort of canopy, shielding our faces from the full force of the heat. "Why don't we work on your next column, Vince," she said.

"Don't call me that," I said. "You'll jinx it. I haven't got the job yet."

"You will," she said and sank against me.

I found a favorite cul-de-sac, just behind her left ear. "What's the topic?" I murmured.

Julie paused campily between kisses, turned her lower lip out, and for a moment looked up at the night sky, perhaps trying to make out the seven stars that form Merrill Lynch, the Bull. " 'Vince Tells Women What Men Really Want,' " she decided finally. Against the dark sky a scored field of cirrus clouds began breaking apart. Before she lowered her face again to mine her mouth was wet and moving. "I like the lead," I said after a few moments.

We were heading the long way back to my car when we came upon the surreal Unisphere. For reasons unknown, a deserted Parks Service truck and ladder stood at the base of the globe. It was simply too come-hither to resist. With sitcom timing, Julie and I turned to each other.

"Let's do it," I said.

In retrospect, I'm sure Julie agreed only to prove (to herself more than to me) that her investment banking promotion hadn't killed her sense of daring.

Now, with the two of us almost naked in the Unisphere, Julie's fingers were pressuring my wrists, her rarely used code to just caress her. But it wasn't simply that she needed time. Something was wrong.

I rolled onto my back and looked up at Greenland, so much smaller and more accurately proportioned than it is on your typical wall map. With my foot I stroked Julie's smooth-shaved calf around to the shin and up until I reached the bump of her knee. In the heat her legs shone like copper, and sweat beaded her breasts, which had always stoked in me a hunger for food. In faint light they resembled loaves crowned by florets of butter.

"What?" I asked.

She exhaled largely. "I'm tense," she said.

You realize, I'm sure, that a woman who wants to give coition in the Pool Room at the Four Seasons a shot is not by nature what you'd call tense. "This is too weird," Julie said.

Where-are-we weird? Or *What-are-we-doing* weird? *Where-are-we* weird I could understand. The sinister bulge of eastern China loomed high above us. Guy wires shot through the Earth's core. We were lying inside a scaled-down planet, with wayward youth and night-owl joggers occasionally scooting by twenty feet below. This was no Magic Fingers bed in a Motel 6, nor the backseat of a '57 Chevy; it wasn't even the stone lion in front of the New York Public Library, which Julie and I had notched right before sunrise the previous autumn, as if we were just children innocently, if overaffectionately, doubled up on a twenty-five-cent bucking pony ride in front of the candy store. All while empty cabs intermittently rocketed by us down Fifth Avenue. It probably took all of eight seconds, I have to confess.

"I just don't think I can keep doing this?" Julie said.

Shit. Definitely *What-are-we-doing* weird. Whenever Julie turned declarative statements into questions, trouble loomed.

"Doing what exactly?" I asked flatly, trying to keep the tremble from my voice. "It seems kind of dumb to climb up here and then do nothing," I joked, or tried to. "After all that, you really think we should leave without doing what we want to be able to say we did?"

It came out far more convoluted and goal-oriented than I'd hoped, but still I thought reason might prevail. No one adored sex more than Julie. The night we first met a year before, she and a girlfriend of hers had come into Scrabbles during happy hour and pulled their chairs and Ladies' Drinks up to the piano while I ambled through my meteorology medley. I was glad it was Julie, not her friend, who'd winked. I played "When the Wind Was Green" for them. Julie told me she was an investment banker who thought investment bankers were scum, and the girlfriend, who appeared not to be a banker herself, exhaled a plume of cigarette smoke at the sentiment and nodded, "You can say that again." I played "Stormy Weather" for them. Despite her earlier declaration, Julie launched, a couple of Fuzzy Navels later, into a strained, byzantine defense of how investment banking *was indeed* a growth industry. Rather than mention my brief stint on Wall Street or share my opinion of the greedy, Ivy Leagued, be-suspendered pondshit at Drexel, I simply heard Julie out; I was, after all, just the piano player. I segued into the opening vamp of "Singin' in the Rain." By the end of the evening, while her girlfriend disappeared long enough to get a fresh pack of cigarettes in Cuba, Julie had volunteered to me that she'd inherited her sex drive from her father. I told her I'd inherited my organ size from my mother and played a smoky, Errol Garner-ish "Blue Skies" for my new pal. We'd been tight ever since.

"Normally I'd go for that," Julie said now in the Unisphere, twisting away from me, "but I can't anymore."

For a moment I calculated the efficacy of whining and puling to get her to yield. It would hardly make a great case for the evolution of men and their feelings, something Vince, the new Vince, the Sensitive New Age Yet Manly Man Vince I hoped to become for millions of women readers, was supposed to personify. But the night was sultry, there was a lovely, accomplished, financially liquid, virtually nude woman inches from me, and I had a lobster in my underpants. Fuck the evolution of men and their feelings.

Julie sheltered my hand with both of hers and brought the assemblage into her lap. If I didn't know better, I thought, I'd say this has all the earmarks of A Talk.

"Neither of us seems brave enough to come right out and say the obvious," Julie said.

I held my breath. Julie paused to corral her strength, though it was an incongruously long pause, I think because she had high hopes that I might break down and say the obvious myself. And I would have, except that the obvious in such situations is always so difficult to phrase.

"So I guess I'll have to," Julie said, regrouping.

"Andrew," said Julie, sitting up, her head neatly framed by western Europe, "we don't go together. Maybe if I had a different kind of job. Or we worked hours where we saw each other more than once a month. I care a great deal for you, I really do. But there doesn't seem to be any point in continuing this if we both know the facts." With her thumb she stroked the pouch my hand made folded in hers. "I can't keep doing these circus acts for their own sake, and I don't believe you can either," Julie said, pronouncing it "*eye*-ther," as if she hadn't grown up in Brooklyn and gone to public school.

In the damp, heavy air, everything around me seemed to slow down. I felt moved to point out that if we were so different, then how did we get to be in this globe together, on a hot Tuesday night in May, nine-tenths naked? If we were so different, then how come you could make up a nice mini *Michelin Guide New York* just of places we'd had sex?

It felt as if a piece of meat were sitting in my stomach without my having gotten to chew it.

"I want you to know how unbelievably sad this moment is for me," Julie said, "but I have to ask you to stop calling. Please."

She began to cry. I was hesitant to touch her but my reflexes took over on this damp night, when we were already losing so much body moisture, and I tried smudging some tears back into the side of her head. The piece of meat I'd imagined sitting in my stomach might remain there, an undigested bolus, for years. Julie was unbelievably sad and I was getting there fast. At least we'd be in synch again.

I managed some vestigial groan halfway between "oh" and "wow." It may have been the most accurate reflection of my feeling, though, since in the sound was a little "ow" and "whoa" both.

"I know, baby," Julie said and sucked my finger, recouping some of the salt of her own tears. "But you were never going to say it, so I had to." Say *what?* Julie gave me a bright smile that I gradually sensed would not crumple into a new frown; already I could sense her getting over me, with the passing of each second. Her resolve made me realize my miscalculation. This wasn't A Talk. It was The Talk.

"You'll always be in my life," she said, presuming quite a bit. "I'll be in yours. Maybe our Significant Others will even become friends someday."

"What?" I said. "Oh, that sounds like fun."

Some pink fragrance wafted through the globe, wisteria perhaps. I closed my eyes and reminded myself that for all our carnal adventures, our union was not heaven-made. Julie was right. We *didn't* go together. I didn't love her, never had, always knew it. The one time she ever wrote me—a rather suggestive birthday card now packed away someplace—she signed it simply *XX,OOO*, and I'd looked at it stupidly for a full minute before realizing it was not a fill-in dollar amount.

Ah, finally: a small epiphany to make me feel better.

For a few seconds after opening my eyes, I wasn't sure where I was. Reality, the exoskeleton of the Unisphere, had all the remote, webby clarity of a dream. I noticed how far I'd tossed my pants during foreplay and that one leg was dangling through a hole in the South Pole.

Then, evolved man that I am, I thought, Of *course:* P.M.S. Q.E.D. Simple as ABC. I began counting backward in my head to the last time I'd seen Julie inordinately cranky; she'd once told me her college roommates called her The Twenty-Eight-Day Alarm Clock. But before I could do the math she announced, "I'm seeing The Consultant."

From time to time Julie had mentioned The Consultant, always emphasizing his cartoonishly yuppie qualities: Richard ran his own financial services outfit, his telephone was a surrogate umbilicus, he wore his beeper even when he ran around the Central Park reservoir so his aides could warn him ASAP if a blindside LBO was about to occur somewhere in North America. The Consultant wore Hugo Boss suits, increasingly wide power ties, and he had a massive crush on Julie. I'd met him once at her office; my mind scrambled to remember how good-looking he was, and how tall. "It's not like you *love* him," I reminded her.

"I could." Julie's voice buckled and she started crying again.

"Why are you crying?" I asked.

"I think . . . I think I will come to love him," she said.

Julie said that for weeks now, she and The Consultant had been "seeing each other," a euphemism that made me wince. She said that their lives were much more compatible than ours. She droned on. I waited for a pause so I could ask her, But, Jule, what do you *see* in him? . . . and then I didn't need to. The Consultant, Julie was now explaining, had just acquired serious equity in a company whose fortunes he'd helped turn around. Any day now the stock would go ballistic, Julie told me (violating S.E.C. law; I was touched), because of a process they were fine-tuning to grow seedless watermelon.

Down below us, the headlight beams of a police car, patrolling the area, wheeled into and across the Unisphere. I imagined Julie and me lying low in a prison yard, waiting to make our break. Perversely, I wanted us to get caught trespassing; maybe an arrest could bring us closer. I thought of couples whose foundering relationships had solidified after they'd gone through an abortion together.

Good, idiot. Now think of the twice as many couples you know whose solid relationships fell apart after going through an abortion together.

"I'm sorry to do this the night before your big Vince meeting," Julie said sweetly. Her attempt to change subjects was transparent but not unwelcome. "I'm so happy for you. You'll make a wonderful Vince for the women of America. The quintessential nice guy with a constant hard-on."

"Cut it out," I said.

"I mean it," Julie said. "Someone should make you a big party for becoming Vince," she said. I had no clue why Julie was persisting on this new tack, and my head spun from the cruel march of her logic. My phantom piece of meat had moved up through my thorax to lodge at the back of my throat. I'd finally reached that unbelievably sad state she'd claimed to be in, then lapped her. "This is the writing break you've been aiming for," she said, rising slowly to her feet.

"Maybe," I said. I felt cleaned out inside, gropy. "If I wanted to run a Vince idea or two by you . . ."

"Sure," Julie said, retrieving her T-shirt, which she climbed into in one sinuous motion, eschewing her bra. "But not for a while. Let's take a wait-and-see. Remember, you can't call me for *a while*," she said, as if I'd signed some pre-breakup agreement stipulating explicitly that I wouldn't call her for *a while*.

"That's right," I said, vaguely. This could actually be sort of funny, I thought, a funny, ironic, maybe-a-bit-too-obvious scene in a movie, say, if it weren't happening to me. In a little more than twelve hours I might be named the next Vince and get my own monthly column in a big, well-respected magazine, where every month I could say whatever I wanted to a base circulation of two point two million American women—ten million in pass-along readership—and my only real qualification would be having some notion, as a man, of how romance and love worked. And on the very eve of all that, as I lolled in the globe in my undies, it appeared more and more as if my relationship—no, that's not right—my . . . my—okay, my *sight-seeing* arrangement with Julie, let's call it—was over.

In her dainty white socks and white panties and white T-shirt, her hair swept back by her bright pink scarf—my, how fast she dressed—Julie arched toward herself gracefully and stepped into her skirt. Dark watery shapes underneath her shirt became visible to me. Her beauty was irrefutable. I was hard at work on a thought to make me feel a tiny bit better: the lines around Julie's taut mouth. They were pronounced, those lines; this, too, was irrefutable. In three years I could imagine Julie, now with The Watermelon Consultant, leading such a consistently smiley life that the creases would have deepened to the point where they tugged at her mouth and made it appear, at rest, as if she were frowning. In three years, I projected, she and Watermelon Man would be married, parents, with in-laws, with a Magic Markered whiteboard magneted to the fridge listing all the emergency numbers the baby-sitter could call just in case; in three years they would be deeply ensconced in exurbia, the owners of numerous lots of community property, and Julie wouldn't even send a card on my birthday. I tried to check the self-pity before it got overbearing. Watching Julie's young image move over me efficiently, inhaling to button her skirt, handing me my shirt and jeans, I could only think, for some reason, of what my friend Lincoln Crye said to make himself feel better. We're all dying, he once told me. We're just dying at different rates.

It was my last clear thought for a while. I'd stood to pull on my clothes. The leaves in the trees below seemed to sway vaguely against their will. A few raindrops may have begun to fall; I think a cyclist pedaled by. Julie snapped the blanket in the air, the sound rising against the curved Unisphere wall and folding back over itself like a wave. She said something I could not make out. She said it again, she claimed later, but I kept looking up at her emptily—even cocked my head to one side as if she were speaking a foreign language—just before I fainted.

❖   ❖   ❖

The first time I ever passed out was during the summer of the moon landing. Maybe the excitement of Neil Armstrong and the small step that was really a giant leap and all that global *esprit de corps* took something out of me. Maybe I invested too much of myself in the New York Mets that summer of '69, or maybe it was the double-dimpled girl in the Cayuga Squaws at day camp who always wore white moccasins. Whatever. Mom kept me home with the flu. After two days of drinking ginger ale and eating challah and watching game shows, I felt well enough to venture out into the blistering August heat. Walking down the street, I crossed between two parked cars and my knee banged a fender hard. I leaned over to massage it and suddenly it began to snow. Next thing I know my mother's head is a religious portrait framed by drifting clouds and the blue heaven and I'm lying in the gutter. "What's happening?" I asked her when I revived. The doctor called it heat prostration.

I fainted when I heard a tumbling skier's bone crack as I flew by him, though I had the poise to make it back to the lodge and play the sound over in my head before toppling into the lap of a Canadian next to me. I fainted, believe it or not, in a movie theater, watching Ingmar Bergman's *Cries and Whispers* (if you care for blood and broken glass as little as I do, you'll have no trouble identifying the scene). And when I was twenty-one, an ancient relative, my great-uncle Irv, the closet pervert, shoved a video camera at me to record the briss of my little cousin—a broiling, syrupy day, a bedroom too small to contain the forty onlookers. "Zoom in," Uncle Irv kept prodding. "He can get married ten times, circumcised once. Zoom!" he commanded, and stupidly I obeyed as the *moyl* prepared the boy's penis for circumcision. I woke up on the floor, tie and belt loosened, collar unbuttoned, a margin of ABC's stuttering in Neapolitan bricks along the upper reaches of the walls. My new cousin's penis, reports filtered down to me, had been splendidly circumcised, thank God.

My eyes stopped fluttering when I realized that what I imagined I was seeing—flecks of light making filigree of the Scandinavian claw over western France, poor silly Australia sitting out there in the middle of nowhere—I really *was* seeing. That's right, I thought, I'm in the Unisphere. It's coming back, if at a few frames per second jerkier than normal.

"Now, what was *that* all about?" Julie was saying, her hand hot and sturdy at the back of my head, which hurt. "What happened?"

"You tell me," I said. "I guess I fainted again."

I started to raise my head but she said, "Nuh-uh. Stay right there. You're not going anywhere."

For an instant I felt strangely content. Maybe I wasn't the picture of mental health, but at least when I hurt badly, something in me knew enough to pass out and draw attention to myself. On some level, my complex system of bodily checks and balances was operating just fine.

"Is something wrong with you?" Julie asked, teetering on the banks of concern. For all our sexual gymnastics—and this is exactly what I'm driving at—Julie had never witnessed any of my numerous fainting spells.

"Must be," I said. "I've let you get away."

She swallowed hard, glands chugging.

"I'm fine," I amended. "Little heat and emotion." She squeezed my hand and I squeezed back. "It's okay," I said.

"Maybe the wine?" she asked.

"Maybe," I said.

She made me lie there a good five minutes, then had me practice walking a few steps inside the globe, as if I were buying new shoes, to get my legs for the climb down the Unisphere. We were quiet on the walk back to the parking lot, then she took my hand. Against the night sky all the park's dinosaurs reared up in silhouette: a bar graph of rockets from over by the Hall of Science; giant microphones that by day were really obsolete exhibits and arcades; the fossil of what appeared to be an immense, sci-fi cupcake but had been, in a previous life, a roller-skating rink. Pale stone water fountains grew gradually brighter and more certain, like Polaroid pictures, as we approached.

I bent to sip and slapped cool water on the back of my neck. "Hey,"

I said. "Give me the next in this series: fourteen, thirty-four, forty-two, *you*, ninety-six." I was trying hard to be upbeat. "That's a big clue there. Give me the next."

"I can't," Julie said.

"Try," I said. "Fourteen, thirty-four, forty-two—"

"I *can't*," Julie said. "Just tell me."

"Express stops on the two-three. Fourteenth Street, Thirty-fourth, Forty-second, Seventy-second—your apartment—Ninety-sixth. The correct answer was One Hundred Twenty-five," I said.

Julie shook her head. "You and your lists," she said.

For the only time I can remember, I wanted to slap Julie. Just once, loud across the face, a movie slap. I shoved my hands in my pockets until the feeling passed.

Oh, you're in the right frame of mind to be the next Vince, all right.

On the drive back to the city the silence was broken only by Julie's turning on the radio. During a commercial I said, "We were going to find an island and start our own country, remember?"

"The national anthem will be a Tom Waits ballad and you pay income tax in sand," Julie said.

"That's right," I said, then neither of us made any more of it.

I double-parked in front of her apartment on Seventy-second Street and we kissed sweetly on the lips, twice. Julie half-jogged into the building because, I was happy to note, she was about to fall apart. With great labor, I ratcheted the car into gear and headed home, the warm air liquid on my face and tongue. Only then did I realize just how late it was, how exhausted I felt. How would I come up with Vince ideas for my big meeting tomorrow?

VINCE: A MAN'S VIEW

Last night, I did not make love in the Unisphere with my now ex-girlfriend.

Nah.

VINCE: A MAN'S VIEW

Last night, when the chance to climax was denied me by a fellow traveler, I passed out inside the Earth. And I'll tell you why.

As if I *knew* why. Snaking deep into Greenwich Village, I cajoled the radio dial with the deliberation of a safecracker so that I wouldn't barrel past the one station that might suit my mood. A breeze drifted through the VW and I could smell Julie coming off of me. I ought to bottle that smell, I thought. I rubbed the lump on my head from when I'd fainted. The bumper sticker on the decked-out, purple van in front of me boasted, DON'T LAUGH. YOUR DAUGHTER MAY BE IN HERE.

Finally I stopped the radio dial at Dr. Ruth, who was talking someone down from the ledge. Whatever else you want to say, she's a good listener, that Dr. Ruth. The next caller, a woman from Armonk who sounded extremely attractive, began her confession with the usual unctuousness. "Dr. Ruth, first I want to say I listen to you *all* the time and I just *love* your show. I think you're just so terrific."

"Oh!" the doctor squealed. "Such kind verds tonight! Vot's your question?"

"Okay, I've been married a week," said the Armonkian, taking a big, shaky breath, "and already I have a problem."

I snapped it off.

At home I shut all the windows, put on the air conditioner full tilt, turned on the TV. It was the Gum Twins—water-skiing side by side, double-dating, testing their aim on a pistol range, shooting up heroin with a shared needle. My thumb got going on the remote. "No wonder the nasal bacteria was forced into the brain," Jack Klugman, as Quincy, M.E., was telling his protégé. On the sports wrap-up, a Yankee lashed a ball to the gap in left centerfield, and beyond I saw Monument Park, the spot where Julie and I first did it. The video on MTV showed an iguana and a barely clad bimbo staring each other down. There's an original concept. Next. Unless I'm mistaken, I got some cats here doing the cha-cha-cha. I boinged off the TV and lay in bed, hours from sleep. The bump on my head throbbed. I thought about catching the end of Dr. Ruth. But I liked the soothing purr of the air conditioner and instead did lists to help myself fall asleep. Hudson, East, Harlem, Mississippi, Nile, Amazon, Seine, Jordan, Volga, Tigris, Euphrates, Ohio, Colorado, Charles, Snake, Salmon, American, Styx, Lethe. Dog, thimble, hat, cannon, iron, boat, shoe, car. Periwinkle, magenta, burnt sienna, raw umber, brick red, peach, her shining copper legs. Copper and the other Crayola metals were always the hardest to sharpen. I wonder if Mom still has my crayons someplace. I wonder if Julie and The Watermelon Consultant are slapping thighs right now.

Dwarves, seas, continents. Brides for brothers. White notes in an octave. Wonders of the World. VHF channels in New York City. Sins.

But it only made me more awake. Every good boy deserves fudge. All cows eat grass. What's the one about the planets? My very educated mother just served us nine pizzas.

What I *should* be doing, I thought, was not listing rivers and Crayola colors but thinking up hip, sexy ideas to present the next day to the editor of the famous women's magazine, and thus ensure myself the Vince column and my new, rightful place in the world. Of *course* Brell Maclaine was going to want ideas; she'd said as much on the phone. Now I'd futzed away my time. Think. Concentrate. Ideas for Vince. Vince ideas . . .

Blue, straw, rasp, black, cran, boysen, elder, mul, lingon, huckle, chuck. Blood, sweat, tears, saliva, lymph, mucus, vomit, wax, pus, urine, semen, bile.

I shot up in bed. The phone shrieked again.

I would have panicked at a middle-of-the-night call like any normal person, but I've trained myself. The room was freezing. I brought the phone back under the blanket with me. "What?" I moaned.

The ensuing pause was excessive, even for him. Finally I was rewarded with the sound of his unhurried, cadenced breathing. "Remember, I'm not only the Hair Club president," he said softly, "*I'm also a client.*"

In reaching for the clock, I knocked it across the room. I peeked out, Kilroy-style, squinting for the time. A four, a six, and another four played three-card Monte out there in the dark. "Jesus," I said. "How do I join?"

"I had a feeling you'd be up," Lincoln said.

"I wasn't," I snapped, laying the receiver on the pillow and trying to fall back asleep.

"I sense anger," he cooed, for maximum sympathy value, "and here I am in a moral quandary." My thorougher explanation that I'd been sleeping received no sympathy. "Zees ees Veentz, zee famous Veentz?" he squealed, Dr. Ruth–like.

"I told you don't do that," I said. "You'll jinx it."

"Is Vince not the man to come to with a problem?" Lincoln asked.

"For women with men problems," I said. "Not men with women problems."

"That's discriminatory," Lincoln said, "and *that's* against the law. I need your advice, Chief."

"I need my sleep," I said.

"I've met the perfect woman," he said so movingly I almost believed him.

"What happened with Renata?" I mumbled. "I could swear the word *perfect* was used in reference to her, too."

"Very nice, Renata, wonderful Florentine body, yes," Lincoln said, "but she'll regret it the rest of her life if she misses Phi Beta Kappa because she fucked up freshman year. I told her we'll celebrate after exams, if she doesn't meet someone. This one, I tell you," Lincoln said, actually sighing, "this one is no voracious reader." "Voracious reader" was Lincoln's euphemism for any setup foisted on him (usually by the matronly colleague at the gallery where he worked) whose sex appeal was, to his mind, wanting. "Voracious reader," I might point out, is *not* a euphemism for "unattractive" or "woof," so please don't write me calling me and my friends boorish, sexist pigs. There'll be time and incitement enough for that later.

"Uta hasn't read *Bleak House* cover to cover, that I'll guarantee you," Lincoln said.

"No *Middlemarch* for Uta," I said, half-awake.

"That's right. She's got a wonderful Danish body. From the looks of it, she's still deep in REM."

"*Mazel tov,*" I said.

He was quiet for a long time.

"*What?*" I said.

"Okay, first my theory," Lincoln said. " 'The Three Stages of Man,' I call it. How a man's view of the world—his *Weltanschauung,* if you will—changes radically in the thirty-second period from right before climax, to during, to right after."

"*Weltanschauung,*" I said.

"I've been testing it," Lincoln said.

"Yay, team," I said, dozing off.

"That's the good news, that I have a new theory I like," he said. "There's also distressing news."

"Lincoln, I have my big meeting tomorrow," I said, mocking a few boo-hoos. "Really—"

"Get this, Uta's a Danish contortionist who rejects all material values, focusing primarily on issues of the spirit," Lincoln reported. "But she's out of work. Chief, this economic downsizing is apparently no joke. She says her muscle tone is nothing like what it was. Still"—he began ponderously to chew something—"she does that business with the head under the crotch."

"Goodbye, Lincoln."

"A spiritually nourished Danish contortionist," Lincoln repeated, as if I hadn't fully absorbed the ramifications. "Pencil me in for hospitalization by next week. If not, something has gone tragically wrong."

"This is me hanging up," I said. "I'm hanging up now."

"Hey!" he yelled in a hoarse whisper, the first inkling that he really was trying to be considerate of his new friend's beauty rest, a courtesy I was at once beneath and above. "Do I hang up when you call me at three in the God knows what A.M. to tell me how you and Little Miss Mutual Fund just made it in the Monkey House at the Bronx Zoo or fucked in a fitting room in Bloomingdale's?"

"I've never done that," I said quietly.

Lincoln took another bite of his mystery food. "Well, you *should,*" he said. "I wish you felt you could."

"Can we please pick this up another time?" I said.

"You haven't heard the disturbing news," Lincoln said.

I rolled over and sighed. "She isn't Jewish," I said.

He seemed to take this in. "What tipped it off?"

"Danish, circus performer," I said, weighing the facts like a cheap detective. "I've never seen a contortionist at my synagogue."

"Outstanding," he said.

"It's not required you find a Jewish girl, Lincoln. You're not Jewish."

"That's where you come in, to keep reminding me of these things. Actually, Chief, there *is* a hitch," he said. "She's not quite twenty-three."

"Twenty-two's a vast improvement for you."

"She's not quite twenty-two."

"All right," I groaned. "When."

"In four years," he said. "Do I worry?"

This time, I think I actually heard myself snoring softly.

"You're right," he said. "Don't worry, eat, drink, be merry. Kibosh on the worrying. But just remember one thing."

I refused to be his straight man.

"Hello?" he yoo-hooed. "Is anybody out there?"

I whimpered. "Lincoln, I really just want to sleep."

Then in a whisper: "I think REM may be *sluttet.* That's *finished* in Danish. Hey, that's funny. Finish in Danish."

"Test your theory," I urged.

"Indeed we shall," Lincoln said. "My next call to you will be a treatise for Vince on the virtues of morning sex."

"No problem," I said, rolling over. "Wait, *morning* sex?" But he had hung up.

Please no. I reached back and several venetian panels buckled under my fingers. The last blue remnants of night were being drowned out by a thick, powdery Crayola gray. Catty-corner, women and men in trenchcoats and galoshes, carrying umbrellas and briefcases, the *Post* and the *Times* and the *News,* scooted in and out of the loudly lit Korean fruit market. The bleat of traffic along Hudson Street was in the ascension.

My friend Lincoln Crye was right. My big day was here.

2/f u cn rt ths u cn gt a gd bl jb

THANKS TO Lincoln's call, I lay awake thinking a lot about Julie, a little about The Seedless Watermelon Consultant. The last thing I remember was hunting fiercely for entries to my most inspired list so far, Famous Second Bananas (jetsam, Friedrich Engels, RNA, Schuster, Nagasaki). Only a truck backfiring was explosive enough to stir me. My eyelids parted reluctantly. I staggered from bed, kneeled by the clock, and was greeted by a particularly obscene sequence of numbers—namely, 12:24.

Why exactly I'd told my loved ones about this lunch that was to start in six minutes, I wondered as I combed, speedsticked, peed, and shaved recklessly, precipitating across my cheeks and neck a pointillist study in blood; why I'd told them anything at all about my candidacy for the Vince job, I wasn't entirely sure. Perhaps so the key people in my life would know at least that I was one of a select group of young men in the running for Vince, even if I ultimately didn't get the job. Perhaps I mentioned it to light a fire under myself. Only by stating aloud that I was in the hunt for the job would I work hard enough to get it—I'm guessing at my rationale here—thus stating it aloud actually gave me the best shot at getting it and avoiding the naked failure of having stated it aloud and not gotten it. You may spit now.

While I hiked on my slacks, stepped into my shoes, brushed my teeth, each activity overlapping several others, an anxiety about being exposed seemed to tap me on the shoulder. *Our hero,* I mused, flying down the steps and out into the gorgeous day-in-progress: Our hero is about to be found out. Our hero has blown it. 12:40. Bad hero. I disappeared into a cab, whipped by remorse. Who knows, asshole, how many opportunities like this come along in a lifetime? I thought of other career paths, jobs I could handle after I didn't get the Vince gig, after the Scrabbles piano bar scene became too tedious: assistant manager at White Castle, graveyard shift; shepherd; freelance pasta writer *nonpareil.* The makings of a new list: Plan B careers. Wonderful.

I sank deep into the vinyl seat of my taxi, a crazed yellow weasel lurching in spasms to Quattrocento, a chichi restaurant on Forty-fifth Street. The armpits of my shirt were spongy, though the heat had broken; the avenue was puddled from the morning thunderstorm I'd slept through. Accordion-pleated minis and neon Spandex leggings and much sleevelessness could be spied. The sky was gem-blue and far-reaching, a perfectly agreeable tent for the circus that is every day my city. It was 12:50, an international double parkers' convention was taking place all up Eighth Avenue, and frankly I deserved whatever I got.

Brell Maclaine, whom I knew only by her husky, commanding telephone voice, had told me I was one of three or four finalists for Vince. In an ensuing call she repeated the phrase "three or four." I didn't know why she wouldn't tell me exactly how many of us were still in the running, but I chose to take this as encouragement; she'd already picked me, I'd convinced myself, and simply hadn't the character to lie with conviction. Hence my lack of preparation. Now, as my overly cautious driver finally turned east, I wondered how I could surpass, or at least equal, whatever I'd done right with my trial column, about an Atlantic City bachelor party I'd attended a month before, an evening corrupt with grain alcohol and our own blackjack table, with Neanderthal practical jokes and rent-a-bimbos named Sundance and Fiir Elise and Bonfire. I'd recounted how much I loathed the bachelor party institution. Hardly time capsule stuff, but it was Grade A Sensitive Tomcat; touchie-feelie and quiche-eating. The magazine's editors had liked it, or at least couldn't *not* like it.

The boys and I surrendered ourselves to a sort of Lord of the Flies *momentum. Just off the beach, the dozen of us, as one, trooped into a club advertising dancers who'd graced the pages of* Playboy *and* Penthouse. *We were given a break on the cover charge, the "bachelor party" group discount. A parade of naked women danced around us; there was much cheering. The emcee announced Big Dave's name and impending marriage with fraternal, "Another one of us is biting the bullet, boys" esprit. More cheering.*

I nursed a beer, watched the women dance, fascinated for a few minutes. Then I started feeling sad.

What else was there to say on the subject of men and women and relationships and romance and love and sex? Lots of things, a world of things. I just couldn't happen to think of a single one. Who the hell was I to describe for millions of women the psychological schematic of a functioning American man? On the other hand, who the hell were the *other* Vince candidates to describe it? Who the hell was the older, stay-at-home, soon-to-be-married "Uncle Vince"—the outgoing title-holder—to describe it?

I closed my eyes and soaked in the Bob Marley playing on the radio and twisted my torso from side to side, cracking my body as if it were one huge knuckle. "F u cn rt ths u wl hv a gd jb," read the postcard Lincoln had sent me, upon first learning I was in the running for Vince, "nt 2 mnshn, frm yr mny fml fns, a vr vr gd bl jb." On the picture side was *American Gothic.*

It was past one o'clock. I had nothing to offer Brell as the new Vince, nothing. I wasn't sure which of us—Lincoln or me—would be more disappointed when I didn't land the job.

At Quattrocento—a bustling dining room and oak bar—any one of three women could have been Brell Maclaine. Each sat alone with a drink at a twotop, gamely waiting for a tardy lunch partner. Pacing until the maître d' returned, I wondered how many blood spots from my brutal shave had clotted on my cheeks.

I studied the youngest of the three Brells, all the way at the back of the room. She was far too young to be the real Brell, who was executive editor. I watched her in profile, bent slightly forward at the waist, one hand collaring a drink, the other spanned across a ringed binder. She sat still enough that I could see her breathe. When a clef of her short, copper-colored hair swung forward, her hand abandoned the drink, and with a graceful dialing motion her finger returned the wayward hair back behind her ear. She then cleared her throat, covering her mouth with the freelance hand, which planted itself again around her drink.

It takes very little to confuse other things with a feeling of love.

VINCE: A MAN'S VIEW

It takes very little for a man to confuse other things with a feeling of love.

She turned and almost looked my way, and my heart made a small throbbing fist. The real Brell Maclaine, I decided, remembering why I was there, was the stouter, more patrician of the two other lone diners, though she had an unobstructed line of vision to me and had made no attempt to reveal her identity. Well, I deserved to squirm a little longer.

The copper-haired woman looked at her watch, then toward the front of the restaurant. I smiled meekly at her.

"Andrew?" she mouthed from across the room.

Certainly it would be easier to date her if she wasn't my boss, I thought, half-waving at her. Suddenly my failure to prepare for this lunch had its upside.

Even before I reached Brell, who was guiding a straw around the circumference of a peach or mango colada, I'd launched into a fully detailed, fully fabricated apology for being late. She accepted it with a shrug, as if she'd been sitting alone for five minutes, not forty-five. "Not at all," she said, looking me over. The question, I thought, was not whether I had blood spots on my face, but how many. "This was actually welcome," said Brell. "It's so rare I get to be alone for more than five minutes." Including, no doubt, when she's in bed, thought evolved-Vince-on-trial.

I slid quickly into my seat and in a burst told Brell how much thinking I'd done about the Vince column, the direction I'd like to take it. "I've got ideas," I lied.

After our order was taken by a frighteningly ebullient actor-singer and I began the healing process necessitated by Brell's wedding band, she told me more about the magazine: the age range of its readers (18 to 34, median of 24), the top national award ———r had just been nominated for, Brell's responsibilities besides editing Vince. Her voice was at once rough and soft, Tammy Grimes proctoring an exam. Brell asked did I mind if she smoked. While she tapped a cigarette from the pack, I picked up my butter knife, turning it nonchalantly in my hands, but couldn't steal a good look at the dried blood I knew was caking my jawline. When Brell bent her head forward to light the cigarette, a lick of her hair—really more a Crayola raw umber than copper—fell forward again and she corralled it with the same delightful motion I'd seen earlier. Our unborn daughters would also have been remembered for the gesture.

Brell revealed that some very accomplished men, ones whose names you probably know but as I said earlier I am legally not at liberty to share, had *been Vince* over the years. Why do I italicize "been Vince"? Because it is important early on to realize the first, most fundamental fact about those who wrote the Vince column. In fact, you do not merely *write* the Vince column. You *become* Vince. You *are* Vince. Vince is you and you are he.

Without that understanding, we have no story.

The actor-waiter brought Brell a warm brie-and-almond salad and me a *prosciutto e melone,* which he kindly translated as prosciutto and melon. Brell took up her fork and knife gravely. "I must tell you we still haven't made our decision," she said in the fantastically sexy timbre of the pre-laryngitic. "We're asking each finalist for one more sample. But it's down to you and another fellow, a little younger."

All right, so now we were two. Brell wouldn't say who was ahead— was the kid getting the free lunch, too? She jabbed at some gooey cheese and twisted her fork several times until the thread finally surrendered. "Okay, I'm yours," she said. "Astonish me with column ideas."

I hadn't quite lied. I did have some ideas, all forgettable. On a whim, I reversed the order in which I'd planned to present them (planned, sure; I'd planned it way back in the revolving-door chamber entering the restaurant) and went with my third lousy idea first. "I'd like to do a column on the contents of my wallet," I told Brell. "Say what it reveals about me in particular and men in general."

Brell made a face, as if she'd tasted something she didn't like. Unfortunately, she hadn't begun eating yet.

"November maybe," she said. "We're doing an accessories spread. It could be thematic there, cute. *May*be."

Okie-dokie. I bit into my dill-buttered *focaccio* which, our waiter had kindly explained, was focaccio in English. "Well, my brother just had a baby," I said to Brell, submitting Stupid Idea #2. "Unclehood as a kind of pre-paternity. It's personal, it's Alan Alda, it's, I don't know, it's, uh, it's . . ."

Brell nodded wanly. "I'd like to wait until we establish the new Vince before tackling kids," she said, making plain that the voice of the new Vince, whoever he turned out to be, was something she planned actively to wet-nurse. "You're not living with anyone, are you?" Brell asked.

Would that be held against me? "No," I said. "But I could line someone up."

Her brow furrowed.

"I live alone," I tried again. "I'm a genial, worldly bachelor."

She flashed a thin smile. For the second time in roughly twelve hours my one-on-one, man-to-woman skills were failing me disastrously. "Jacqueline thinks there's much charm in your spec column on bachelor parties," Brell said, referring to the magazine's editor-in-chief. "Of course, I do, too. Frankly, most of the other men I was trying out"— here Brell leaned forward from the waist, theatrically playing up the strain—"asked if they could make their first column a how-to on the perfect blow job." She scrutinized the room conspiratorially, then shook her head. "No thank you."

I drowned some focaccio with Diet Coke. "Giving or getting?" I finally asked.

"Giving or getting?" Brell pondered. "*Oh.* Women *giving*, of course. The ultimate service piece."

Evidently this was the first shift in our waiter's career, because all the food seemed to arrive at once. He brought Brell a half-order of *fettucine e salmone* ("fettucine and salmon") and a side of broccoli. I swallowed a curl of my cantaloupe just as he repositioned the plate and dropped in front of me some prenatal carrots and a sirloin three fingers thick. Brell and I oohed and aahed over the meat for the benefit of our multilingual waiter.

"I think Vince is a carnivore," I said to Brell. "I think he would approve of my ordering this."

"Me, too," she said. "I like boys who eat meat."

It so happened I liked girls who liked boys who ate meat.

"Is that it?" Brell said. "Any more ideas?"

"More ideas?" I echoed a bit too loudly.

Not a list, please. Not now. Don't undermine yourself now—

UNCLE IRV THE PERVERT'S
FAVORITE KAMASUTRA POSITIONS

(deduced from bent pages in a copy found in his basement strongbox; in no order)

X—When she raises both legs and places them on her lover's shoulders, it is called the "yawning position."

XI—When biting is done by all the teeth, it is called the "line of jewels."

XII—When the lingam is held with the hand and turned all round in the yoni, it is called "churning."

"That is," Brell shrugged, "only if you have something. If not, not. I can't compete with that steak."

I felt caught in the netherworld between tact and frankness, self-possession and wit, the circle Dante neglects to talk about. How about Uncle Irv's favorite Kamasutra positions?

"How about the three stages of man?" I blurted.

"Stages or ages?"

"Stages. Seven ages but three *stages*," I said, scrambling to remember the gist of what Lincoln had served up to me in the wee morning hours.

There was a pause, then Brell tilted her head. "You . . . want me to guess what they are," she said a bit wearily.

"Not at all," I said. "I'll tell you." I cut into my steak and stabbed a cube of beef for some sense of fortification. I pointed the forked meat at her, as if in accusation. "One," I said, "just before a man climaxes. Two, during. Three, just after. What the column would be about is . . . It would be about the radical change in a man's world view—his *Weltanschauung,* if you will—over the, say, the sixty-second sequence that spans all three stages. Don't quote me, but maybe even thirty seconds."

The only remaining question was whether Brell hated this idea more or less than my previous two. "Just out of curiosity," she said, "you don't expect to get away with a word like *Weltanschauung* in the magazine, do you?"

"Couldn't hurt to try," I said, resignation already creeping into my voice.

"I'm just wondering," Brell said.

"What?" I asked.

"Well . . . if you thought a word like *Weltanschauung* was for us, maybe it would be useful for you to read a few more back issues of the magazine. Get a better feel for the previous Vinces."

I nodded. We ate briefly in silence.

"Before you turn in that other sample," said Brell.

I nodded again. Masticated, nodded.

"And that's your idea," she said flatly.

With my fork I maneuvered a pile of baby carrots around my plate like a croupier herding casino chips. "During sex," I said, "there are three discrete stages of a man's worldview—"

"I think you just explained that," Brell said.

"That's right." I put my fork down. Damn. Here I'd had a chance at a job that afforded celebrity, though without fame; the escutcheon of wisdom without the armor of knowledge; the chance to say whatever I wanted, as intimately as I wanted, every single month, to a base circulation of two point two million women, an estimated pass-along readership of *ten million women,* women roughly my age, all across America, a one-thousand-city verbal rock-and-roll tour from the comfort of my own desk; I'd had a chance at money, exposure, fabulous clips, and I'd thrown it away, or at least seriously risked it, because of a belief that I was so good I could just wing it. Where did this confidence come from, this misguided ego? For God's sake, I was playing cocktail piano four nights a week for mid-level managers who staggered after work to an Upper East Side fern bar to get shitfaced before catching the PATH train home to Jersey, I was going nowhere as a novelist, I knew by heart the 800 numbers to report late payments for all my credit cards. The woman I'd long been in like with, and whom I still lusted after, had just blown me off for a man who was going to set the watermelon industry on its ear. And now I was going to lose the Vince job to some precocious high-school junior (I imagined him) with windwhipped hair, drunk on his own testosterone, impressively endowed, a literary whiz owning a fluid way with a sentence that would've made Zelda ditch F. Scott just as fast as she could hop out of the rumble seat. I was living out a bad anxiety dream; garden-variety fear of professional success.

I had—there was no way around it—fucked up royally.

Act pissed.

"You have to trust Vince a little bit here," I told Brell. "After all, if this is the *man's view*—which I was under the impression it was. I happen to be a man and that's something I think I should talk about, the way a man feels before, during, and after he makes love. It's something I think a woman would want to know about a man. But then I'm not a woman so I can't really say what a woman would want to know. But if Vince is really supposed to get down here, I mean, to be *sensitively* active, that is, a youth, a tomcatting closet youth, a sensitive, youthful cat, I mean . . . young, that is, active . . ." You know that feeling when you're trying to park in a space that's obviously too small but you keep pulling in and out, in and out?

From Brell's expression I knew none of that had worked a bit. Might as well go for broke. "I'm sorry I'm not prepared but I think I may have broken up with someone last night and it's just been a really rough two weeks," I spewed, generously extending the last twelve-plus hours to cover the whole period I'd been allotted to drum up ideas.

"I'm sorry to hear that," said Brell.

"Thanks," I said. "I'm not exactly clear on what happened. *Did* we just break up? Did she break up with me or did I break up with her? You know how ambiguous those things are. Do I really care that we're finished or is it, like, Hey, thanks, I know where your mole is, have a nice life? Have I really slept with her for the last time? It's been a long night and morning. And I'm sorry about being late. You don't know how disgusted I am with myself."

Brell picked up a broccoli spear. I started daydreaming about the explanations I'd need to make to my parents, to Lincoln, to my bartender pals at Scrabbles, about why I hadn't won the Vince job. Probably I shouldn't have quit my job at ———'s so rashly, I thought. Butter dripped in a long yellow tear along the broccoli stalk and down Brell Maclaine's pinkie. She caught me looking and bit the treetop. I felt a dim sadness for the extinction of the stegosaurus, who, I remembered from fifth grade, had subsisted primarily on leafy vegetation.

"Why don't you write about that?" Brell said. "I think our readers would be very interested to hear about a breakup from the other side, the man's side. And all that stuff about the ambiguity."

"I don't want to betray anyone," I said.

"Who said anything about betrayal?"

For an instant her response froze in the air and took on a tone of hand-rubbing, Judas-inspired mischief (*Who said anything about betrayal?*). "You're human," Brell continued. "Your girlfriend—or maybe ex-girlfriend—is human. What happened to both of you is human."

"I don't know that she'd appreciate my writing about her," I said, "human or not."

"Whose experiences were you planning to write about, anyway?" Brell said. "You have to write about your own, in some way. You were at that bachelor party you wrote about, weren't you, with all those strippers—Für Elise, and Cloudburst—?"

"That was different," I said.

"Well," said Brell, "then don't tell her you're writing it. Don't tell anyone. The last Vince didn't want a soul to know. He was positively paranoid anyone would find out." How was Brell to know I'd already dropped hints to everyone I knew that I was up for the job? "That's the whole essence of Vince," said Brell, picking up her fork and harpooning the last divot of salmon. "It's really been a remarkably well-kept secret for more than a third of a century and you—Vince, that is—Vince is our point man among the male species. Anyway, consider writing about what happened between you and your friend."

"I will certainly do that," I said.

She lit another cigarette, inhaled vigorously, then turned her head politely to exhale but without averting her stare. "But now," said Brell, "I want you to tell me something about yourself that has nothing to do with all this. Something I couldn't possibly guess."

For the first time I noticed just how forcefully green Brell's eyes were, turtle-green. The irises weren't clear but milky, and finely ringed by a much brinier green: Scrabbles' Super Key Lime margaritas, salted, $6.95. Faintly, from outside the restaurant, came the throbbing sound of jackhammering on Forty-fifth Street. I watched the second hand on the huge antique black-iron clock across from me move in tiny but palpable increments, and I sipped my Coke. Our waiter stood over a neighboring table, no doubt translating dessert. Brell waited for my answer. She'd hardly asked my opinion of Special Relativity. How about: *You're seriously considering hiring a guy to write about love who's never been in it.* How about: *If you've never done it on the Wonder Wheel at Coney Island, a warning—absolutely NO Nathan's hot dogs beforehand.*

"Well, I play piano in a joint uptown," I said, coming to. "Happy hour, dinner, late-night drinks."

"Is that right?" Brell said, the business end of her cigarette a glowing nib the color of jack-o'-lantern light. "So what was all that hemming and hawing back there, then?" she said, nodding behind her as if the past were something you could actually point to, even touch. "A lot must happen to you around that piano. I bet you've broken a busful of hearts. And you worked with all those women at your old magazine . . . ———'s, no? Why should you be so strapped for ideas?"

Excellent, excellent question.

✿   ✿   ✿

During a break that night at Scrabbles, John the bartender asked me about Vince. "Hey, big shot, how much do they pay? I could do that shit."

"I bet you could," I said, lining cheddar cheese–flavored goldfish across the bar. "They want me to write another one." Since I planned on squeezing maximum juice from my Vince candidacy if I flopped, I didn't add that the job was still very much up for grabs; that it was still me versus the *Wunderkind*—*mano a mano, tête-à-tête, prosciutto e melone.*

"What's the next one?" John asked as he drew a beer for a heavyset customer a few stools over. "You know I loved the bachelor party."

"I can't decide," I said. "I have this idea about the male orgasm. But she made some remark about men being obsessed with sex. I think she wants me to do the ambiguity of breaking up."

"The job is yours—final, over?" asked John.

"Actually, no," I said.

"So you're still auditioning?"

"Yes," I said.

"This one's a no-brainer," said John.

"Which?" I said.

"Breakup ambiguity. She's hiring, right?" John said in his bartender-mellow best. "Then, after you write a bang-up column on the ambiguity of breaking up and you sign the contract—then you write about orgasms till the cows come home."

I looked at my watch. My break was up in five minutes. "I could do something on women and tipping," I said. "How women are worse tippers than men, but men tip much better in the presence of women than when we're not."

John dropped into my glass a few pillow-shaped ice cubes and spritzed more soda. "Breakup ambiguity," he said.

"You want my opinion?" asked the heavyset customer three stools over. John and I looked at him and John raised his chin at the man.

"What's that?" asked John.

"Orgasms," the customer said.

"Why?" John asked.

"He should go with all his guns smoking," the customer said.

"Do you know who this is for?" I asked the man, and realized it came out funny, as if I were trying to terrorize him with the information.

"Nah, I don't know," the customer said, "but I can sorta figure it out."

I named the magazine, which of course he didn't read; his girls read it, he said, sometimes his wife did. I told him the column was called "Vince: A Man's View" and that this was for the plum chance to become Vince. John listened as he held the soda gun over four glasses. It looked like he was watering window plants.

"If they want a kissy-kissy piece," the customer said to me, "screw them, let them get someone else." I admired how quickly the stranger had taken up an interest in my career and, more touchingly, my integrity. "In that case, you don't want to be writing for them anyway," he said. "What they want is you should write what a woman *thinks* a man thinks."

"I want to write what a man thinks," I offered.

"There you go," the man said, draining his beer. "Hey, it's your choice. Do what you feel is, you know, safe." With the back of his hand he erased a thin foam mustache. "*I* vote for orgasms." He dug his hand into his coat pocket for his wallet and I told him not to worry about it.

He stood and tucked in his shirt. The restaurant was beginning to fill. With each ensuing set during the evening I had to play louder because the extra bodies soaked up the sound. By the end of the night, as the place thinned out again, I had to play quieter or Garth, our subtle manager, would walk over to the piano, stand over me, and stick his fingers in his ears as if he were blowing his brains out.

"Well, thank you," the customer said and saluted me.

"And to you," I said.

"I got a wife, three sisters, two sisters-in-law, two daughters, five, six nieces, a secretary," the customer said. "So I know what I'm talking about. You got a girl?"

Why was everyone so curious about that all of a sudden? "I'm not sure," I said.

"Jesus, I don't know what the hell that means," the customer said, bending to pick up his briefcase. "But listen. Whenever any of mine start moanin' and bitchin' to me that I'm acting like a man, I tell 'em this. I tell 'em, 'If women were men, they'd behave exactly the way men do.' "

"Biology is destiny," said John.

"Bingo," the customer said. "Hey," he said to me, "I love the way you tickle the keys. Good night, and repeat after me: Orgasms."

"Orgasms," I said.

3/So Much for Uncle Vince

VINCE: A MAN'S VIEW (spec column #2)

The Three Stages of Man

What's his world view? Depends. Is he
a) about to have an orgasm?
b) having one?
c) just finished having one?

A lot can change in a minute.

*A city is leveled by an earthquake. A basketball team
snatches victory from the jaws of defeat. A raw egg gets one-
third soft-boiled.*

*But perhaps no single-minute change is as startling and
profound as the one going on inside the mind of a man hur-
tling from the land of Immediately Preclimax to Climax to
Postclimax. It's a dramatic psychological journey, taking
roughly thirty to ninety seconds; for argument's sake, say a*

*minute. At times it's difficult for men and women alike to
believe how radically a man's personal philosophy can
change in that time span—and all because he's muscled a
tiny spoonful of semen from the testes to the epididymal duct,
through the vas deferens and the ejaculatory duct, and finally out of himself! If you think there's something deeply
incongruous about this phenomenon—that a major shift in
Weltanschauung should be triggered by such a sensation—
you're right.*

But there it is.

*In the tradition of Kinsey, Masters and Johnson, and Dr.
Ruth, I wish to endeavor my own study of what the male
psyche goes through during the three stages immediately
surrounding, say, a fun-filled Saturday-night coition.*

Stage 1 (Just Before Orgasm): I am a conquistador.

In the midst of writing "Three Stages" I panicked that what I was
about to say might be imprecisely observed. Before I delivered Brell
my thoughts on the inner man, I thought I should experience lovemaking once more before refining my thesis. It would hardly help my
chance of becoming Vince if in only my second audition column I
sounded derivative or overly nostalgic.

I called my love safari partner.

I braced for Julie's reproach; she'd been quite clear that I wasn't to
call her for *"a while."* But the businesslike tone she used to greet callers
warmed immediately ("Well, hello to *you*, Steinbeck") and she even
turned a couple of calls back to her secretary. Armed with confidence,
I thought it would be awfully mature of me, not to mention improve my
stock further, to ask after Watermelon Guy.

"Richard's fine," Julie said. "So there's this Oktoberfest in the park
this weekend." As if it were one continuous thought. No mention of
watermelon, seedless or seeded.

"Oh, yeah? In May?" I said, fondling the glass paperweight dome on
my rolltop desk. "Open tents, beer, bratwurst?"

"Oom-pah-pah, the whole deal," said Julie.

"Where did I see something about that? Maybe the Weekend Section." Genial, worldly bachelor to the *n*th.

"I asked my brother to go," she said. Julie and her younger brother constantly made plans to do fun weekend things together and constantly blew each other off. I couldn't remember whose turn it was this time. She was giving me an opening a Sherman tank could drive through.

"Hey, how *is* your brother?" I asked. "I liked him that one time at the concert on the pier."

"Where we wanted to slip onto the Intrepid?"

"Was that the same night?" I asked. It pleased me that Julie was keeping the flame of our brave history alive. I recalled my enthusiasm that evening the previous summer when it appeared we might actually get to do it on the deck of a real live, if retired, American aircraft carrier, the U.S.S. Intrepid Museum off the West Side Highway. Our hopes were later dashed when we found the old girl locked up for the night. "Yeah, I guess maybe it was," I said.

"So it was just going to be the two of us, little Stevie and me," Julie said. "But if you're free you could meet us—oh, shoo. You play piano Sundays."

"Actually, I was thinking of taking the day off, let Marcel sub for me," I said. "I haven't had a free weekend in a while and thought maybe you and I could, you know, maybe touch base," I said, punching up for Julie some corporate Casualspeak, the *lingua franca* of the white-collared. "F.Y.I., I've got a column to finish."

"Yes? You're Vince now?" Julie sounded genuinely excited, as if my professional life was, when you got right down to it, inherently more entertaining than hers. Evidently the thrill of the Lucite cube chase had worn off some.

"Just about," I said. "It's my second and last trial and I need to make it a good one, so I was going to take the weekend off. But when I'm done I'll want a break ASAP." If it meant spending all of Sunday in bed with her, after a brief and obligatory swing over to the Oktoberfest with her little brother Stevie, whom I disliked, then fine.

We made plans to go. Rubbing my glass dome paperweight, I wondered if Mr. Seedless Watermelon had failed, or if he and Julie were still together and she'd simply had to seek certain satisfaction elsewhere. Honestly, I couldn't have cared less.

It wasn't quite what I'd fantasized. On the other hand, it was better than nothing. While Julie and I waited at her apartment for her brother, Watermelon Guy phoned three times, just to chat. Then Julie's brother called to say that his Saab, which the genius had parked on the street, had been broken into and he needed to take care of it. When it came time for Julie and me to leave for the Oktoberfest, she didn't want to go. I could see she wanted me but . . . not *quite*. She wouldn't let me in. In fact, she wouldn't touch me anywhere "funny," she said in a distracting little-girl voice, because it wouldn't be right; but she'd be more than happy to let me serve her. Which I'd begun doing when the telephone rang. She crossed the room and brought the cellular phone back with her to the opened futon. It was Watermelon Fella again. I listened to Julie lie to him with such breathtaking matter-of-factness that I had trouble not smiling as I continued, and she writhed and adjusted and stroked my hair. I would go and then pause, go and then pause and look up—until her small, perfect mouth broke into a new smile, the International Yes, Please Continue. She turned her head to the side, and tucked her chin against her collarbone in a violinist's sort of half-slumber and watched me. From below I could see the nutted pink frosting at the center of her breasts rise and clench. Periodically, Julie "hmm"ed into the phone for him to keep talking. She closed her eyes and listened to Herr Watermelon, whose deep, nonsensical syllables wafted out of the telephone receiver and hovered, then died, in the air above us. It was something about assumption of long-term debt and money supply and Fannie Maes, but I knew pidgin econ at best and the point was lost on me.

Her breathing became audible, pained even. Her thighs against my face felt warm and creamy buttery; she flapped, she squirmed. She moved the telephone to her other hand, briefly raised her free arm above her in that way of hers, then slowly, lovingly, rested her hand back on my head, an almost priestly gesture. *S.E.C. intervention;* I specifically caught Watermelon's use of the phrase *S.E.C. intervention.* Julie's fingers slowed in my hair, their trail thickening. This is when sex is the most exciting, I made a mental note to note in some future Vince column, when she loses you, when after a certain point you are merely a vessel and she's far off by herself on a pleasure cruise somewhere. In such moments I think of myself less as a lover and more as a sort of, I don't know, travel agent.

Briefly Julie opened her eyes and mouthed "I love that" to me. Watermelon *über Alles.*

"Yes?" I whispered.

"Keep doing," Julie mouthed, then mouthed oh, and oh again, nostrils dilating, oh oh, the gun lap now, a plateauing familiar to me, a friend, I slowed, briefly broke contact, *Once we were slaves in Egypt,* I always thought right about this point, then suddenly there was a big oh, a huge oh, and finally, with startling speed, her legs scissored my head and she clenched her muscles until, after a series of brilliantly noiseless spasms, she was done.

A new strain in Julie's telephone personality with Mr. Watermelon— baby talk—fortunately made its presence known to me only after she'd finished with her second installment of climaxes and I was toweling off. Then she started fairly gurgling into the phone. I wanted very much to leave. Unless, of course, she'd changed her mind and was in the mood for returning favors.

Finally, Julie hung up—remorseless, I knew. She crossed the room to turn up the air conditioner next to the giant-screen TV, which was topped by a burgeoning skyline of yet more chunks of Lucite. She placed the cellular on the windowsill, then stretched her entire wonderful naked body, hands behind her head, elbows pointing at opposite walls, a spectacular impression of a weather vane with a libido. Her whole being seemed to yawn. "That was nice," she said.

"I had fun, too," I said. I was not at all sarcastic and she understood that. Julie would always understand that.

"I'm sorry I can't offer you more," she said, sitting on the edge of the futon and brushing her hand across my stomach, symbolically tapping my belt buckle. Somewhere down below I felt nascently Himalayan.

"That's okay," I said.

"I miss making love with you," Julie said.

And I couldn't believe I'd gotten to such a point of self-consciousness, or un-self-consciousness, that I uttered the following: "Did we used to make love?"

Her expression was a cross between puzzlement and hurt.

"I mean, you *say* that," I went on, "but what about it exactly is making *love?* Sure, there was always a lot of *affection* involved, but love? Maybe it was making like. Yeah, I guess we made a lot of like."

"Stop it," she said.

"I'm sorry," I said, quickly recanting.

The phone rang. Julie strained to lean forward, knots pebbling up her spine. She let it ring a second time. "How many times a day do you guys talk?" I asked. It rang a third time.

"Maybe you should go," Julie said. It rang a fourth time.

"Why don't we just admit you were right, Jule. We need time apart. We belong in our own tax brackets for a while." I smiled sheepishly. Julie stood. "You'd better get it," I said. "People rarely let the phone ring more than a few times anymore."

Julie glided to the phone in a way she hoped would appear nonchalant, but she was covering ground fast. She reached the phone, lifted it just enough out of its cradle, and covered the mouthpiece. She smiled at me.

What I meant to say, I realized as I waved and quietly let myself out, was, Yes, of course we made love, but did we ever make *love* love? That would have been the more accurate, not to mention politic, thing to ask.

Outside Julie's apartment I listened for a moment at the door. More baby talk.

With little official fanfare I became Vince. Brell, my new boss, called to say that everyone at ———r had liked "Three Stages" very much, had found it refreshingly raunchy, and that she was looking forward to working with me. My contract was for one year, a thousand bucks per column. Brell never said anything more about the other finalist, my younger competitor. Wherever he is, I wish him well.

Within days I got my first official "put-through"—the version of the article that's typed into the magazine's network and read by the senior staff. I was supposed to read it over for errors, then call Research or Brell to make changes or clear up questions. I was surprised and pleased to find that various editors had scrawled curly comments of praise in the margins of the put-through.

"So much for Uncle Vince!" howled one.

Instead of phoning in my changes, I told Brell I was going to be in midtown anyway so why didn't I just come up to the office? She made noises of approval because she wanted to talk to me about something.

I was *not* going to be in midtown anyway. That part I'd made up because I wanted to see the magazine's office and perhaps get caught up, seemingly nonchalantly, in the swirl of the staff, which (I knew from my ———'s experience) would largely consist of eager women recently out of good colleges who strode purposefully down the carpeted corridors between the Production Department and Art, Editorial and Fashion, Research and Beauty and Health.

I walked into the off-white building on Madison Avenue, three blocks north of the lion on which Julie and I had had, the previous fall, perhaps our most daring tryst. The lobby newsstand prominently displayed the next month's issue from my new employer, as well as the several other magazines owned by the same publishing giant. I rode one of the eight elevators (express, 11–21) to eleven and introduced myself to the receptionist. The greeting area was very white and bright and clean and cozy.

I'd come here to do nothing more or less than flirt, and now that I was in the employ of the magazine, I could flirt with some degree of impunity, so long as I remained within the officially designated flirting areas. The receptionist told me Brell would be out as soon as she was off the phone.

I sank into the couch. The name of my new magazine, in cream-white block letters in *mezzo-relievo* behind the receptionist's desk, was adorned with colorfully wrapped Hershey's kisses. I picked up a copy of the current issue from the low glass coffee table. A hum issued from the bank of elevators behind me, then a *ding!* and a whoosh as the doors opened. A fashion model with short auburn hair, sharkskin cowboy boots, and a polka-dot miniskirt announced herself timidly to reception. She leaned her black grain portfolio against her endless brown leg. Stealing peeks over the magazine, I saw she had the hot new cheek mole that was sweeping the modeling world.

"I'm here to see Annie?" the model said in what I guessed was a New Zealand accent. While the receptionist waited for her contact to pick up, she asked the model for her name. "Sony?" the girl offered, as if she herself needed convincing. I doubted she was related to the electronics juggernaut. I knew that most fashion models worth their day rates went by one name only, but didn't that make it difficult dealing, say, with the Department of Motor Vehicles? Oh, yeah, I'd like to see you use that one as an icebreaker.

Sonie sat down on the couch opposite me. She nodded shyly, assuming I was safe and spoken for. Generously I pinned her as eighteen, which meant she was only half a decade younger than my baby sister. Models like Sonye prepared all morning to meet sittings editors. I realized I'd prepared for part of that morning just to meet people like Sonee.

Brell came out dressed all in white, including a white headband that made her strawberry-gold hair look positively incendiary, and her green irises were flecked with gray. She introduced me to the receptionist.

"Meet the new Vince," Brell said. "Our resident sex expert." I smiled and noticed Sonjie look up, her expression darkly serious. Did she have an attitude about sex? Was my sexperthood so clearly a joke?

Before the receptionist could offer official welcome, the woman I guessed must be the fashion sittings editor appeared, causing something of a greetings bottleneck in the reception area. "Oh, Annie, good," Brell said. "I'd like you to meet the new Vince."

Annie took my hand and pouted. "I'm mad at you," she said. "I just read that story on . . . orgasms. Now no one's working because all my people are stealing over to Production to get a look."

Excellent, I thought. The building was overflowing with sexy women's magazines and their sexy, predominantly female staffs. Word travels. Excellent.

Sjonee stood, shook hands with Annie, then looked at me. "Vince?" she said.

"It's a pseudonym," I said. "For . . . the column . . . I do." Suddenly I didn't know if this information was classified under all circumstances or not. Was I, too, allowed to acknowledge it? *Should* I? Perhaps disclosure was discouraged everywhere but here on the eleventh floor, where I enjoyed something akin to diplomatic immunity.

"I'll look for it," Soney said, with Kiwi cheerfulness.

"Do," I said.

My friend Lincoln Crye would love this. Too bad I wasn't going to mention any of it to him.

Meanwhile, the receptionist was scrutinizing me, and finally offered her hand. "Pleased to meet you," she said. "I guess."

As we walked back to the editorial chambers, I said to Brell, as a test, "What do you think about all that 'our sex expert' stuff? I don't know."

"No?" Brell looked at me weirdly, one eye half-closed, as if perhaps I hadn't yet come out of the closet.

"I'm flattered, don't get me wrong," I said. "But—"

Two women approached. I was introduced to a senior and an assistant editor. "Vince?" said the senior, examining me foggily as if I were a nephew she'd last seen before the start of a war years earlier, and who'd grown several inches since. "At your service," I said.

"Terrific," the senior said. "Our resident sex expert."

I give up.

"I know you were only trying to tell the truth about boys," the senior editor said in a voluptuously patronizing tone, "but I can't tell you how many times reading that orgasm story I wanted to break your little neck."

I elected not to thank her for this. When she walked away, the assistant editor, Monica, who had a sensational tan and looked to be maybe one week removed from any of a number of top-shelf New England liberal arts colleges, rolled her eyes. "Anyway, *I* liked it," Monica said, "especially Stage Three." She leaned in and modulated. "I can't tell you how many times I wanted to get up and leave but then had to lie around for two hours so I wouldn't hurt his feelings."

Back in her office Brell put her fingers together, steeple-like. "We're doing an issue devoted to love, romance, and sex," she said, leaning back in her chair, "and the deal is this: Now that Jacqueline sees what kind of a Vince we have on our hands—sensitive *and* active—she'd like you to write something, under your own name or Vince's, called something like—this is a working title now—'What Men Want to Tell Women About Sex but Can't,' or something. Of course, if you use the Vince byline, it could boost readership for the column—"

"I thought everyone read Vince already," I said.

"They do, they do," Brell assured me. "But we want people who don't even *read* the magazine to hear that Vince is up to new tricks, and want to find out about it."

"Aha," I said.

"Yes," said Brell, eyes a high-voltage green, tubed inert gas, M-O-T-E-L. "Where was I . . . working title . . ." She gripped the desk. "Oh! Yes! If you use the Vince byline, you can say certain things under the cover of pseudonymity. Though it seems pretty clear you have no hesitation writing about fairly intimate subjects. Do you think using your real name would inhibit you?"

"I think I might like to try it under my own—"

"But the important thing is, you're interested," Brell said.

"Sure, it could be fun," I said. "I'm not getting pigeonholed here, am I, as some kind of sexpert?" I thought of Psonyie, the premier up-and-coming New Zealand fashion model out there somewhere, roaming the magazine's cool vanilla halls. Six months down the road I'd meet her at a party and the hostess would warn her off me because I was America's premier up-and-coming pervert.

"No, no," Brell assured me, without basis. "Not pigeonholed. And if that *should* happen—which it won't—would it really be so terrible? To be known as our all-purpose sensitive, sexy guy? A handsome, single fellow like you?" The expression on Brell's face was hard to decode, but I'd narrowed it to two possibilities: utterly sincere or utterly mocking. "I'll just assume, of course," Brell went on, "that you'll continue to keep a tight lid on who knows you're Vince, outside of those of us here at ———r and *maybe* your parents." She smiled. "It's remarkable what a well-kept secret it's been for a third of a century."

"Vince and I make a lovely couple," I said. "If people knew, that is."

Because of the magazine's three-month lead time, my first Vince column wouldn't appear until mid-August. But it seemed downright profligate to let the whole summer go by without exploiting the coup of my becoming him. I didn't come to this opinion by myself. It was called out to me at two in the morning, from a bullhorn on top of a car parked a few blocks north of the Fifty-ninth Street Bridge, as I was leaving Scrabbles.

"Vince!" Lincoln Crye's voice boomed from the speaker on the roof of his '75 canary-yellow Chevy Impala. He sat inside his car waiting to meet me at the end of my shift, a welcome service he sometimes performed after an evening out or when he simply had nothing better to do. "Your signature doesn't actually have to *be* on the contract for you to abuse Vince's privileges," Lincoln admonished through the bull-horn.

"Shut up," I called out, my voice echoing down the cavern of First Avenue as I moved quickly across the street to get at him. Lincoln's car differed from other non-law-enforcement vehicles in the speaker he occasionally affixed to the roof. When he felt sure no police were in the vicinity, he took the speaker from the floor of the passenger's seat and clamped it to the top of the Chevy, exactly the way TV cops in unmarked cars slam on the Mars light when an A.P.B. comes in. Then Lincoln would pull out his hand-held mike and simply chat with people on the street. He might ask an old woman walking her dog a philosophical question, or pose a *two-on-two-outs*-type baseball scenario to a little kid. Sometimes he just spewed facts ("Swedes and dentists knock themselves off at an alarming rate") or the day's news, entertaining those lucky few who happened to be out on the street at that moment. When Lincoln did this on the freeway, he was mostly a public servant for driving safety: He might announce to the car in front, "That was an unbroken line, sir," or "Ma'am, you can shut the directional off now." People smiled, sometimes they cursed. It was obnoxious, if it wasn't against the law it should have been, it was almost always fun.

"Shut up," I repeated, standing over Lincoln now, the ramp to the crumbling Queensboro Bridge looming black behind us.

"What?" his voice boomed, a Cheshire smile tugging at the corners of his mouth. "Your column needn't have *appeared* yet," he said, re-newing his public advice to Vince.

I reached inside the car and shut off the mike. "People are sleeping," I pointed out. He continued his assault over cheeseburgers at Florent down on Gansevoort.

"No girl's going to ask to see Vince *clips*, for Christ's sake," Lincoln said. "Stop being such a slave to the truth on these matters. It's some-what inconsistent, if you ask me."

"I didn't think I had," I said.

"You're so in, if you were in any more you'd be out," Lincoln said. "I despise people like you." He took a swig of his Dos Equis.

"And what kind of people is that?" I asked.

"People on a roll," Lincoln said. "Guys on a roll. Straight guys on a roll. Straight, non-viral, non-short guys on a roll. The speed with which you can get laid exploiting this Vince thing is frightening. I'm frightened for you. Aren't you frightened?"

"But I'm not that kind of girl," I said. "I never have been."

"Um?" He raised his arm, a schoolboy all of a sudden. I called on him.

"Miss *Michelin Guide New York*?" he said.

"That was different," I said.

"Or perhaps," Lincoln suggested, "you never were that kind of girl because you never *could* be? Be, all that you can be." He shifted his weight in his chair and, subtly, his agenda shifted with it. "And in case you've forgotten, I *am* that kind of girl. If you won't do it for yourself, forget it and *I'll* use the Vince line. All your best quotes and ideas are mine, anyway."

"Oh, right. I forgot."

"You'll be owing me for this," Lincoln said, picking up his cheeseburger and burrowing further inland. "For my experience and wisdom. For access to my Type A personality."

He hardly looked the Type A. Lincoln was soap opera–handsome, with curly dark blond hair, one dimple, and pale brown eyes that seemed slightly astigmatic, giving him the same faraway look that launched James Dean to stardom. With his athletic, if somewhat slight, build he was perfectly poised to exploit the opportunities his face allowed him. In winter his cheeks even turned pink and ruddy. He was American-looking, great-looking, girls loved him. "You're hardly the only friend whose opinions I solicit for the column," I said. "Anyway, most of the time I call on my own experience, thank you."

"Three stages of man—remember?" Lincoln said. "*Weltanschauung*? You have more friends and I have more sex, remember?"

"I said that half-jokingly."

"Freud says there are no jokes," said Lincoln.

"Freud's dead," I said. "Rebuffed. We now know how wrong he was much of the time. It should have been a woman who fathered psychoanalysis."

"You are so sensitive it's almost scary," Lincoln said.

I asked how things were working out with his extremely young, spiritual contortionist. Despite her wonderful Danish body, Lincoln said, Uta wasn't turning out to be quite so wonderful after all, or spiritual. For starters, he reported, his great Dane shopped at Saks, I. Magnin, Banana Republic. Uta had bought herself a ten-coupon book for facials at Georgette Klinger, her friends hung out at the Vertical Club. At the tender age of eighteen, she was having her résumé laser-printed for a possible summer internship at Goldman Sachs, where Daddy knew, like, the managing director. She dreamed of someday going to business school.

"It turns out she was only an *intern* with the circus, she's only Danish on her *grand*father's side," Lincoln told me, cracking his neck, then shaking his head partly in disbelief, partly in sorrow. "The Uta's a front. What happened? She was organic, my nature girl. A month ago she was making her own envelopes."

"You gotta keep the faith, pal," I said.

Though I'd known Lincoln for three years, I can't say I understood him; mostly, I found him entertaining and perverse, quixotic and uncontrollable. He'd grown up in Michigan, I knew that much; I knew his mother had remarried a hateful man and that Lincoln had severed virtually all contact with the family. (One of the only things he'd ever said about his former life—and by far the most revealing—I'll never forget: "My family had money, that's all. Then I cut that off altogether, so I essentially have nothing." Said with a smile and a punctuating crack of the neck.) In piecing together his history, I found there were always a couple of years that remained unaccounted for. Lincoln loved being the center of attention, and had a dangerous thing for young girls. He was a broker for a prestigious Soho art dealer, though it never struck me that Lincoln loved his job, or art, nor did he work particularly hard at it. He was a classically handsome WASP who loved Jewish things and people because, he claimed, they "gave off a heat." But I couldn't tell you what any one aspect of Lincoln's life had to do with any other, what was the manifestation of what void.

My friend Lincoln Crye seemed like nothing so much as one of those people raised by wolves—a wild man who licks people's hands but could just as well eat out your entrails.

"Dream interp time-out," Lincoln said now, over our 3 A.M. supper. "I'm in church, I'm praying, Protestant girls are running around just in socks and crucifixes. It's the third time this month."

"Yeah, it's a Jewish dream," I said, "very typical, nothing to worry about, only I don't know why *you're* having it."

"Who knows the human mind?" Lincoln said, raising his brown bottle of beer in toast. "Just you keep sucking their dicks over there at ———r, Chief, and playing it cool. Keep up the naive act no one does quite like you and I'm telling you, there's no end to the possibilities Vince affords you. Keep telling yourself this gig is just a nice professional stepping stone and not that singular event that comes along to change your life. Next thing I know you'll be a gold-chained, hairy-chested asshole celebrity and you'll have your machine on when I call late at night." Lincoln leaned forward over the table and stuck out his thin tongue so that it looked like pink glass piping, a frightening sight. "And when that day comes, pal, I'll be there to spill the beans and tell everyone what a complete fraud you are when it comes to sex. Seat belt fastened?"

I raised my bottle and we clinked.

4/I Am of Two Minds

OVER THE summer I cut my playing at Scrabbles to three nights, which made my piano alternate, Marcel, happy; worked sporadically on notes toward my ambitious, unpublishable novel; wrote three Vince columns—on why men prefer Mary Ann to Ginger on "Gilligan's Island," on the monetary rules governing early dating, and on women who constantly eat off of men's plates (*"Couples would do well to spend less time on how they relate in the bedroom," says my friend John, a bartender, "and more time on how they relate in the dining room"*); and did little to exploit the gold mine of being Vince. In late August, walking near the Plaza Hotel, I passed a newsstand that had a row of September issues of ———*r* lining the top rack. I was in there; the Vince in there was *me*, my first printed installment. I'd expected to get my copy early, in the mail, but I was actually sort of glad that my initial encounter with my bound, pseudonymous work was out here on the street—suddenly, almost haphazardly. There was a seemliness to it; it *should* take me a moment to recognize myself in another form.

I flipped open the magazine and scanned the table of contents. Thar she blows. "Page 184 . . . Vince: A Man's View: His orgasm, his world view—An inside look at the three stages of man." I fished out the two-fifty and sat on the edge of the Plaza fountain.

> **Stage 1 (Just Before Orgasm): I am a conquistador.**
> *We're fast approaching the precipice, the other side of which a man can no longer hold back, where evitable turns to inevitable. What's he thinking? If a man was asked at this precise moment to free-associate and name those he most identifies with, he might grunt some of the following: Caesar, Air Jordan, Uebermensch.*
> *"You achieve a certain philosophical state of mind only conquerors feel," says Brian, a budding screenwriter. "You're atop the tallest hill." The feeling that most permeates a man's soul at this juncture is invincibility, even superiority and arrogance. "At that moment, you feel as if nothing can be taken away from you," says Lincoln, an art broker. "You've gotten what every boy, every man, struggles his whole life to get. Why do men really want to make money, or pursue pro-fessional success? We're doing it all for the woman. When-ever you have penetration, it reassures you you're on the path. The minute you're inside her, you're as good as or bet-ter than any man. At that particular moment, maybe one percent of the population is making love. Almost all other guys in the world are asleep or doing something else."*
> **Stage 2 (The Orgasm): Iloveyouiloveyouiloveyou . . .**

As I fed into the pedestrian traffic along Fifth Avenue, so bright in the noon sun that it seemed like a movie-set boulevard, it struck me that I was on the verge of becoming part of a world at once bigger and more exclusive than the one I'd been living in. I sensed that I was on

a path, an invisible conveyor belt, and it would transport me someplace else until I was somewhere else—some*one* else—almost despite
myself. *I was the new Vince.* Unable to bear the idea of going under-
ground and taking the subway home just yet, I walked the city. It was
the thick of lunchtime and the air was crowded with summer smells.
I walked on the balls of my feet, drummed the rolled-up magazine
against my thigh. Fifth Avenue was a Nile of femininity—calves and
hair, muscle and eyes, knees and nostrils and asses and yellows and
blues and cottons and rayons; Fifth Avenue was a fucking all-girls
school. Their odors were honey, lilac, hot coconut, French perfume; I
would need a nose plug to get through the season in one piece. Each
woman was a valentine to New York diversity and American ingenu-
ity, each parcel of blocks its own nation-state of feminine virtues, only
now I was being paid to study it, ruminate on it, write about it. In the
upper Thirties, hard by Lord & Taylor's, loitered youngish mothers
with overpriced strollers; women of means, wise, cynical, overbur-
dened, abloom with the fact of their sexual prime, several wrapped (I
made a mental note to note in some future Vince column) in the sen-
suous nimbus of late third trimester. Around Twenty-third Street,
with the Flatiron Building looking svelter and more beautiful all the
time, a flash flood of tourists, models, a policewoman engaged in the
theater of directing traffic, businesswomen in terrific shoes and
alarming hurries. Today I am just a body stocking with a penis sticking
out. Down at Washington Square, NYU women—or "co-eds," as
Vince would have called them back in 1956—favored black and
leather, high-tops that hugged round calves, meticulously ripped
jeans. Young, smart, fresh, bird tattoos, hip-hop, nose rings, lots of
Lennon specs. No voracious readers out on this street.

Soon a healthy percentage of America's female population would
know my name, if not exactly the one my mother and father provided
me. And the magazine had European editions. Ah, Europe: Continental *panache*, the beaches of the Lido, the *après-ski* and *après*-schnitzel
of Innsbruck. Parisian hemlines, Swedish saunas, ladies of the British

Isles with cheeks the translucent flush of Cezanne's summer peaches. Italian women with skin smooth as mozzarella, eyes busy as the Sistine, Tuscan olive-and-coconut-oiled and sun-dried in a light cream or garlic sauce. *Ah* is right.

I sat in the Bleecker Playground. Sometimes I lunched here, and at least a few minutes every day I watched it from my apartment window. A premature, late-summer flurry of white petals drifted down around the mothers chattering and the children waddling and the homeless men sleeping. I spied a fabulous au pair and her cherubic charge I thought Vince could be very happy with somewhere in the Hebrides maybe, fake mommy, fake daddy, someone else's baby. My eye was drawn to the half-opened third-floor window of the apartment building above the Korean market opposite the playground. The Candy Woman, as I'd some time ago dubbed her, nibbled on her usual confections, then stepped out of her skirt and disappeared, leaving the square suddenly barren and pregnant with possibilities. To a man with a hammer, everything looks like a nail. The squeals and giggles of little children in the sandbox uncoiled toward me like the leaf of a spreading beanstalk. I opened the magazine and read over my lead, as if it were some portentous fortune-cookie fortune.

VINCE: A MAN'S VIEW

A lot can change in a minute.

Why none of them at ———*r* warned me about the temptation to reveal everything, I can't say. Then again, they were all women, so how were they to know? The sidewalk at the Hudson–Bank Street crossing glittered in the sunlight, as if paved with flecks of gold. It could have been a trick my eyes were playing on me, but I didn't think so.

A lot can change in a minute.

It was my lead. I'd written it. I turned out to be absolutely right.

*　　*　　*

For my big Brell-assigned article, "What Men Don't Tell Women About Sex but Want to, by Vince," for the special upcoming love-and-sex issue of ———*r*, I needed to consult other men, and not rely simply on my own experience and that of my friends Lincoln and Brian, as I'd mostly been doing lately. I began by calling old college buddies. "Tell me," I asked Rick, an upbeat if predominantly out-of-work actor, "what would you like to tell women in bed but don't?"

"What would I like to tell women in bed but don't . . ." said Rick, the speed of the sentence decelerating word by word. "Got it," he said finally, and I began typing. "Okay. If I could tell them *anything?*"

"Anything," I said.

"If I could tell women only one thing about the penis, it would be this: the little place underneath, about an inch below the military helmet? That's the most sensitive. That *is* the G-spot."

"That's good, Rick," I said.

"Okay, most women don't understand that, orally or manually, they need to focus most of their energies on that half-inch-wide band just south of the head—not down around the base," he said. "You can't grab the base and wiggle the skin and expect a man to climax. I'm not entirely sure where they got this idea . . . a porn movie maybe?"

"Personally," mused Dan, a stockbroker, Deep Throat #2, "I'll take a finger up the ass any day of the week, twice on Sundays. I want women to bite me but I don't feel there's, like, this convenient point in the evening where I can really come out and say, 'Bite, go ahead and bite me.' I'm a kinkmeister, Andy, always have been. But you knew that about me, right?"

"I've heard," I said. I dearly hoped my life's work would not be as archivist of the banal, *Penthouse Forum*-esque, polymorphous perversities of men, even if they happened to be men who held respectable jobs, used Polo aftershave, had aced their SATs.

Perhaps one of my poker buddies, Big Dave Navinsky, a New York copyright lawyer who'd married recently but had been a terrible scoundrel, would have something profound to add, though I wouldn't bet on it. "You mean," Big Dave said, "what do you discover in bed that you couldn't predict beforehand?"

"That's not really what I was asking, Big Dave," I said, but already I could tell it was to no avail.

"Being on bottom gives me a view of The Wife that most closely resembles the classic MTV video shot: the beautiful rocker riding a horse or in a car, her head and hair flipping every which way. All that and her breasts hanging above me. I find that enhances her beauty."

"Sounds like it," I said.

"When I'm inside The Wife," Big Dave continued, "it's always surprisingly, perfectly snug. Especially when I've been away a week on business. Tits, too. Deceptive. They always feel bigger than you'd think they would from what they look like. Probably because they feel so good, period. From the clothed perspective, tits always look smaller than you think they'll look—feel bigger, look smaller—because naked she's usually lying down."

A woman in America is raped something like once every three minutes; or is that three times a minute? Domestic violence continues to climb, and that's only the fraction that's reported. Women in this country didn't win the right to vote until this century. When I phoned my friend Zachary, an environmentally correct artist with a thousand-square-foot studio in Long Island City, he asked, "Is this off the record or on?"

"On," I said.

"Good," said Zack, his tone of voice full of darting glances. "Mention how during intercourse we think about falling in water, getting good gas mileage, hitting jump shots." Zachary volunteered that he came from a family that had no real interest in sex, and his desire had always made him feel like an outcast. "And the double whammy is, Andy? The double whammy is I worry someday soon I'll lose my drive like all us Boones—Dad, Mom, Sis, my older brother. None of them has sex or wants to. My kid brother is even starting to show symptoms. All he talks about is volunteer work, volunteer work."

"This stuff now, I assure you, is all off the record," I said.

"Oh, no, not at all," Zack said. "You ever need to write about me and my family's little problem—quote unquote—go right ahead. For example," he said, "the other night I go out in this big group and sort of hit it off with this one girl who just moved to the city. Check this out: Harvard undergrad, Stanford law. Great personality, good sense of humor, listens. Ex-diving champion. The Botticelli hair, the alabaster skin, shithouse bod. On paper, perfect. Right?"

"Yeah?" I said. "And?"

"And I have zero interest in her physically," said Zack. "So already I'm starting to worry. I end up walking her back to her place and I suck it up and near her house I go to kiss her. And she goes, 'I don't kiss on the first date.' And I go, 'This isn't a date.' I mean, I'm really trying to make myself into a cad. I want someone but I find it hard. And it's not latent homosexuality either, damn it. All I care about right now is painting. You want to know what I really, truly think?" he asked.

"Absolutely," I said.

"It never works out," Zack said. "Not in the end. For a while maybe, a year, even three years maybe, but in the end, no. How can you have the intensity of being in love *and* the never-endingness of a close marriage, and still be happy years later? I don't care how much you once wanted her, at some point down the road you're going to stop and think, I wish I'd never kissed her, slept with her, gotten down on one knee."

Both John, my bartender buddy at Scrabbles, and Mike, his meathead roommate, gave me trouble getting off the phone. They each spoke for over half an hour, handing the phone back and forth between them, then finally got on separate phones and regaled me in stereo with sexual conquest after sexual mishap, most of which were not fit for the men's column of a women's magazine—or were they? Might that be my legacy to the Vince column? That I would find the crack in the genteel code, work smut into the column, and perversity, and all the truest workings of the male mind? "It's a woman's world—and thank heavens," read "Vince: A Man's View of Girls" eons ago, or 1956, whichever came first. But them days was long dead. Maybe history would remember the era during which I served as Vince—my Vince Administration—as a watershed of filth and lack of restraint.

John the Scrabbles Bartender thanked me for including him in my research and I told him I'd be happy to change his name and occupation in the article. But it was his roommate Mike who was particularly useful. "Everyone has physical imperfections," said Mike, "so your attitude toward these imperfections is important. Even if a woman's body is disappointing in some ways, she can be beautiful and compelling to me as long as she doesn't make a big thing of her flaws. I went out with a woman who had a cellulite problem. She did all these self-conscious, faux cool things to cover it up—sitting on the bed instead of lying on it, turning her butt away, a certain amount of posing and refusing to let go. Always a robe at the foot of the bed. That turned me off in a way the cottage cheese did not."

In the third-floor window across the street, I saw The Candy Woman doing what she does best, nibbling away. It's been said no woman in America has an entirely healthy relationship to food, or is allowed to. Mike went on and on—about the secret to shy women and the need for groinal muscle tone and how "kissing is more intimate than intercourse, and kissing the genitals is the most intimate act of all," and how peoples of all nations may be different but in the end a French virgin is like a South African virgin is like an Israeli virgin is like a virgin from the Five Towns. I typed furiously and could only get him off the phone by telling him I thought I smelled smoke. After hanging up, it struck me that Mike's sexual résumé—not its quantity so much as its variety, the thrilling, breathless reach of his demographic net—made him, on one hand, far the worthier Vince. On the other hand, from all he told me I guessed that the needle on his ethical barometer had broken off somewhere around toilet training, which perhaps made *me* the better Vince. Let's face it, a lot of guys out there could have done what I was doing.

In the middle of the night—three, four—the phone rang. "What?" I said.

"I appreciate a woman who doesn't work at sex too hard," volunteered Lincoln, whom I'd already interviewed at length for the article, "who recognizes that it's neither art nor science, just fun. Also, it should never be biting, always nibbling."

"No, I wasn't sleeping," I said, clearing my throat of phlegm. "Are we quite finished?"

"Also, I view sex as a weakness," Lincoln said. "Occasionally it's a crime, usually just a misdemeanor. Sometimes, if she's innocent enough, sex becomes a Class D felony. That's when it's memorable."

"You always have to have the best lines," I said.

"I always *have* the best lines," Lincoln replied.

Once again I decided to hand-deliver my latest creation, "What Men Don't Tell Women About Sex but Want to, by Vince." Back in the high-ceilinged lobby of the Madison Avenue building that houses America's sexiest magazine empire, where the hottest, coolest, shiniest women's publications are gestated, spanked, fed, and burped into being each month, I scanned the covers of all the issues on the newsstand rack. "Shape Up Your Thighs in 30 Days—Or Less!" our latest installment threatened.

Pacing until the next elevator, I studied one of the many fashion models waiting for a local. The weighty metal cross draped around her neck was of a size sufficient for a small crucifixion—a grasshopper's, perhaps a salamander's. *If you brought this girl home for a Seder, sure, Mom might be horrified, at least initially. But, boy, to see her in just that cross . . .*

Hey, hey. You're regressing. Hundred bucks says society has forced her into a desperate binge-purge cycle to stay that way.

I must have forgotten to avert my stare because the model's customary ennui now warped into something much pissier, and she flashed me the nastiest amber-eyed glare, that yeah-you-and-everyone-else expression they learn their first week at the Barbizon Modeling School. *That's a demerit, young lady,* Vince thought. *A sentence in my next column. Clean Up Your Act in 30 Days—Or Else!*

Upstairs in the reception area, as I waited for Brell, a woman sat beside me. Wedding ring, no religious jewelry. I did not start anything. She did. Let the record show that the reception area contains at least two other sofas and a Danish Modern metal-tubed chair, any of which the woman might have sat in.

"So," the woman began. "What do you do?"

A winning opening gambit. Have it your way. Two can play.

I told her I was a writer. From her reaction, it was hard to imagine a more appealing career choice. What did I write, she wanted to know.

"Freelance," I grunted.

"Yeah? For whom?" I named my old magazine, ———'s; another famous women's magazine for whom I once wrote some eleventh-hour, seafood-based copy ("Of peppercorns and scallops I speak, of clams and shallots"); and America's two most impressive-sounding newspapers, both of which had once published a couple inches of mine. I smiled shyly at the woman and concluded my biography with the phrase "and, you know, places *like* that," a flourish at once pardonable and totally untrue.

"Do you write about anything special?" she asked.

"I do a monthly column," I said.

"Yeah?" the woman said. "For?"

I nodded my head at the front desk, made a vague sweep with my hand of the écru couch, the coffee table, the vacant Danish Modern metal-tubed chair she might just as well have sat in.

"What's the column?" asked the woman.

"Oh, it's all about men, women, men and women, women and men, relationships, romance, love, dating," I said. "That sorta thing." I was working to a fine pitch the Huck-and-Tom-feet-dangling-off-the-pier innocence; I'd graduated beyond Remedial Aw-Shucks mode. "Sex," I added bashfully.

"Wait," the woman said. "Don't tell me. You're not Vince. Do *not* tell me."

I looked down, scratched my nose, humble as pie gets—cross-strip topping, rhubarb-peach, twittering birds come to sit on Grammy's sill, the works.

"Actually," I half-whispered, "I am."

"Oh, my God!" the woman blurted. "The man behind the myth!" Her wedding-ringed hand slapped down on my knee. "I've always wondered about Vince. I can't wait to tell my girlfriends." Brief cloud cover darkened her expression. "It's all right if I tell my girlfriends . . . or . . . maybe just—my *best* friend?"

I nodded. For a moment we were both silent, refueling. Suddenly I wished her gone. I was sorry I'd weakened and exploited the line with a complete stranger. Frankly, she didn't appear that intriguing or unmarried.

"Wow, *Vince*," said the woman, who seemed to have rebounded strongly after the time-out. "The man behind the advice. That's really something."

"It's been interesting," I said cryptically.

"So you're *the* Sensitive New Age Man of the Nineties," she said, checking my posture, scrutinizing my footwear, studying me for signs of lice eggs. "You talk openly about feelings, you do the dishes without asking."

"Do the dishes, do the windows, read up on prenatal-care legislation, even put in the diaphragm," I said. "Whoops. I'm sorry. That was crude and uncalled for."

"Listen," the woman said, ignoring this, "I have a friend who'd . . . basically sleep with you once she found out you were Vince."

I emitted a kind of hum. Evidently, the woman read my mind. "She's adorable," the woman said, "totally cute, an actress on the rise, very sunny." Crap; I'm a sucker for any woman described as "sunny." "Here," she said, "I'm going to give you Cheryl's number"—in her deep concentration the woman's brow furrowed like a tilled field as she copied Cheryl's phone number onto a pink "While You Were Out" slip and tore it from its pad—"and you do what you want."

I thanked the woman, a cosmetics P.R. rep named Sue. We talked briefly, then retreated somewhat antisocially to the magazines on the table. I was glad when Brell came to whisk me away into her chambers. *Come now, Sue, this woman whose number you gave me—she's a voracious reader, no?* Vince and I both wanted to ask before leaving the reception area. *Sue, this friend of yours, this Cheryl person—has she just read* Middlemarch *cover to cover?*

In her office Brell and I batted around topics for future columns— what guys mean when we say we'll call but don't, what we mean when we close a letter with "Sincerely" when "Love" really seems the more appropriate sign-off, what we mean when we don't write altogether, what we mean when we just grunt. How the hell should *I* know what we mean? Personally, I thought a road trip for Vince might be nice, maybe a Club Med deal. I would be willing to model for an art class and write up the experience if I weren't so positive Vince would get an erection. Maybe he could have an affair with a married woman? How about it, Brell? I'm sure he'd get insights you couldn't begin to imagine. Or he'll have a sex change. "I'd give anything to get inside the mind of a woman," I said.

"The mind, you say," Brell nodded.

"Yes," I said.

"I think you've been indoors too long," said Brell.

"No, really," I said, "there are so many things I wonder—all men wonder—what it would really be like to do. Have a baby, breast-feed. Talk one's way out of a speeding ticket."

Brell sucked some cranberry-flavored seltzer through her straw, licked a tiny knob of cream cheese and sprouts off her finger. She and her fantastic green eyes nodded at me. If you don't watch it, Brell, I'm going to do a column someday about your eating habits. I'm going to do a column about women with strange, deeply unethnic names.

Remember: *I'm Vince now.*

"So . . . I'll do something about traveling together for next month," I said. "Or maybe men on the telephone." Forget how we city boys really think, Brell—what say a column about farm boys? There's a whole sector of American men out there whose needs and desires Vince is not explicating. And I have the perfect title: "Some Count Sheep, Some Fuck Sheep." So maybe that was Brian's idea, or Lincoln's. Or how about this one, Brell, and stop looking at me like that: If women were men, and women could enter men the way men enter women, women wouldn't get so excited about walk-in closets.

No? Well, it wasn't my idea. It was my buddy Big Dave's, I think. One in four women in American emergency rooms has been injured by a husband or boyfriend.

I refrained from pitching Brell *all* my column ideas, such as "What If Vince Abused His Title and Position—Then What?" or "Suppose Vince's Frame of Reference Was in Fact Extremely Narrow?" or "Would Vince Ever Totally Fabricate Quotes?" Brell and I agreed on the next few topics ("How Might Vince Spend 24 Hours as a Woman?"; "Vince as Uncle"; "Lovers Traveling Together"). On my way out, I stopped by Research to pick up from Monica, the perpetually tanned assistant editor, my first batch of letters to Vince.

Dear "Vince: A Man's View":

About your "Why Men Prefer Mary Ann to Ginger" column (October) on "Gilligan's Island": Well, I am a sweet Mary Ann and not a sexy Ginger and I can tell you ninety-nine point forty-four percent of men all want big tits and someone who will go to bed with them no questions asked. You do not represent the mainstream of American men, Vince. I find you're "sensitivity" phony. I hope the women of America know what a phony you are.

Vince,

My father never physically touched me, even as a child. So I let the wrong men near me rather then risk never being held. When I was little I cried in the mornings when I woke up because I was still alive . . .

I have a shaving disability. I am facially challenged. I am differently follically abled.

By the time I was to show up at the Upper East Side apartment of Cheryl—the sunny actress who would, in the words of her friend Sue of the ———r reception area, basically sleep with me once she found out I was Vince—not only would my cheeks and throat be prickled by blood dots but, because I'd overdressed for what was turning into one of those greenhouse-effect December evenings, I'd be sweating like a pig. Cheryl and I had talked briefly on the phone. She sounded sunny, all right, perhaps a touch wacky, possibly a space cowgirl. Her interest in my Vinceness was more subdued than I'd been conned into believing by Sue; maybe it was Sue who was thrilled by the idea of meeting Vince, but she herself was spoken for, yet ever on the matchmake for her friends.

Amazingly, though, Sue's assessment had been accurate: Cheryl *was* adorable and totally cute. My whole body relaxed as soon as she opened the door and smiled. Cheryl had large blue eyes and a shade of red-gold hair Crayola has never perfected, a tint even more aflame than Brell's. What was still more encouraging, when I shook Cheryl's hand I noticed on the back of it a blurred purple splotch, some downtown club stamp, mark of the eternal party girl.

What Sue had *not* told me was how petite her friend Cheryl was. I berated myself for not planning for this possibility. Extra time and care should have been spent clipping nostril hairs, not fluffing my hair to cover my bald spot.

Light bulb. "What Men Hide from Women." Only make the person with the bald spot "a friend."

Does my friend Scott, an air-traffic controller and pos-sessor of a slowly but inexorably expanding flesh-covered lake on his head, do anything for his condition—the Hair Club for Men, baseball caps? "I stay in the sun a lot. When my hair turns blonder, my baldness is not as apparent," he says. "So big deal, I'll die two years earlier of skin cancer."

Two kittens ran through Cheryl's legs and into the hallway. I hoped that was all; it's up to New Yorkers with more than two four-legged pets to prove they're *not* loony. The kittens tuned their tails up into hooked pipe cleaners, circled and sniffed Vince, like tailors checking fit. Cheryl wore a peasant skirt and a shirt the color of raspberry sorbet, and she had on those old-fashioned pointy lace-up shoe-boots—is it a shoe? Is it a boot? Her apartment was lit dimly, warmly. Wood floors, exposed brick, faux Tiffany lamps, *Playbill* covers from old Broadway hits framed on the wall. All in all, her home perfectly caught that hearken-back-to-a-more-innocent-era, turn-of-the-century-Coca-Cola-advertisement feeling.

Cheryl bent to pick up the kittens. "What are their names?" I said, nodding at the feline bundle in her arms.

"Cee and Encee, for Cat and Not-Cat," Cheryl said.

Damn. I hate when people try Zen out on their animals.

"N.C. is so easygoing," Cheryl said, nuzzling the calicos. "He's somewhere between a pet and furniture. No *Sturm und Drang* with these fellas—isn't that right, boys?"

To make matters worse, a copy of Leo Buscaglia's *Love* lay on the coffee table in front of her floral-upholstered, antique-looking couch. When Cheryl saw me eye the book, she cocked her head to the side, a soul sister, all of a sudden, in the appreciation of fine literature. "It's nowhere near his best," said Cheryl.

Strike two.

We made our way to a nearby international beer garden, a regular U.N. of beers. Behind the bar, each of ninety-nine varieties stood at sparkling green or brown attention, eleven rows across, nine bottles down. I ordered Mamba, an Ivory Coast brew, while Cheryl quickly knocked off beers from China and Wales. Now she was on a Dutch pilsener and vowing to make her way through the Benelux nations. I hold the record for nursing one drink.

"But wait, I don't understand exactly," Cheryl said, running a finger along the rim of her emblazoned pewter stein. "You can totally support yourself from your Vince column?"

"Pretty much," I lied. "But I also have another job, a music job. Because I love music."

"Oh, yes?" Cheryl said. "Something in the entertainment venue?"

"I'm a piano man," I said. "At a bar-restaurant."

"No kidding," Cheryl said. "And do you sing?"

"They wouldn't pay me if I sang," I said.

"I always wanted to know—how do you decide what to play next?"

"That's why the medley was invented," I said. "You can just tune out. I do a Gershwin medley, a Fats Waller medley, a World War Two medley, a fruit medley." The waitress came by and I ordered another Mamba.

"Wait," Cheryl said to her and tapped my hand. "I think you want to try another country, don't you," she said.

"I liked that one," I said.

Cheryl considered this but said nothing, while the waitress stood stiffly monitoring the briefly poisonous karma.

"I just can't imagine ordering the same country twice," Cheryl said once the waitress had left.

"Oh. Well," I said. "If it ain't broke."

"There are fifty-four more I still need to try," Cheryl said.

"Fifty-three," I said. "Here, take a sip."

"No, I want my own Mamba, thank you," Cheryl said.

Maybe Vince shouldn't have been so hard in his current column on women who share men's food, I thought; at least that wasn't a sign of hostility. *"Please don't diet on my dinner,"* advised "my friend Hugh, a chiropodist," in the Vince column fresh on the stands. *"I say this especially to those of you whose version of saying grace before meals is 'I'll just pick.' "*

Cheryl talked about what plays she was up for and the Off-Broadway callback she had the next day. After her extraordinarily prehensile tongue scooped up the last bead of foam from her beer head, she asked, "So, tell me. Why are men such shits?"

"Are you sure you want one of us to answer that?" I asked without, I'd like to think, missing a beat. "Maybe there's a little conflict of interest there."

"No, go ahead," Cheryl said with a strange mix of enthusiasm and resignation. "Vince is supposed to understand women so well, you and Ingmar Bergman. And he's pretty much retired. I just rented *Persona* again. God, is that on. Anyway, Bergman and you. So if you know women, I assume you understand your own sex a little bit, too."

"I'd hope so, but I'm not sure," I said. "And I'm not trying to be modest. Maybe it's just easier to understand whichever sex is more remote to one's experience."

"Men are always the more remote sex," said Cheryl.

"That's funny, Cheryl."

"Will you use that line in a column?" she said. "Will you credit me if you do?"

"If I use it I will credit you," I said.

"What I want to know is," said Cheryl, "why such male *Sturm und Drang* in terms of making a commitment? Are guys so horny all the time they feel they need to leave their options open in case something better comes along? In a shorter skirt and no bra? Is it as simple as that? Is it more?"

"I don't think we're really that much hornier than women," I said.

"Phooey," she said.

Phooey? Wait, Cheryl, let me go get my beanie. "I think the gap in sex drive is considerably smaller than most people think," I said. "Though as teenagers, I admit, so much blood is re-routed from the male brain to the groinular area—for months, even years at a time, without relief—that the insanity plea is really justified there in covering a cornucopia of behaviors. You've never been a teenaged boy. Take my word for it. We're rapists. We're animals. We know only one law."

"It's all biology," Cheryl nodded.

"It *is* all biology," I acknowledged. "I always say: If men were built like women, we'd behave exactly the way you do. And vice versa. I mean, how would you feel if you had to go around all the time with this thing between your legs?"

"Thrilled," said Cheryl.

Time for a sip. "You're something, Cheryl," I said.

"What?" she asked, touching my arm, perhaps tenderly.

Cheryl said I should pick the dinner cuisine. I'd had Japanese the previous night, so I ruled that out first. "Why, don't you like eating raw things?" Cheryl asked lasciviously.

She tossed back the last of her beer and smiled over her pewter stein as the check came. I turned it over to examine the damage and Cheryl excused herself to use the bathroom. Apparently she hadn't read Vince's November column on men, women, and money, or she would have made a token gesture to split costs, at least kick in for the tip.

At one of those seafood restaurants where the menu is a wood panel, Cheryl ordered a dozen Cherrystones, extracting a promise from me to help. As the clams slid cold and wet down my throat, I reminded myself I was eating for texture, not taste. I washed them down with my third beer of the night—American, lite—while my date burrowed deep into her second six-pack. Add to this the fact that Cheryl was so petite and it mightily impressed me that she hadn't yet slid under the table.

As I listened to Cheryl drone on about which actresses she admired for the choices they made ("and let's for the moment leave Streep out of this"), I grew enervated—somewhat due to my extraordinarily low tolerance for alcohol, somewhat due to the idea of listening to Cheryl for even five more minutes. I realized that for all my supposed indifference to what was, first and last, a blind date, a Vince excursion for material, I (that is, Andrew) had basically come into it with way too much optimism.

By night's end, Vince whispered to me, *you'll drop a hundred bucks on the gossamer provocation of "adorable and totally cute," not to mention "sunny." Sucker.*

Cheryl was describing how her ex-boyfriend, an NBC production grunt named Vladimir, had given her an engagement ring, then refused to set a date, then set a date, then backed out, then backed back in, then asked that the ring be returned. "Would you call that normal?" Cheryl asked.

"Sure I'd call it normal," I said. "For a guy who's unsure about his professional and financial station, who isn't quite ready to go all the way but yet who's in love and has no compelling reason to leave the woman he loves just because he can't take that final—"

"No, no, you're wrong, you're all wrong," Cheryl said. "You and the rest. It's really so sweet how little you all know. Men are just so full of . . . *Sturm und Drang.*"

I found it increasingly hard to concentrate. I spun a Cherrystone around the platter, making the shell clack against the side.

ACRONYMS WITH B IN THE MIDDLE

NBC

ABC

CBS

BBC

IBM

FBI

PBK

PB&J

I. B. Singer

E. B. White

Jack Be Nimble

"So Vladimir's still bugging you?" I asked, tuning back in after Cheryl had ripped off a list of her own—Complaints About Vladimir in Particular, Men in General.

"Yeah," Cheryl said. "Why should that surprise you?" She shook her almost carrot-colored hair and pulled at her lip. The faraway look in her blue eyes was part beer, part Vladimir nostalgia, part my own glazed perception.

"He still calls," Cheryl said softly and I wondered if I was still forbidden to call Julie, or if the embargo had once again been lifted because, according to my backward-counting menstrual cycle calculations, any day now my former love safari pal would be thoroughly estral. "How do I forget about him?" Cheryl was asking. "Where do I put . . . *it*? You know *it*? You know what I mean by *It*?" Crescents of water trembled at the rim of Cheryl's lower lids. "You're Vince," she said, blinking wetly. "Tell me."

Somehow, in some subtle nocturnal hall of mirrors I'd missed, I'd been transformed from date to therapist. "You definitely need resolution here, Cheryl," I said, "and you need to get it on your terms. Maybe surprise Vladimir, catch him off-guard, tell him you're finished with him, he's a buffoon, he's indecisive, poorly endowed, lousy in bed, and he's not to call anymore. Be firm. Vince says: Tell him not to call for . . . *a while.*"

"Yeah," Cheryl said. "I want to get my licks in, too—if you know what I mean." Her eyebrows arched. She bit the bottleneck and bared her teeth in a simian way.

"Cheryl," I admonished, my beer alighting on the table with more vehemence than I'd planned, "you're going to have to stop the double and triple entendres."

"I do do that, don't I," Cheryl admitted. "My life is just so full of *Sturm und Drang* these days—"

"And the *Sturm und Drang* business, Cheryl. Find a new expression. We won the war."

She ignored me. Good for her. "What sign are you?" she asked.

Oh, crap. Not that. Not now.

"Taurus," I said.

"Damn," said Cheryl. "That's Earth. I'm Gemini. Air. Earth and Air don't go," she lamented.

"Don't I know it." I tried to sound deflated. "Maybe we should . . ."

"Listen, maybe we should cancel the dinner order," Cheryl said, reading my mind. "Cherrystones are *so* filling. And really, I should work on this Shaw monologue for tomorrow's audition. And maybe turn in early. And maybe think about Vladimir. He's Libra, an Air sign, too."

"Probably you should go, then," I said.

But just then the waitress showed up with our blackened fish dinners and Cheryl and I pretended we'd never had this exchange.

"Do I," Cheryl asked halfway through her charred red snapper, "or do I not know good seafood?"

Though Cheryl had acted indifferent to my ordering the Mississippi Mud Pie, when it arrived she shifted her chair closer to mine. As the first chocolate forkful headed for her mouth, she froze. "Uh-oh," said Cheryl. "You're probably going to write about how girls do this, aren't you? Scarf food."

"Don't be silly," I said. I already had, so why should I do it again?

Afterward (this check we split), a few blocks from the restaurant, Cheryl stopped abruptly in front of Carl Schurz Park, gazed up at the sky, and, without looking at me, put her hands out to be taken. It seemed the gesture of a young, blind ice-skater: floating by herself across the frozen lake toward some human destination, legs wobbly at first but not weak, speed and equilibrium building, and now coming home to rest on the far side, the goal met, putting out her hands to be taken. Cheryl's tongue had Magellan's love of exploration, and its texture reminded me of the topmost meat of overripe honeydew. Her breath tasted beery, though had I been more of a connoisseur I might have appreciated the truly international stamp of its flavor. After ninety seconds she left my mouth feeling very large and very raw.

"It's so quiet," I said as we unclinched and looked up at the three stars visible in the Manhattan night sky. "For New York. Listen."

Cheryl took a deep breath. "People mistake oxygen or the atmosphere or unconsciousness for silence," she said, her small, strong hands kneading the area just above my collarbone. "Nothing could be further from the truth. Is that Mars?"

Back at Nostalgia Central, Cheryl poured herself a double vodka and made tea for me. From the kitchen she talked about how she'd been thinking about applying to the American Conservatory Theatre in San Francisco but the money she'd been counting on had recently been squandered by her alcoholic father, who was now in the twelve-step program. "For him it's always too much and it's never enough," Cheryl called out flatly, as if asking did I prefer Earl Grey or Darjeeling. Meanwhile, I sat on the couch while her Zen calico kittens, C. and N.C., roamed all over me, exerting with their rubbery legs a not-unwelcome pressure on my swollen groin.

Cheryl sat down and took off her shoe-boots and I liked the careful way she tucked the laces inside the bowls of the shoes. Together we flipped through a coffee-table book of Doisneau photographs and before I knew it the raspberry sorbet–colored shirt was unbuttoned and I was fumbling with some primitive snaps at Cheryl's back, finally releasing her as if from some antique holster. What exactly do I have in mind here? I wondered. What exactly does Cheryl have in mind? Am I not an Earth, she an Air?

Go with it, Vince advised. *Deadline approaches.*

Near the pebbled middle of each breast were two or three stray red and gold hairs. They were fine shoots, dignified, fiery, anachronistic hairs; I was put in mind of the last of the great American farmers who stubbornly and proudly refuse to yield their land to condo developers even for ridiculous sums of money. It is precisely metaphors like this one that remind me how poor my tolerance for alcohol really is.

This is not what I'd call being in the moment, I thought. Are you Vince now or are you you? One of us whispered to Cheryl that we liked red and gold.

"Believe it or not, they were my school colors," she said. Not-Cat moved slinkily over my feet and along the floor to the kitchen, its shoulders moving so liquidly as to appear snake-like. Cat gurgled in a low, tensed, almost human voice. Cheryl flipped off the Tiffany lamp beside the couch and we were left in the grainy light from the moon in the window. You had to hand it to Cheryl, I thought, the way she did not check both ways for cars, did not look for passersby, how *in* the moment she was. She was a regular ball-spinning seal, a thief with the tongue. With her thick-lashed eyes closed, her pretty face calm and serious, Cheryl looked quite touching, actually, but for some reason I could not stop myself from making silly expressions at her. I stuck out my tongue and made the rubbery monster face I called on to get my niece to laugh. This is definitely not in the moment. I certainly hope this doesn't become an occupational hazard of being Vince. I watched N.C. tightrope across the arm of the couch, then stop to attend, with its paw, to an itch behind its left ear.

Ssh, sssh. The moment. So Cheryl is just this night's Miss Congeniality. So she isn't going to be the grandmother of your grandchildren. So what. The moment. Concentrate. Try to stay in the moment.

JEWISH HOLIDAYS OR PIZZA TOPPINGS

Hanukkah
Pepperoni
Rosh Hoshanah
Green Pepper
Yom Kippur
Mushroom
Pesach
Canadian Bacon
Shavuos
Fresh Garlic
Purim
Sausage
Tishah B' Av
Double Cheese

Somehow Cheryl had removed all her clothes, though her underwear caught around her feet and it was a moment to free her of the nuisance. She held her arms out to me stiffly, as if waiting for a drenched and muddy football jersey to be pulled off. Her mouth said, Yes; her eyes, Did you hear what my mouth just said? There's nothing more arousing in a woman than aggressiveness, even selfishness, I thought. If nothing will get in the way of her pleasure, it's the most incredible turn-on. To me. To Vince. Ergo, to all men. A pen, I need a pen, damn it.

The rolling hills of her backside launched, the scraped meadow of her lower back plunged, the sharp young mountains of her shoulder blades strained to knock against each other. She twisted over onto her back and exposed to the elements her entire milky geology. The trail that led from her navel down glinted in the moonlight like splayed sparks. "Do you have something," Cheryl said.

I mumbled.

"Take everything off," she said. "I don't want your fingers, piano player."

While I was busy pondering the implications, Cheryl deftly un-hitched my belt with one hand while with her other she relieved me of my shirt, undressing me faster than I can myself, completely lucid. None of the age-old game of I go, you go.

Of all the words I'd ever read in books, of all the words I'd ever heard or spoken or seen or copied down, one came to mind now, over and over. *Yikes.*

Just like that: *Yikes.*

"Cheryl," I said. Yo, Cheryl? *Yikes.*

I stroked her hair. Her middle climbed toward me, the back of an animal. "Vince," she whispered.

Yikes.

"I mean *An*drew," said Cheryl. She aborted the giggle. "Really, I meant Andrew." A soft snap of waistband.

From the kitchen the hot water whistled, a maniac's cry in the night. Stroke of twelve, glass slipper hour, Cinderella must go. Bless you, Earl Grey.

That night, while sitting at my rolltop desk and explaining to my read-ers how Vince hadn't really wanted to do anything with Cheryl (though certainly I could have used her beside me for warmth, even on that tepid December night), how he'd uncomfortably (but honorably, of course, sensitively) used the tea break to extricate himself from deeper involvement ("Not all men are pigs *all* the time"), I shifted in my chair and nudged the desk with my leg. I put down my pencil, cracked my knuckles, my back, my neck, stretched my whole body, yawned like a big cat, a six-foot N.C. I swigged my Tropicana, picked up my pencil, and returned to next month's column. On a dare, Vince, sensitive tom-catting Vince, was trying to tackle the question of what makes a man fall in love. It was the ultimate man's-point-of-view column—Vince's Rose Window, his *Great Gatsby*, his Ninth Symphony—but since the hand inside the puppet had no clues, no promising leads, he bagged the idea and scribbled out some thoughts instead about the contents of his wallet and what it meant about him in particular, men in general. The column was slowly materializing on the white legal pad before me (*"behind the cash we find three fortune-cookie fortunes"*) when I realized that, like a dog bracing himself to scratch, I'd pinned myself up against the desk. My legs had gone wide to make a muscular V that embraced one edge of the desk.

Fantastic, I thought. Now you're getting horny just *writing* the column.

Ooh, the phone. Bet it's the neighbors complaining about the racket my desk and I are making.

"The Eagle has landed," Lincoln said.

Oh, damn.

Lincoln amplified on what I am always dreading. "Not only is she legally a grown-up," he said, "not only is she smarter than I am, tall, Jewish—"

"Lincoln, *you're not Jewish,*" I snapped.

". . . wait, with arms like straps," he continued, "she's—are you sitting down? Anj, she's willowy."

"No," I said, feeling slight nausea. "Not willowy."

"Yes, a truly wonderful Westchester-American body." Then Lincoln said, "There's only one thing I worry about," and my heart sang—or hummed, anyway. It was always something with Lincoln's women—or girls, because they were almost always alarmingly young. The fact that he buried his reservation under four or five resounding endorsements meant the worry was significant. "Where are you?" I asked.

"Subway," Lincoln said. "I just dropped her off. Hold on." There was a long *whoosh*, then a *basso profundo* thumping. It was the goony, yellow maintenance train that crawls and sneezes along the subway track after midnight, holding up everyone's train. I felt a native's smugness that I could identify it merely by its sound over the phone. "I just left her," Lincoln said when the plodding train had passed. "I tell you, there's nothing like the approbation of your fellow man. Suddenly everyone's got a comment, everyone's *shtupping* us with flowers. One guy got so aroused when we walked by I had to punch him for harassing us. One of those insane Vietnam vets who looks like ZZ Top. Ouch. What's the rule again about a broken hand?"

"What's the hitch?" I said. It's going to be okay, I thought. He's too manic. He can't have found her, he simply can't. In the background a deeper rumble began building.

"Okay, it's her profession," Lincoln said, "which—say this for her: At least it keeps her humble—oh, here's my train. But listen, this afternoon at the drugstore? I read the new column about sharing food. That doesn't sound like you at all, you *love* sharing food. That sounds exactly like Big Dave and The Wife, with a little bit of me thrown in. And I notice you've started making up names and nutty professions. Scared we'll get credit for your pithiest observations? You really should give us a cut. Who else knows that Vince is a total fabrication, an amalgam of all of us? Everyman and no man? I loved the title, 'Entree Nous.' Vincent, I'm afraid I really must go." By now he was yelling to be heard over the roar of the train.

"What's the hitch?" I said.

"I can't hear you!" Lincoln screamed. "We'll talk soon, V-Man. Bye."

In the shower I needed increasing imagination: Julie in just a mesh New York Knicks jersey, center court, Madison Square Garden. Julie and me atop the Chrysler Building. Julie and me on the floor of the New York Stock Exchange, at the four o'clock closing bell, a day's worth of buy and sell slips strewn about us like lily pads.

Cheryl and me on the kitchen floor, the tea whistling, her twelve-step father reading an old *Playbill* by the Tiffany lamp in the next room.

Julie and Cheryl and me forming a strange, horizontal isosceles. Good, we're getting there. Stumpy, but getting there. Now the other way around. Cheryl, you here; Julie, you there.

How about with long, beautiful Soney, the New Zealand fashion model who'd shown up at the magazine office, in a big open field, some fresh kiwi, gingham picnic blanket, wicker basket, under the Southern Hemisphere stars?

How about I bump into Sue, the P.R. rep, on a run around the Central Park reservoir, she invites me back to her place to look at press releases? No, that won't work.

How about watching tanned Monica in Research do it herself? Stop, you had it, now you're losing it. Too abstract.

How about me and Diana the Scrabbles waitress atop the piano during Sunday brunch (Scrabbled Eggs Benedict, your choice of Mimosa or Bloody Mary, $9.95), Marcel my alternate tickling the ivories beneath us, doing his moronic Body Parts medley ("Those Lips, Those Eyes," "I Left My Heart in San Francisco," "He's Got the Whole World in His Hands")?

How about Colonel Mustard, in the study, with a lead pipe?

Wonderful, Andrew. Recording your own jerking off for posterity. Your parents should get great *naches* from this.

And congrats to you too, Vince. Just look at yourself. You got the whole world in your hands.

5/Helen Gurley Brown Has the Hots for Me—I Mean, Vince

At this moment, I do not have an erection. Writing about sex does not give me an erection. Perhaps it would if I were seventeen, but if I were seventeen, flossing would give me an erection.

—"What Men Don't Tell Women About Sex but Want to, by Vince"

EXCEPT THE Magazine ran the lead using in-your-face 13-point type:

AT THIS MOMENT, I DO NOT HAVE AN ERECTION.

Beneath the article's accompanying artwork—a typically licentious, sepia-toned photo of a semiclad female and male model, their limbs wrapped around each other like vines—it was suggested that readers would do well to pay particular attention to *my* advice since pseudonymity freed me to tell the real truth. (*"Because no one knows who he is, Vince can say things other men can't."*)

My "What Men Want" article hit the stands one sunny frozen day in January. In its first week, ———*r*, like all but one other magazine in America, was ignored: The *Sports Illustrated* swimsuit issue came out and women all over town made jokes about suicide. By early February, the competition was gone.

Happy Valentine's Day, readers, I thought. To all my subscribers and newsstand purchasers, and especially to all my friends at hair salons and on the non-express lines at supermarkets around this great big beautiful mall-laden country of ours: May all your orgasms be multiple.

If we seem unaware of what we want, it's because we're reluctant to spell it out for women. We're worried that if we share with you the nuts-and-bolts of our fleshly desires, you'll think us any number of wonderful things: selfish, misogynistic, controlling, perverted, homosexual. As Roy Blount, Jr., says, men think "it is better to keep one's mouth shut and be thought a pig than to open it and oink."

The first desires a woman should consult are her own. But if getting him excited is part of what gets you excited, I'm ready to oink.

And Happy Valentine's Day to you, too, Vince. Everyone read the story. Every time I left the house I came home to an answering machine blinking its maximum load. Pumped, I turned on MTV, clapped my hands once, hard, as if signaling to myself that the next stage of my life had begun, that Sensitive Guy (Andrew) was being rewarded because Tomcatter (Vince) was letting it all hang out. Or maybe I had that backward.

Before we begin: There is no one act, position, body part, or fashion that all men love or hate. *Some men like to be spanked, some don't. I don't; my friend Jason, a NASA nutritionist, does. Some men prefer a woman to wear black satin panties, some prefer those white cotton Calvin Klein deals. I prefer the white cottons.*

I rewound the answering machine, settled into the couch, hugged a couple of cushy throw pillows to my chest, and waited for another round of kudos. "Can I have your job?" my old college roommate Brian asked on the machine. "I would like your job."

Give him an inch. *"If I could tell women only one thing about the penis," says my friend Douglas, an actor, "it would be this: The little place underneath, about an inch below the military helmet, is the most sensitive. That is the G-spot." Kurt, a computer programmer, concurs: "Most women don't understand that, orally or manually, they need to focus most of their energies on that half-inch-wide band just south of the head—not down around the base. You can't grab the base and wiggle the skin and expect a man to climax. I'm not sure where they got this idea—a porn movie?"*

"Holy, moly," said Brian's kid sister Alison on Message #2. "Little Andy Pandy. Please call sometime. I'm Xeroxing your article to give to girlfriends. I didn't know you liked white cotton underwear. Brian just called to say he wants your job."

"You have an X-rated mind," said Diana the Scrabbles waitress. It began to dawn on me just how many people I'd told I was Vince and that he was I.

Act confident. *"Confidence can make up for every lack of physical endowment," says Roland, a private investigator. "It may be the greatest aphrodisiac of all." Conversely, he points out, "Fear and lack of confidence are frightening to a man who, after all, sometimes goes to a woman for the reassurance of being held by someone who knows what they're doing."*

"Did *you* write that raunchy story," asked Big Dave Navinsky on the next message, "or did Lincoln? The Wife and I are at his gallery yesterday and he tells us *he's* Vince. Which is it? Good work, either one of you."

Get into oral sex. *You knew I was going to say it, and I knew you knew, so let's dispense with it now: Virtually every man* *responds to this form of stimulation. While some men may have problems with intercourse for its inherent performance pressures, others with masturbation, kink, and sustained foreplay, oral sex is, year in, year out, the carnal Honda of consumer satisfaction.*

If you love oral sex, that won't surprise you. If you don't, and can't imagine why we do, here are some clues.

"That was some . . . article," my mother's message announced. "Very provocative. Call us when you get in."

Sooner than later. *"Sex, and anxiety about it, can be a waste of time needed to develop other dimensions of the relationship," says Trace, a quantum mechanic. "Therefore, it's sometimes very liberating to have sex before dinner, so you can actually enjoy the date activities and the conversation. It also buoys the bond because of the reassuring foundation of sex early." This schedule alteration may strike women as going about things backward, but might be welcomed by those whose men habitually fall asleep right after late-night sex.*

Rock music pulsed from the TV. My pseudonymous celebrity was spreading. In the apartment across the way, there was no sign of Candy Woman, but her TV was going. I couldn't help but think she was somewhere just beyond the square, committing Vince-recommended acts and eating chocolate, all while blue light flung itself against the walls, headless men climbing, cavorting. The phone rang, a living thing. More good news?

"Hi," she said simply.

"Hi," I said.

"How about I come over there right now—that is, if you'll write about me sometime," she said. Over the phone I could tell she was applying lipstick thickly, strategically. What fiber optics. "But I don't want you to change my name or make up these ridiculous professions. Since when do you know a NASA nutritionist?"

"I don't," I said.

"No, I didn't think so," she said. "So, what do you say? By cab it takes no time, door to door." I'd never heard such coyness. I felt the Great Pyramid forming. "Just say the word," she said.

I took a big breath and muted the television.

"Who is this?" I said.

***Don't try to make every encounter one for the storybooks.** As my friend Lee, a tractor salesman, puts it, "I appreciate a woman who doesn't work at sex too hard, who recognizes that it's neither art nor science, just fun."*

Somewhere deep in the engine of Gotham, Helen Gurley Brown, that Cosmo Girl, read my article. The First Lady of women's magazines, Queen Mother of self-esteem between the glossy covers and between the satin sheets, Dalai Lama of the Cleave-Age, High Priestess of Slaving Away Over a Hot Man, Madam of hard-hitting feature stories like "Penis Size: Does It Really Matter?" ("It's always enough, and it never is," says Jeannette, 24, a flight attendant) . . . somewhere, H.G.B. finished my article. She sat back, picked up her phone, and put out an All Points Bulletin.

Find out who Vince is, she commanded. *I want Vince.*

"How can I end up with a dentist?" boomed Lincoln. I could hear him through the Walkman. I pulled out my earplugs and saw the Talking Car gliding beside me on Sixty-first Street as I walked to the subway after a long night at Scrabbles, a measly twenty-three bucks in tips, and five—count 'em, five—Andrew Lloyd Webber requests. "Why not just say undertaker?" Lincoln announced over the bullhorn. "Or exterminator?" It was after one on a cold February morning and I gestured for Lincoln to turn the bullhorn off.

He had a point, though. Dentist was a tough one. Exterminator, undertaker, dentist, corporate tax attorney: the problem professions. The needling that Lincoln and his new willowy dentist-lover would face at parties would certainly take its toll on him—on them—over time. There was no finessing any of these occupations. Lincoln had already gone through it four girlfriends ago, an exercise I knew he'd found frankly exhausting: Gupti, an Indian schoolgirl ("a wonderful Hindustani body"), stateside for three months while her father counseled Union Carbide in its defense against the residents of Bhopal. But even there Lincoln could sort of slime his way through. Told people—if the topic was unavoidable—that Gupti's dad worked in environmental law.

"So she's a dentist," I said, not slowing my walk.

"I can't end up with a dentist," Lincoln's voice thundered, as a homeless man sleeping on a steaming grate looked up at the voice filling his street. The homeless man pointed to the car, as if he'd just spotted a UFO. Lincoln waved and the man waved back stiffly, as if it were both beyond his will and also of the gravest importance. "Hey," Lincoln's voice called out to the homeless man. "Can I end up with a dentist? Sir?"

The man nodded yes, no, then in drunken exhaustion his head slammed down against the grating.

"Sure you can," I said. Since learning of the occupation of Lincoln's latest soon-to-be-ex-girlfriend, I'd felt—I cannot tell a lie—my spirits lifting. Oscar Wilde was right, it's *not* enough to succeed; your friends must also fail. "It's not the dentistry, Linc," I called out. "All fingers now point to you. It must be you. Call me a nut, but I think maybe you can't be with *any*one permanently."

"Can't or don't want to?" he announced, a touching curiosity audible even in the crackling, amplified voice.

"I'm ending this conversation if you get semantic on me," I said at the corner of Second Avenue. "You know what I mean." There was a pause as we crossed the street, Lincoln in the car, I on foot. It grew into a longer pause. The Talking Car weaved and almost clipped a parked Jeep Cherokee 4x4. "You drive like a blind man," I said.

"You may have something," Lincoln finally said, responding, I think, to my previous point.

"Not that you have to go ahead and make it work with the dentist just to prove something," I said, backtracking, as a small wave of guilt washed over me.

"Oh, not to worry about that, 'Vince: A Man's View,' " Lincoln's voice boomed as he coasted along. "I'm not getting involved with anyone to prove any points, especially not to you, my good friend who is so very wise and active that once a month he tells America what to think and how to love and which time of day it's best to bone."

"Please," I said. "There are major magazine editors sleeping all over this neighborhood."

"I'm ending it with Remy," Lincoln said in explanation, "because already I know I could never be around tooth rot and gingivitis and gum disease on a regular basis. That's just too much, sorry."

Lincoln drove me home. He and Remy had been going out for almost a month before I learned the last three letters in her name were D.D.S. Lincoln had held on to the secret of her spoiling profession as long as he could. The first week he told me she reminded him of a sabra from the kibbutz (Lincoln has never been to Israel). The second week he told me that she gardened, that she listened to German opera while doing the laundry, that she loved to sail. The third week he mentioned how talented a painter she was, what a beautiful black Lab she had. Right before I learned she was a dentist, I was sure he'd just gone and described the woman he'd been looking for as long as I'd known him, though she was a good decade older than the ones he usually went for. Correction: He'd just described the woman *I'd* been looking for. According to him, she was perfect. That's how I knew something was wrong.

> *Dear Vince,*
> *I don't usually write letters to the editor, but you've woken me from my slumber. Your column used to be somewhat be-*

nign and sprinkled with platitudes, but not unamusing. I've noticed that lately your column has turned puerile, even Neanderthal, in its view of women. One question for you, Vince: Did you and your friends sleep through the eighties?

"If you're gonna stay with the same woman," Orson, bassist in a jazz quartet that played up the street from Scrabbles, was telling me just before a snowy happy hour, "you gotta be creative." Periodically, Orson, the lone married man in his combo, would tell anyone at Scrabbles who hadn't already heard (a category none of us fell into) that he wanted no one feeling sorry for him because he wasn't, in his own words, "getting enough fresh." His wife and he played games, he said.

"I come home from work," Orson described for me, for the tenth or twelfth time now, "put on my dark suit, I say I'm with the I.R.S. I inform Nanette she owes Uncle Sam forty thousand dollars and just what exactly does she plan to do about it? Her books are a mess, she keeps a bunch of napkins and matchbooks in a shoebox and calls them receipts. I tell her we're putting a lien on the house, taking it over as assets, at which point she gets all flustered. I put my hand over her hand and soon enough she gives me a whole sob story, about how her 'husband' is out of town looking for work. She asks if there isn't some other way she could work off the money. 'Other way.' I love that. I'm a lucky guy, Mr. Andrew. Or maybe Nanette's a doctor and I'm the patient with a terminal tumor the size of a casaba and there's only one way she can leech it and pull me back to life." He laughed slowly, musically.

"A casaba," I said. "That's good, Orson."

Garth, the manager, stood from his bar stool, which was Orson's cue also to stand. Four heaping plates of free happy-hour cold cuts and tricolored fusilli were the limit.

"Hey," Orson said to me, "you ever want to write something about me and my wife in your column, let me know. I got the stories."

I looked at Garth and Eddie, the bartender, then back at Orson. "What are you talking about?"

"That thing you do for the magazine—what's it called? Victor?"
"Vince," I said.
"Yeah," said Orson. Guy the Waiter walked by with refills for the happy-hour cart and Orson was able to snare three wieners-in-blankets and a fetal gherkin.
"How'd you hear about Vince?" I asked him. Oh, come on: You told two friends, and they told two friends, and they told two friends, and so on and so on. You've been treating what was supposed to be a professional secret like it belonged in a Publishers Clearinghouse mailing.
"One of these guys here," Orson said.
"I guess maybe I told him," Eddie volunteered. "I didn't know it was privileged. I'm sorry."
Why should Eddie be held to a standard of discretion I myself had by now flouted dozens of times? "That's okay," I said.
During my first set, I played my Northeast Corridor roundup ("Rhode Island Is Famous for You," "(I'll Take) Manhattan," "Moonlight in Vermont," "Boola Boola," etc.), and hoped none of the patrons would request any of the dreaded contemporary classics, my definition of musical vomit: "Tomorrow" from *Annie*, the theme from *Love Story*, "Feelings," naturally. I love the Beatles, but not on cocktail piano. Don't even talk to me about "Memory" from *Cats*. "Send In the Clowns" used to be a pretty tune before I had to play it nine hundred times.
In my trance I surveyed the crowd, the cashier's area. The fatter the guy, the more likely he'll take a toothpick. Only anorexic or naturally very thin women take a single mint, the rest of us take a handful. Do something with. Column possibilities.
It looked as though it might be a slow evening, so I snuck a few more dollars into my tip glass. I segued into a Cole Porter tune, "Miss Otis Regrets," one of my favorites because I do this voluptuous quasi-*glissando* during the bridge that fakes listeners (customers and even some of the Scrabbles staff) into thinking I'm capable of such cascades all the time. A customer sat on my bench and sang into my ear, a quarter note off-key. His breath stank of alcohol. I turned to him, smiled. It was

all I could do not to swing my hips over and knock him to the floor; I can be terribly proprietary when it comes to my bench. The man's elbow came dangerously close to knocking the keyboard cover and smashing it closed, which drives me crazy. It was hard to concentrate with him crooning in my ear like a weepy hound, and harder still to reach my left hand over for chord changes. His expression was pure driver's license daze. "You play beautiful," he said.

"Thanks . . ."

"Morty," he said.

"Thanks, Morty," I said.

"Just beautiful," he said.

"Thank you, Morty." When I talk while playing, I say people's names a lot not to be chummy but to help keep the rhythm.

"Can you play something for me?" Morty said.

"I can play anything, Morty," I said. "If I've heard it or even if I haven't, Morty, and you can hum it, Morty, I can play it." A waitress trainee went in the out door to the kitchen and crashed into Diana. Glasses shattered, everyone applauded.

"Could you play the beautiful tune Barbra sings," Morty asked me, "the one Frank sings, 'Where Are the Clowns'—"

" 'Send In the Clowns,' " I said. "Sure, Morty."

Morty hit my knee. "Beautiful song," he said. "Could you play 'Bring On the'—"

" 'Send In the Clowns,' Morty," I said.

"Right," he said. "Could you play that for my wife over there?" With his drink leading the way, he pointed out Mrs. Morty, who smiled an insanely wide smile at me.

"Absolutely, Morty," I said. I swung into the opening arpeggios and he watched my fingers.

"Beautiful song," he said, and winked at me.

"It's lovely," I agreed. Before standing up, Morty squirted a fresh Alexander Hamilton into my palm, penance for his singing off-key and requesting rehash. "Hey, thanks, Morty," I said.

When Morty sat down with his wife, who smiled again to acknowledge I'd sent in the clowns, I did a run with my left hand, with my right placed the ten in the snifter, and quickly abandoned Sondheim for "My Funny Valentine," heaping on the Miles Davis inflections. Diana refreshed my ginger ale and laid across the piano top a curving trail of cheddar cheese–flavored goldfish. She wore the clown outfit that all Scrabbles employees but me have to wear: pink buttondown, argyle pink-and-gray vest, bow tie, chinos. Diana always introduced herself as a divorcée from Jackson Heights. She smiled toothlessly while stealing a few quick puffs on a cigarette.

"You have enough to write about in your Vinnie column?" she asked.

"Vince," I corrected.

"Vince," she conceded.

"So far, yeah."

"Your love life is so fascinating, is it?" she asked.

"I can't complain," I said.

"The one from Wall Street," Diana asked.

"Julie," I said.

"Julie. Nice-lookin', rich bitch, I bet she had a little hard-on all the time," Diana said in her endearingly dentalized Queens accent. She leaned across me to get at the ashtray she kept hidden inside the piano. Her breasts weighed against her vest like pouches of not-quite-ready pudding. "Is she still in the picture?"

"She's around," I lied.

Diana studied me. "When're ya gonna write a column about me?"

"When you start dating again and come up with a specific complaint about men," I said.

A far-off smile danced in her eyes. "You mean like, All you guys are pigs?"

"*Specific,*" I said. "You know what the word *specific* means, Tortarella? Come up with something more pointed. Tell me something we don't know."

"Excuse me, Leo Tolstoy," Diana said, exhaling smoke forcefully in my face. "You know, you could do worse than write about a character like me." Across the dining room a thick-necked brute waved his arms at us in a lunatic arc, as if his family had all been shot and he was desperately flagging down medical attention. "Fuck," Diana said. "Motz sticks. I knew it was too good to be true." She stabbed out her cigarette and disappeared into the kitchen.

The frantic customer sat with a woman far more captivating than he had a right to be paired with, even for a night. I segued into my medley of songs with the word *blue* in the title.

Light bulb. How do men *get* certain women? Vice versa? Poss. Vince idea. What does it say that men think of women as *get*table? *Have*able? Column idea.

As always, I ended the evening with Gershwin's "He Loves and She Loves." I walked home with Guy, our singing waiter. New York was beautiful out. The snowflakes were glistening and tumbled down in slow motion. "Where troubles melt like lemon drops," Guy sang, without warning, as we slid down Fifth Avenue.

"Away upon the chimney tops," I recited, à la Rex Harrison.

"That's where . . . you'll . . . find me," Guy sang. He told me he'd recently moved from the Upper East Side to the corner of West Fourth and Twelfth Streets, everyone's favorite Village conundrum. Guy was sweet and clear-faced. He elliptically described his upbringing outside Philadelphia, neatly refraining from actually using the term "Main Line" while still conveying the idea that his family had serious jing. If I hadn't caught on yet, he clinched it with an embarrassed allusion to his vintage MG Spider parked in some overpriced Village garage.

When we got to his corner I said, "Well, this is you."

"You want to come upstairs?" he asked. He undid the bottom two buttons of his camel-hair coat to get at keys.

I started to walk away. "Thanks, but I'm about to collapse."

"Maybe if you could just come upstairs and help me off with my pants," he said.

"I don't think so, Guy," I said, remarkably in stride.

"You want to fool around?" he said.

"What?"

"You want to get sucked?" Guy said.

"I'm not interested, thank you," I said.

A look of such pain crossed Guy's face that I felt as if I'd struck him. He lifted his foot to examine the bottom of his shoe, as if maybe he'd stepped in something, but it was only so that when he replanted it he would be closer to me. My diligent nostrils took in a snort of his breath and the quick licorice smell.

"Better take nightcaps *after* you've refilled the ketchup bottles, Guy," I said. "For your own sake. Diana says Garth calibrates the expensive stuff with Magic Marker."

"You don't like to get sucked?" Guy asked.

"Guy, I'm talking about the alcohol," I said. "I can smell your breath from here."

"But only by girls," he said.

"Listen, Guy, I'm straight," I said. "You know that. I'm not interested."

He nodded in defeat. "I wasn't sure," he said.

Gorgeous. "Come on, Guy. Me? *Moi?*"

He plowed on. "So you only like to get sucked by girls?"

"Hey, now," I said.

Guy took out his keys. He exposed the fleshy inside of his lower lip to indicate how-do-you-like-them-apples incredulity. "You're Jewish?" he asked. In a sad, awkward way, it was rhetorical.

Guy looked past me, as if he saw someone he knew, then turned and opened the door to his brownstone lobby. "See ya," he called out without turning back, and held on to the railing as he took the stairs one by one.

> *Dear Vince,*
> *While not the World's Greatest Mom, I would put my*
> *children up against anyone's. They try their hardest in*

school, Dian the older one has just started tutoring men-
tally handicapped children and Deirdre the younger one
has her daddy's blue eyes and thinks he's just the best. Both
do some kind of athletics. Ron, whose promotion was long
overdue, and I have had our problems, esp. since his
mother came down with Alzheimer's but I'd give our mar-
riage a solid B, B+, esp. in this day and age.

   Why am I telling you all this, Vince? Because your lovely
piece about breaking up ("Who Broke Up With Whom?")
made me write my first "letter to the editor." When you wrote
about how your breakup with your girlfriend was "100%
50-50" and how different you both were professionally, and
that maybe sex clouded the issue, you made me feel as if you
shared a part of yourself, and so I hope others will share with
you. I don't know who you are, Vince, but if someday you
"come out of the closet," I want you to know my home is open
to you for tea and a chat. I will gladly push my work aside.

With warm regards,
Mrs. Ronald ——d

My reading of the latest batch of Vince letters was interrupted by a
call from Monica, in the ——*r* Research Department. Was she still
deeply tanned, I wondered, even in late winter?

"Someone just called the magazine trying to get in touch with you,"
said Monica, with what sounded like three nights and four days in St.
Maarten buttering her voice. "She only knew your first name and that
you write Vince. I didn't give her your number."

"Good. Thanks," I said. "You guys look out for me."

". . . and I told her I'd pass on the message," Monica said. "Her name
is—shoot, it was here a second ago . . . oh, I'm sending you another
batch—where *is* that?—batch of letters, canceled subscriptions are up
to nineteen from the orgasm column, talk about delayed—here we go.
Remy Kleinwort," Monica read. "She says she's a dentist-friend of your
friend Lincoln Crye? Does this make sense?"

"Sure, give me the number," I said. Why was Lincoln's ex calling *me*? I dialed the number.

"Hello, Dr. Kleinwort?" I said when Remy Kleinwort, D.D.S., picked up. "This is Lincoln's . . . writer-friend."

"I'm sorry about calling your magazine but I didn't know your last name," the dentist said. "The only thing I knew was that you and Lincoln collaborate on some men's column there."

"Yes, we do fine work together." I rolled my eyes for no one's benefit but my own.

"Lincoln had only good things to say about you," the dentist said. "Probably you're wondering why I called."

"I guess I am," I said.

"I'm just sorry it didn't work out with your friend—*our* friend," Remy said. "And I suppose I wanted to understand what was going on with him."

"Okay," I said, nodding like a doctor listening to a list of symptoms.

"I tried with him," the dentist said. "At least I thought I did. You want to know what I think? I think I'm just too old. I think Lincoln wants a little girl."

"Please don't feel you need to explain to me," I told her. "I'm nobody."

"I may just want to," Dr. Kleinwort said. "Explain, I mean."

"Okay," I said. That's two noncommittal *okays* in my last three utterances. My Vince license should be revoked right here, right now, I thought. "You want to know what *I* think?" I offered up in compensation. "I'm not certain Lincoln *ever* wants these things to work out."

"I'm sure you're very busy," the dentist said, "but I was wondering if I could take you out to dinner and pick your brain."

Just don't pick at my salad, Vince thought. "Okay," I said. Three *okays*. You really are one of the conversational giants.

"Good," said Dr. Remy Kleinwort. "Great. By the way, what *is* your last name?"

I told her.

"Do you always ring twice?" she asked. "Does just everybody say that?"

"No, no," I said. "I've never heard that one before."

Let's say I have a dinner consultation slash date. Let's suppose my date and I buy wine, then dine at a small, West Village bistro without a liquor license. No, I got it: Suppose my date is a dentist. Yeah, let's say I'm a half-assed piano player slash adviser to the lovelorn who doesn't know shit about being in love or in lorn, and my date, as it turns out, is an extremely appealing cleaner slash fixer of teeth, though not at all my type. And just suppose my date is the girlfriend, sort of—practically ex-girlfriend, really—of my best friend.

"Kleinwort?" I said as Remy tipped the bottle of California Burgundy against the rim of my glass and poured me another. We sat at a twotop nestled toward the back of our Bleecker Street hideaway, safely away from the roving accordion maniac. "That's an unusual name," I said.

She's perfect, Vince pointed out to me. *Court a couple months, have some heart-stopping sex at a Vermont B&B, introduce her to the fam, maybe she comes to a Seder, things look serious, follow up with the inevitable "I'm not ready to commit, it's me, Rem, not you, me," because you are, after all, a man—a.k.a. a pig—and she is, after all, a dentist . . . that's what? Three, four, five columns right there.*

Remy said before dental school she'd done graduate work in literature at Yale but grew disillusioned and bailed before earning her degree. Excellent. Grew tired of Deconstruction, she said, that critical theory by which out-of-shape, balding French guys say things no one understands, thereby getting lots of anorexic American grad students to sleep with them.

Can you believe the gem your friend Lincoln has ditched? Vince whispered, barely able to contain himself.

Remy said that after much soul-searching and a stint in the Peace Corps she decided to become a dentist because her father was one and because, well, believe it or not, she *liked* it. "People laugh a lot in our business," said Remy Kleinwort, D.D.S. "Though not for the reason you'd think."

"Laugh," I said.

"Sure, laugh," said Remy Kleinwort, D.D.S.

I nodded and pretended Remy and I were on identical wavelengths, pretended Remy was not from, say, the Crab Nebula, pretended I, like everyone, knew the obvious reasons why dentists and dental hygienists are out there splitting a gut eight to five-thirty, Monday to Friday.

Don't her gray eyes put you in mind of winter? They do me.

"Your friend Lincoln just never wanted to give it a chance," said Remy Kleinwort, careening somewhat randomly to the next topic.

"These things happen," I said. "It wasn't meant to be."

It wasn't meant to be? These things happen? Now my Vince card *definitely* should have been revoked. A tidy collection of columns under my belt and this is the most insightful solace I could manage? *It wasn't meant to be?* Next thing you know I'll be comforting the dentist with the ever-popular *There, there.*

"You have a great smile," said Dr. Kleinwort, who looked something like Jane Pauley, but without the TV varnish. "Your teeth are exceptionally well-spaced."

I offered the doctor some spinach gnocchi, which her mouth plucked eagerly from my held-out fork. She told me more about her brief affair with Lincoln. This is good, I thought. I'm getting both sides of the breakup. Column idea.

"For instance, one night we got into an abstract discussion about babies," Remy said, "and Lincoln reacted in just the most banal, male way, the kind of behavior you only read about in trashy women's magazines. Oh. Sorry."

"That's fine," I said. "Keep going."

"Then Lincoln starts in with his own theory," Remy said.

"He has many theories," I said, and the Vince in me stared down into my gnocchi bowl for a moment so that when I looked back up my face would be bright with color from the blood rush. "The man's a big theory guy," I said, flush and hale as an Irish schoolboy.

"His theory," Remy said, "was that a woman couldn't conceive unless she was in love and maybe not even then—maybe *both* parties had to be in love." The dental scientist/dental surgeon helped herself to another one of my gnocchi balls. "Mind you, I didn't say it was a *good* theory," Remy said, shaking her head.

Normally, I would have gone home immediately once the delicious Italian dinner with Remy was over; normally, I'd have gone home, called Lincoln, and tried to break him of his resolve to end things; would have advised him to give it another shot with her and if it didn't work out *then*, to give it still another shot. I really *do* want my friends to be happy; I really do.

But because Vince found Remy to be so interesting, I didn't go home and talk anyone out of what they were feeling. Our internalia and genitalia were drying up. I hadn't had Biblical knowledge in the many months since the night of the Unisphere, a fact you know as well as I since I most certainly would have informed you of its occurrence, probably in boldface. Vince? Vince was Vince. Vince has an appetite. Vince needs material. Without it he dies. I'm not proud of what I did with Remy but I also offer no apologies. Let's just say I made no effort to help Lincoln—who, after all, was a grown man perfectly capable of making his own rational decisions and anyway how do we really know what anyone else wants, or needs, to be happy?

What I'm saying, basically, is Vince, my mass-market *Doppelgänger*, was terribly curious to know what nookie with a D.D.S. was like.

"I'd love to get a real tour of a dental office," I said over cannoli and coffee, certain I must be blushing at the transparency of Vince's machinations. "A behind-the-scenes look. What goes on when no one's in the chair, no holds barred. What goes on below the gum line, if you will."

With the point of her napkin, Dr. Remy Kleinwort dabbed the corners of her seemingly clean mouth, a gesture I'd only ever associated with WASPS. "That's quite a line there," the dentist said.

"I didn't mean, please understand, I thought—"

"I didn't say no," Dr. Kleinwort said.

Her office was in the Bronx. This was no Julie love safari spot. On the other hand, Remy did show me the lab with shelves and shelves of plaster impressions of teeth.

In the dark corner of her partner's examining room, or "operatory" (you learn something new), stood a huge Styrofoam sculpture that was either a tooth or an albino Red Delicious apple. All around Remy's operatory were Dental Awareness Month pictures for the kids—Ms. Flossie, Mr. Gum Abrasion, Phrenum the Dog. I sat down in Remy's extremely comfortable green leather chair. I laid my arm on the armrest while Remy Kleinwort, D.D.S., stood over me explaining all manner of dentition-related issues. I learned that the apple is considered "nature's toothbrush" because its juices clean away whatever sugar the apple deposits on your teeth. I put my hand on her arm. Dr. Kleinwort, a reckless and exciting conversationalist, then asked me what my most treasured dream was. I took her hand and told her I'd like to see and do everything in the world I possibly could; hence the need to check out a dentist's office in the Bronx after hours. *I'd like to sleep with several women at once,* Vince thought.

"I'd like to ride in a hot-air balloon, perform a successful Heimlich," I said.

I'd like to sleep with a black woman. I'd like to have a position named after me.

"I'd like to maybe write a novel someday," I said.

"Lincoln also tried that one on me," said Remy, lightly stroking her knuckles against my jaw, then suddenly clamping my mouth shut and ordering me to smile to make sure there was no malocclusion. "The writer bit," she said. "It didn't work. He thought he could coax me into bed."

"But Lincoln's not a writer," I pointed out. "I *am.*"

"Of course you are," she said. "The great Vince."

I pretended to be taken aback. I was sure that Lincoln was sharing

Vince-classified information within hours—*moments*—of talking to any woman in the eighteen-to-thirty-four age range, probably younger. I just wasn't sure how often he was faithful to the truth and pointed out that he was merely Vince's *friend,* and how often he passed himself off as the real thing. "So you never let him?" I asked. "I take that back. It's none of my business."

"No, it isn't," said the Doctor of Dental Science and, according to the framed degree on the wall, a highly decorated graduate of the New York University College of Dentistry. "But we only slept together twice. No, three times. Never in my office. And never in the chair. He kept dressed. He's like a grown boy."

Remy squeezed into the chair with me. I could feel where her thumb had paused to check for swollen glands. "Push the button," I said.

Electronically, the chairback slid down. The leg rest extended.

"I hope you don't take this the wrong way," I said, "but can we do the gas?"

Remy looked at me for a very long moment, then left the room. I heard her rooting around in her partner's operatory. I wondered if a miniature tape recorder was a worthwhile professional investment. Dr. Kleinwort returned with the fun.

She hooked up the mask and put it on herself first. Minutes later, I was licking her cheek and staring past her at a statuette of Molar Man across the room. Remy moved her hand from my thigh to my fly. Naturally, I had trouble getting it up.

"This has never happened before," I giggled.

"Never?" laughed Remy. There seemed an urgency to her voice I hadn't expected; I'd expected complete understanding. Column idea.

"*Never,*" I confirmed. In between giggles my words sounded slurry to me.

"Well, Vince, what can I do to help?" I heard in her plea the voice of generations of decent Americans—grass-roots organizations, splinter political groups, founders of food co-ops, just plain Good Samaritans. Well, Remy, I was moved to suggest, you could recycle. Adopt a refusenik. Send food shipments to Africa. Either this is some powerful fucking nitrous or I am once again losing my mind.

"I don't know," I said. "It's just not working. It's got to be the laughing gash."

She started to laugh.

"Why are you laughing?" I laughed. "Don't laugh at me."

"You said 'gash,' " she laughed. "Laughing *gash*." She was practically in hysterics now.

"Listen, I'm really sorry about this . . ."—I made rabbit ears with my fingers as I felt a smile creeping up—*"problem."*

"Well, don't worry about it," said Remy Kleinwort, D.D.S, calming down a bit. It sounded through her giggles as though she was trying to convince herself as much as me. My hand blazed a slow trail over and under her shirt. She squeezed my hand tight, the old pressure-on-the-wrist warning. Yikes. "Please," she laughed. "Really, it's okay."

Remy gently kissed my closed eyelids and I had a sense of déjà vu. Why did I recognize the technique she was using? Had Julie done that? Cheryl? Someone else? Did I dream I wanted it done to me? Then it dawned on me: Luther, a university provost, quoted in my upcoming April column, "25 Things That Make Men Feel Secure." It was *he* who had craved the tender eyelid-kissing, not me.

But Luther, a university provost, is you. Isn't he?

I can't remember anymore.

While I continued to laugh, nothing continued happening below. Even though Remy was no longer touching me, I sensed how knotty things would get if nothing continued to continue happening. The worse I envisioned the aftermath, the worse my attempts at performance got. I didn't spend my energy thinking of Remy, of sexual turn-ons, of women I'd been with (or, more likely, never been with), I didn't spend it flexing and relaxing my muscles; rather I spent it considering the imminent damage control necessary. I laughed at the image of the *National Enquirer* headline: "I Slept with Vince . . . and He Went Soft." I laughed at myself, five years down the road, my once good life and career shattered; I was now working the graveyard shift at the main post office on Thirty-third and Eighth, on my forehead a mole had newly erupted and a thick, wiry gray hair drooped out of it, I carried in my back pocket a pilfered copy of *Soldier of Fortune* magazine, or *Juggs*. When people found out what my last name was, and that I'd ended up doing the job I was doing, I'd giggle at it too, and my supervisor, a certain Mr. Gum Abrasion, would yell at me to wipe the drool off my shirt and get back to sorting letters.

Remy must have thought of something that struck her as extremely funny, and each time she quieted down to try and share it with me, she started laughing again. While I laughed intermittently at her little show, I attempted again to manufacture a cheap erection, but it was more tensed quads and glutes than anything else. *Yikes.* Remy abruptly abandoned her funny thought and did what she could. What exactly does "missing-limb syndrome" feel like? I wondered. Dental Awareness Night was not going well. Come on, concentrate, be one with your body. Foods You Mispronounced as a Child. *Pasketti. Frankittuh. Hayngubooger.* I couldn't decide if it was the guilt of being with my friend's ex that was holding me back, or something else. *Saynguhwitch. Eye screen.* I went the highbrow route, gunning for sympathy.

"I guess I don't feel completely unencumbered to do this," I chuckled, astounded that I could use the word *unencumbered* ripped on N_2O. "You know, with Lincoln," I said. Remy's head rested against my chest and I think her eyes were closed. She had a big, pre-laugh smile on her face and I was a little hurt that she wasn't listening carefully to everything I said. Also, it made me laugh. "I think it's the mood in here, a mood of . . . antibiotics," I whispered. *Can we go in the teeth room again?* I tried saying next, but I don't know if it ever made its way out of my mouth.

"It happens to everyone," Dr. Kleinwort laughed, matter-of-factly. "That's probably why this is happening to you." She patted me, indelicately. "That's what they all say once they get in the chair."

"You said you'd never been in the chair," I pointed out, deeply confused now by the laughing gas.

"Maybe I have," said Remy. "Once."

Her deceit excited me. She squeezed.

"You seem to respond to suggestions of betrayal," she said. "Why not imagine I'm a married woman."

You got it, Sarge. So say she's a married woman. Say The Husband is away for the weekend. Say The Husband's out of town and I'm with the I.R.S. and the books are a mess and The Wife keeps a bunch of napkins and matchbooks in a shoebox and calls them receipts, and just what exactly does The Wife intend to do about it? Say all that.

I got a little harder, a pneumatic presence snaking its way through me. Then dumbly I thought: Wait, *is* she married?

"Wait, *are* you married?" I giggled.

But several tantalizingly obscure cerebral events seemed to have occurred without my knowledge and again Rome toppled. I wondered if dentists go to a special furniture store to buy the swiveling circular dental table my hand was now resting on. Naturally I found this a scream.

The D.D.S. said, "I'm legally separated."

If she was trying to get me aroused again, through deadpan delivery of a provocative untruth, then it was sweet of her to say so. But still it was no dice. What was my problem? Excellent question. In fact, I didn't know what my problem was. If I wanted reasons I certainly had enough sound suspects. Guilt. The morbid setting. Hygienic fragrances in the office that evoked the precognitive past. The N_2O.

She gave a gentle tap on my fly and kissed my cheek maternally. "I guess we won't have to concern ourselves with ringing twice," Dr. Kleinwort said, a particularly gratuitous witticism at the time, I thought.

And, then again, maybe the source of my problem was something completely different. Maybe it was something I hadn't seriously entertained—that I wanted more than just to be inside.

As I tucked in my shirt, I realized, *Wait:* Has there ever been a moment in your life when you *didn't* feel like that?

I made two extremely authentic pig oinks. Remy fell to the floor laughing.

6/All Men Are Pigs

THE FIRST Thursday every other month the boys gather for a poker game. I liked the camaraderie, the ordered-up food (chips, pizza, Chinese, a four-foot sub), the mock showdowns over an especially rich pot. But for the first time since college I considered missing a game I was in town and free for. The group's changing dynamics had begun diminishing the enjoyment. The games started later (too much work) and broke up earlier (increasingly demanding relationships, burgeoning families). One of our core eight now had kids; one, Big Dave, was finally a newlywed after a stormy three-year engagement; one was gay and living with someone; another was virtually living with someone; another, a guy who worked for a think tank, was one of those right-of-center, good all-around wonks born without a penis. Then there were Brian, Lincoln, and me, who apparently had complete license to tomcat/scavenge, with periodic interludes of sensitivity.

The game was in Brian's East Village loft. In an hour I'd split the

pot on one small hand. I wondered where Julie, my love safari partner, was right at that moment and I wondered, too, if you can make
yourself fall in love with someone after knowing them for years and
not being in love (though magnificently in like) with them. Was the
very fact that I was turning this question over in my mind a sign of ma-
turity? Or was it a sign I'd thrown in the towel on finding love—*love*
love, I mean? Was it an idea for a column? Is some form of self-
hypnosis possible, I wondered, whereby you can live happily but de-
ludedly with a not-quite-right partner into your golden years? Is
compromise what my friend Big Dave, all six feet six inches of him,
finally yielded to by tying the knot a year ago after threatening countless times to ditch The Fiancée (now The Wife) and law partnership
both and move to Katmandu and give up altogether on the notion of
connubial yuppie bliss?

I anted once more as two others divided the previous pot between
them. Lincoln sat back from the table, spinning a basketball on his fin-
gertip. Fred scooped a chip from Lincoln's fattening empire and put in
for him, then continued to read my big sex article in ———*r*, occasionally quoting aloud from it. Fred told me that on his way over for the
game he'd stopped at a newsstand and plunked down the two-fifty to
buy the magazine, just to read my story. I was not unmoved.

"You really should be better at this than you are, Vincent," Lincoln
said to me, skimming the basketball with his free hand, rotating it on his
index finger faster and faster until it was an orange blur. "Piano players
have highly developed fingers."

"The fingers of history's great pianists are characterized more by
strength than length," I said. "Brahms had relatively squat fingers. You
just love calling me Vince, don't you."

"Can you get your name legally changed?" Brian asked me. "No last
name—just Vince."

"Andrew's been good to me," I said.

"You realize, of course, there's a movie in this," Brian said. "Young
man as Dear Abby-ish type, how it helps and pollutes his sex life. Matt

Dillon or Keanu Reeves could play you, maybe Cusack. Just sit down and write the damn treatment."

" 'Oral sex,' " Fred said, quoting me to the group, " 'is, year in, year out, the carnal Honda of consumer satisfaction.' Too much."

"I think now *Consumer Reports* says Nissan," George said.

"Do fish spit?" asked Jeremy, stacking his red, white, and blue chips neatly in front of him. Jeremy worked hard at maintaining his reputation as the human being most likely to ask totally irrelevant questions. No one ever answered him, mostly because when we play poker no one really listens to anyone else. Usually it's just ante, deal, talk trash, bet, declare, bet. "When a television network advertises a show," Jeremy asked, "is it free, or do the show's producers buy commercial time from the network itself? Anybody?"

Lincoln stopped spinning the basketball when it became obvious he could go on forever. His fingernails were rimmed with ball orange.

"The Wife showed me your piece, and I do mean that," Big Dave said to me, his baritone reaching to the far walls of the loft apartment. "It made me sad."

"Sad? Why sad, Big Dave?" asked Lincoln. He put one hand under his chin, the other at the back of his head, and cracked his neck, producing a gruesome machine-gun crunch.

"I used to think it was my God-given right to try and screw every woman in America," Big Dave said.

"Whose deal?" asked Sandy, holding up the blue deck and finally offering it to me. Sandy was the most intent of all the players and the most frequent loser. "Deal, Andrew, or Vince, or whatever the hell you're going by these days."

". . . and now that I'm married," Big Dave concluded self-importantly, nodding at Lincoln and Brian and me as he tossed in a blue chip, "I have to leave the screwing to you boys, I suppose." Big Dave's collegiate discus-throwing career was cut short when he tested positive for steroids. In a much-publicized case, he argued before the amateur athletic governing body that he'd never used steroids and just had an unusually high level of natural testosterone. Apparently there are such men in the world. Personally, I take Big Dave's word. "You seeing anyone, Lincoln?" Big Dave asked.

"Yes and no," Lincoln said. "This week, yes. A wee, wonderful Scottish-American body. But she's just too damn perky. You know the type, Chief?"

"And how," Jeremy said, cryptically.

"Cards, let's go," Sandy said. I dealt the next up card in five-stud.

"What about you, Vance?" Big Dave asked me.

"Vince," I corrected.

"Whatever," Big Dave said. "You must be living the good life these days."

"I'm no priest," I said.

"Be careful," Fred warned. "Old Chinese saying: 'You only as germ-free as your most recent pudendum.'"

"Let's go, money in, money in," Sandy said. "Brian, your bet. Less talk, more action." I could envision us as eight chimpanzees sitting around wearing visors and starched shirts with armbands, smoking cigars.

"Brian?" Big Dave asked. "You still a Peeping Tom? You have any mushrooms I can buy off you? How's it hanging these days?"

"Yeah," Brian said distractedly, checking out the cards dealt so far, before tossing in two red chips, each worth a quarter. "I got a nice one. Fred's met her. She's nice, right, Fred?"

"Nice," Fred said.

"Nice, but a little moody," said Brian. "She's got too many personalities."

"Think of it as going out with several women at once," Jeremy offered. "Hey, whatever happened to the one who always wore black? Vanessa."

"Oh, forget Vanessa," Brian said. "Jeremy, I wouldn't fuck Vanessa with your dick."

At age ten, the average American boy and girl display roughly the same measure of self-confidence; by age twelve, that girl is hard at work on a state-of-the-art self-esteem deficit. The anorexic, according to studies, *knows* her behavior is foolish—she will say so on a questionnaire, for instance—but she will not act on this knowledge.

Fred looked up from my article and threw down his personally bought copy of ———*r*. "Okay, which one am I?" he asked me. "No fooling now."

"You're Kurt, a computer programmer," I said, pushing in two red chips.

"But Kevin, a Seeing Eye dog trainer, also," Fred offered.

"No, you're not," I said. "That's Dave. Not Big Dave. Another Dave."

"Dave, your friend the physics graduate student?" Fred said.

"Does anyone here know if fish spit?" Jeremy asked. "Really."

"Yes," I said.

"They do?" Jeremy said. "How can they possibly spit?"

"No," I said. "I was answering Fred. Yes, 'Kevin, a Seeing Eye dog trainer,' is my friend Dave, the physics graduate student Dave."

"Then who's Trace, a quantum mechanic," Fred asked, "and Jason, a NASA nutritionist? And where do you come up with these names and occupations?"

"Actually, those are both Frank," I said.

"Frank Frank?" Lincoln asked. "The one who was arrested Frank?"

"No, another Frank," I said. "You don't know this Frank. This Frank is a teacher."

"But Kevin's quote sure sounds like me. Come on," Fred pleaded, picking up the magazine once more. "I think maybe you're confused. 'Kissing is more intimate than intercourse, and kissing the genitals is the most intimate act of all'?" Fred read. "That's me. 'It's a deeply reassuring thing when a woman says, "I want to eat you . . ."'? That's me to a T. I say stuff like that. I think I said that. Are you sure it was Kevin? I mean, the other Dave, the graduate student?"

"No," I said. "You may be right."

"The fact is, they're all me, all the quotes," Lincoln said, flopping over his cards and abandoning his hand. "Let's go, Vincent, your call. I want to get in the next hand already."

"Is it illegal to get braces if you're over twenty-one?" asked Jeremy.

"Ask Vince," Lincoln said, looking straight at me. "He knows a lot about *teeth*." I'd told him about Dental Awareness Night with Remy Kleinwort, D.D.S., and he couldn't have cared less. I hadn't felt it necessary also to tell him of my little problem that night.

"Ask Lincoln," I said, looking straight back. "He knows a lot about child law." I dealt the last card. "I appreciate your interest, Fred," I said. "I really do. I think of you and Lincoln and Bri and one or two others as the sort of bird's-eye view from the penis."

"What about me?" Sandy asked, for the first time looking up from his deep study of everyone else's cards. "What am I?"

"Listen, Sandy," Brian said, "you'd better start sleeping with someone soon or you're off the A-list entirely."

"Can animals be gay?" Jeremy asked.

We played two more hands before Brian telephoned for Chinese. Lincoln knelt next to Brian's stereo and pulled out *La Bohème*. The search for the right woman, Fred was telling all of us now, was very much like Showdown, the five-card game we played at the end of the night in which we each toss ten bucks into the pot and the first guy turns over a card, then the second guy keeps turning over his cards until he has the first guy beat or runs out of cards, then the third guy keeps turning over *his* cards until he has the first and second guy beat or runs out of cards, the fourth guy does the same, and so on. "Two years ago I was with a woman who was good, not great," Fred said, "and when I found one who was better—"

"Danielle?" I asked.

"Danielle," he confirmed, "I dropped the first one. And if I find one who's better than *that,* and I can get her, then I'll drop Danielle. It's a can't-lose system because I keep trading up."

"I like Danielle," I said.

"Me, too," said George.

"Be that as it may," Fred said, "it's a can't-lose system."

"Look, Anj," said Lincoln, nodding at Fred, and I was pleased to note that for once he'd called me by a non-Vince moniker, "someone even more fucked up than me."

Fred gave Lincoln the finger. Diana was right, Cheryl was right, women are right. Men really are pigs. A new hand was being dealt.

"Alison tells me she loves your column," Brian said to me, referring to his little sister. "I think she's really getting to like you."

"That's Vince she's hot for, not me," I said, charitably. "Anyway, can we please talk about something besides women and sex? It's a little like a busman's holiday."

We played awhile to the strains of Puccini, the only other sounds the sporadic, soothing click of chips and Lincoln's expert shuffling of the red deck. The Chinese food rang from downstairs.

"Hey, Vince," Brian said to me, standing to buzz the guy up, "how about this for a column idea, or maybe a short story: It's the Garden of Eden, Eve has just gotten the first orgasm. She's totally flying, she's wrapped around Adam content as hell, but Adam is scared shitless because he doesn't know what just happened and he doesn't know if he can do it again. All you need now is a title and some funny dialogue." Brian walked over to his window, picked up his binoculars, and looked into the apartment of the woman who stir-fries topless.

"What does it mean, 'I love you'?" asked Big Dave at—for him—an unnaturally gentle volume. I looked up and saw he was looking right at me.

"What does it *mean*?" Sandy asked, about to wisecrack. One by one, the others looked to our huge friend, imagining his question was just more of the same, playing around, kidding—and one by one we saw the frantic, pleading look in Big Dave's damp, boyish eyes.

So. Things with The Wife were even rockier than any of us had thought.

"First of all, Large David," Lincoln said, gamely trying to defuse the moment, " 'I love you' is a question, not a statement, especially when lovers say it, *especially* for the first time. No one says it to hear what it sounds like. They say it to hear what kind of return they can expect on their investment."

Big Dave yawned hard, and the bunched pain and redness of a long workday at a prestigious, cutthroat Park Avenue law firm made his face look all of a sudden grotesque. He saw Sandy's bet. Everyone folded but Sandy and me. "Big David," Lincoln said, "I know this guy in my gallery? His father died last year of a heart attack during sex, and now he can't climax—the dealer can't—because he's afraid if he does, he'll die just like his father. I know a curator, after he quit smoking he stopped screwing because he realized he only did it for the cigarette afterward. You know what Sophocles said when they kidded him that he was too old to get an erection?"

"What?" Big Dave asked bloodlessly.

" 'Thank God that's over with,' " Lincoln said.

"Where do you come up with this shit?" Big Dave asked.

"I'm out there in the jungle," Lincoln said. "Every day. Like you used to be, Chief. I'm out hunting and gathering, at Knicks games, downtown, the Soho galleries, I'm at pro-choice rallies at Columbia and NYU. Sometimes I sneak upstairs at Orthodox synagogues, a great way to meet Jewish women."

Big Dave, it turned out, did not have the flush he was going for. His sadness had only bought him a pair of jacks. Neither that, nor my trip fives, was good enough to beat Sandy's straight. I stood and followed Big Dave into the kitchen for a drink. "Is it just me," Big Dave asked me, "or does every man fear at some point that right at the ejaculatory moment, what is about to shoot out is not semen but blood, or some sickening mixture of both?"

I scratched my head. Come inside off the ledge, Big Dave, there's help for things like this, even for giants like you. "That's a new one on me, Dave," I said, "but maybe we should open it up to the gang."

"No, they don't know anything," he said. "None of them knows a fucking thing."

I didn't know what to say to this, so I busied myself with a carton of fried rice. My fortune-cookie fortune read, YOU HAVE YEARNING FOR PERFECTION.

"You want to talk about it?" I asked.

Big Dave pulled a beer from the fridge, unscrewed it, and swigged. From the butter bin he took a tinfoil packet, undid it, and stared miserably at the mushrooms inside for a long moment, then closed them up and put them back. I shook my head at him. *I know,* my head shake was supposed to say. He nodded back. *I know you know,* I think his nod said. I should have given him one more gesture, a follow-up, but I didn't know how to mime *I don't know shit.*

As if his huge right arm were not part of his huge body, he reached back stiffly and lifted the receiver from the wall phone. He made no motion to suggest I should leave, then typed in a phone number. "Hey, there," he said into the phone, not taking his stare off me. "Duh widdoo boy is woozeen his widdoo shirt," he said. "Howz duh widdoo girl?"

Oh, crap, Dave. Not you, too.

I raised my eyebrows and started to walk out. Big Dave gripped my arm as I moved past him. "Wait," he said to me.

What, I mouthed.

"Does duh widdoo girl," Big Dave said into the receiver, "want to speak to Mistoo Vince, who know *awwwl* about dese tings?"

I felt my face flush. Big Dave's own face looked completely lifeless. Fred walked into the kitchen. "Um?" he said quietly to Big Dave, holding his fist to his ear. "Danielle could call any minute."

Big Dave nodded. Fred smiled, took a beer, looked at both of us, and walked out.

"All right, then," Big Dave said into the phone now in his deep, suddenly ridiculous grown-up voice, then shrugged his shoulders at me. "So where was the little baby doll all fucking afternoon?" I heard him say as I slipped from his grasp and walked out.

Work on my going-nowhere-and-not-particularly-fast-either novel was thankfully interrupted by a call from Monica at ———r Research.

Monica, outrageously sun-kissed Monica. Heat of my heart, fire in my groin. Mo. Ni. Ca. "What can I do for you, Monica?" I asked.

"Your article got the most letters last month," she told me. "According to our reader survey, 'What Men Don't Tell Women About Sex but Want to, by Vince' was, quote, 'extremely divided between those who thought it was incredibly honest and helpful, and those who were irate that we published it. There were thirty-one canceled subscriptions, two marriage proposals, and several other kinds of proposals.' Unquote. Forty-nine percent of those who read the article would like to see more big features like it by Vince, twenty-two percent thought it was sexist, twenty-four percent thought it was sexist *and* want to see more, three percent didn't know or care. Two percent had never heard of Vince even though they're subscribers. There's a four percent chance of sampling error. So I guess women love you and hate you."

"Thirty-one cancellations," I said. "Not bad."

" 'What Men Don't Tell Women' may qualify as one of the first truly great post-Crash essays," Monica said.

"Is that you talking or the reader survey?" I said.

"Me," she said.

"Thank you, Monica."

"The reader survey also says 'What Men Don't Tell Women' may turn out to be one of the most widely read articles in the magazine's history."

A wonderful document, that reader survey. I could use it for leverage when negotiating my upcoming contract.

"Anyway," said Monica, "I'll send you a big batch. A few of the letters say you're just like every other man and really hate women."

"Hate women?" I said. "How come any man engaged in observing and analyzing and discussing women eventually gets accused of hating women?"

"I'd tell you," said smart, tanned, cynical Monica, "but my lunch date just arrived. Ciao."

Dear Vince,
After reading "What Men Don't Tell Women About Sex but Want To," I tried some of the suggestions on my boyfriend, and was he surprised. I thank you, my boyfriend thanks you.

To ——r Subscription Dept:
Re: Vince's "What Men Don't Tell Women About Sex":
I have returned my renewal form marked "please cancel."
Disappointed in the editors,

The most enthusiastic responses were from younger readers, often ones with girl-boy names (Dani, Terry, Dee, Nikki) who wrote in scooped, overwrought script—circles floating above *i*'s like stringless balloons, *g*'s and *y*'s like expectant mothers reclining on propped pillows. The strongest criticism came from older readers. They had preteen daughters scampering about the house, they claimed, and my article was a cold slap in the face of innocence—or, more aptly, a forceful hand to the back of the head.

Brell phoned to ask if I'd write another article ("5 Ways Men Have Changed") above and beyond the call of column duty. Only this time, for the first time, I could—cross her heart—use my own name. I prevailed upon my usual cadre of buddies for insight and undergrowth, while also manufacturing the occasional quote from the occasional sorry sap (Percy, a fur trapper; Ignatius, a freelance Egyptologist) when I couldn't get any of my friends to say something I thought needed to be said. When I turned in the story, Brell flipped quickly through the manuscript, her green eyes flashing over the pages. We were in her office overlooking Forty-fifth Street and her lunch was the usual fruit salad, oat-bran bagel, and cranberry-flavored sparkling club soda. "You certainly get colorful quotes," Brell cracked.

"What does *that* mean?" I asked.

"Nothing," said Brell, with a lupine twitch of the nose. "Just that I know you also had the column to do this month and whatever else you have, and I know what it's like writing on deadline."

So my weird occupations and . . . *lively* quotes had bothered her. "I'm lucky," I said. "I have colorful friends."

"I'm sure you do," Brell nodded. "I can't imagine why you wouldn't." Listen, Brell, I wanted to tell her, it isn't so much what I put *in* as what I leave *out*. Trust me. That first Vince I wrote, the column about the Atlantic City bachelor party that helped me land this gig? I conveniently left out the part about how any man who's been to such a shindig knows the cruel math: There's a 25 percent chance a happily involved single man wants to do the stripper. If he's happily married, add another 25 percent. Has kids? Add another 10. Single and *un*involved? Add 10 more. What are we up to now, 70 percent? If he's involved and *un*happy, add 20 more, if his wife's more than three months pregnant, another 5, and if he's in his first year of medical residency, married or not, kids or not, happy or not, it's a lock.

"Probably we can get you on TV talking about this article," Brell said. "Would you like that?"

"Sure," I said. "Why not."

"Of course," Brell cautioned, "you can't say anything about being Vince."

I laugh at your suggestion, Brell. "What," I said, "you think maybe I'll, like, panic and blurt it out?"

"No, not at all," said Brell, slightly apologetic now. "It's just . . . our P.R. folks may use the fact that you're Vince to help get you *on* TV, so you might just run into people at the studio who know you're Vince. But we must all always remember it's a state secret."

"I was meaning to ask you about that," I said, growing needlessly righteous. "Don't you think readers who know that Vince has been around since 1956 might have an inkling that an actual man is writing it?"

"Of course they do—"

"—and that this man is not one man but many men who've been rotating over the years?"

"Yes, of course they do—"

"—and that this man might even be subject to the kinds of desires and vulnerabilities that an individual man, and not Everyman, is subject to?"

"All right, all right," Brell said, nodding. With her finger she poked a pellet of chive cream cheese from the corner of her mouth inside. Her beautiful green eyes sparkled. It really was a shame Brell was blissfully married. "You've said your little piece," she said. "I apologize. Just prepare yourself to go on TV when this comes out. And, yes, of course, I know you'll keep it secret that you're Vince."

Damn right I will.

Blind date.

Vince had just written soberly about the institution for the upcoming issue ("25 Things Not to Do on a Blind Date"). *Don't hold your breath (#24)*, he'd suggested. Then again, *Don't give up hope (#25)*. (*#14: Don't plan to meet in a place that's heavily trafficked. #19: Don't proselytize or hand out promotional literature.*) And we always needed material, we'd been hired to be active and tomcatty, so we agreed. Lily, a friend from college, had called to suggest this woman she'd met at her gym. "Sasha's really smart, really funny, really beautiful, and tall." Yeah, yeah; they're all really smart, funny, beautiful, and tall. "I can't tell you how many times I wished she were gay," hummed Lily.

"You could wish you were a man," I suggested.

"That's right, I could," she said.

"Sasha's profession?" I asked.

"She works in the publications department at MOMA," Lily said, "but she's sort of in flux on that. What else, let's see . . . she's got brown hair, blue eyes I'm telling you you won't believe—oh, she's a runner, like you. Very athletic. She's a voracious reader."

"What? Why did you say that?"

"Say what?" said Lily.

" 'She's a voracious reader.' "

"I said she's a voracious eater," Lily said.

"Oh," I said. "Oh. Recent relationship history, please?"

"Well," Lily said, "she was on and off with someone wrong the better part of, like, eighteen months. One of those mythical beasts that just refused to die."

"And did it die?"

"Yes," said Lily.

"You're sure?"

"Yes," Lily said.

"Lily . . ."

"Yes, I'm sure," she said. "Six months ago, at least."

"Because we don't want any rebound situation here," I admonished. "I believe Vince's 'Are You His Transitional Woman?' column explains very clearly why they don't work, how they mess with your head. If you want, I can look up the month it appeared—"

"Okay, Dr. Freud," Lily said. "Now, I know she loves the Naturemax movies at the Museum of Natural History, hint hint. I think *The Grand Canyon*'s playing, and the award-winning *Beavers*."

"Thanks for the tip," I said. "And she knows I'm Vince?" At this point, who didn't?

"I may have mentioned it," said Lily.

I called up Sasha, my blind datee, at the Museum of Modern Art and asked if she'd like to see the two Naturemax documentaries. Her manner on the phone was extremely brisk, and I could quickly rule out her being stupid. It was harder to confirm over the phone if she really was everything else Lily had claimed—tall, for instance. We made a date for a Saturday afternoon—nice and nonthreatening. I'll suggest a drink for after the movies, I thought. (*#8: If you have no idea who it is, do not make it for dinner, but drinks.*)

"Maybe we could have dinner afterward," I said.

Just before hanging up, Sasha asked, "Which movies are playing?"

"One's about the Grand Canyon," I said, "and the other . . ."—*Beavers*, it's called *Beavers,* not everyone's mind is in the gutter like yours, just say *Beavers*—"I forget," I said. "But I know it won an award."

Oh, Mr. Puritanical all of a sudden?

Saturday I walked uptown to the Museum of Natural History in the rain. Sitting on the stone bench at the top of the museum steps, I started the Blind Date Watch. Maybe this wasn't such a good idea. For Christ's sake, a *blind date?* Next thing you know you'll be buying Lotto tickets, answering chain letters. As each woman walked by who was brown-haired, somewhat tall, and conceivably in Sasha's age range—and *not* in her age range, and *not* brown-haired, and *not* tall, come to think of it—I remembered: *Don't hold your breath (#24).*

On the other hand, *Don't give up hope (#25).*

Now here's a very large lady but she's got to be at least thirty-five, forty . . . no, she moves on. God be with you, dear.

Here's the right age, sort of brownish hair and rather frantic-looking, but that doesn't look nearly tall enough to reasonably be called tall . . . she stops, looks around. So this is Sasha, then—another complete misrepresentation in the ongoing nationwide blind-date scam. *#11: Special note to women—"Six feet" is a euphemism for "five-eight." #12: Special note to men—"Bubbly" is a euphemism for—*

She moves on.

A middle-aged couple.

An intriguing woman, right height, right age, wrong race.

An old man walking his dog.

A couple walking four dogs.

I wondered if perhaps I could no longer find whatever I might be looking for because something clinical, corporeal had actually snapped off; because boyhood was no longer an isthmus at the far end of my consciousness but an actual island, and the submerged land bridge between then and now was sinking fast.

Junior-high-school girl, Tartan skirt, saddle shoes, Lincoln's speed.

More couples walking dogs.

Two boys walked by in shoulder pads and helmets, carrying a football, real rich Manhattan private-school kids, grimy, well-fed. One of them walked with his right foot on the bottom-most museum step, his left foot on the pavement, so that he limped Quasimodo-like. I called to him to toss me the ball. At first he hesitated, suspicious. I clapped for him to throw it already. He spat in his palm. He found the laces. He cocked his arm. A tall, graceful woman wearing blue jeans, an oxford shirt, and a thin black cloth jacket looked up as she passed the museum steps. Wind filled the back of her jacket so that it swelled like a parachute.

Though the football hit me flush in the face, I still wish those two private-school boys well in life, along with the young man I beat out to become Vince. I wish my second cousin Stanley and even the investment banking community well. All the couples and individuals and dogs who walked by, I wish well, too. Vince predecessors dating back to 1956 and Vince letter-writers? I wish you all well.

After the woman's obvious amusement at my non-catch ceased, she put out her hand. I did not look at my watch to note the exact time, but I'd say it was roughly 2:22 in the afternoon. In Moscow it was 9:22 at night, in Tokyo 4:22 the next morning.

"Sasha?" I said. She nodded and we shook hands.

Toto, I don't think we're in Kansas anymore.

> *So when exactly does it happen? At what point does red turn pink, gray black? When is it time to call twilight the end of day, when the beginning of night? When does a flipped coin stop going up and start coming down? When does not being in love suddenly become being in love?*

I'm no movie critic, but you can skip the Naturemax film *The Grand Canyon*. It's really quite disappointing; most of the images—and let's face it, you go to Naturemax for the images on the four-story-high screen—are stuff you've seen a hundred times on TV, just bigger. As the closing credits rolled, Sasha leaned over in the dark. "I kept expecting it to degenerate into a Jeep commercial," she whispered.

We roamed the museum until the next movie, the award-winning *Beavers.* I confessed to her that I couldn't bring myself to say the title over the phone. She said the beaver was the mascot at her all-girls school and you can imagine what *that* had been like. She had a frank ease, a way of keeping the crude dignified—which, I thought, was sort of what my life's work as Vince was mostly consumed by. Or did I again have that backward?

"I really know nothing about you," Sasha said as we walked past Allosaurus, cousin of T. Rex, attacking Barosaurus and her kid. "Except that Lily thought we might like each other." In the Diorama Room, Sasha and I looked upon the well-crafted underwater habitat of the Penrhyn Pearl Divers, amid beautiful coral and giant clams and sea stars and colorful fish. At least, that's what we were sup*posed* to see, and I gather that's what Sasha saw. What *I* saw was myself on the ocean floor with Julie, me on top, basic missionary. I turned to Sasha guiltily, smiled into her deep, swimming-pool blue eyes, then turned back to the diorama, where my X-rated life of the mind now faded to black. The underwater habitat of the Penrhyn Pearl Divers returned.

We walked past the sea otter lying in a kelp bed where, instead, Remy Kleinwort, D.D.S., was flossing me in the nude. Maybe I could get it right this time with the dentist, though I think we all agree it was the N_2O's fault. Believe it or not, I think this afternoon with Sasha is going well. I blinked, the dentist disappeared, the otter returned.

By the time we got to the great walruses ("the noisiest of Arctic mammals"), my hallucinations had grown much less pronounced and I could only sense the outlines of what looked like Brell and tanned Monica and the people in the Art Department at ———*r,* all for some reason in Crayola magenta Lycra bicycle shorts, holding their arms out, beckoning to me. Or maybe it was just a reader with a question for Vince. She faded, whoever she was she faded, they faded, the walruses are return-

ing, return, time moving with labored little breaths through the itera-
tions. Never in my life had I so appreciated walruses.

I showed Sasha my favorite exhibit on the upper landing, the sorry
little rainbow parrot fish that sleeps in its own nocturnal mucus envelope. She appreciated it as much as I hoped she would, and as Vince
feared she would. Before our second documentary began, Sasha, who'd
let me buy the movie tickets, insisted on treating me to an apple and a
cruller, whose pronunciation we pretended to fight over. She rubbed
her apple against her shirt, just above her heart, until the fruit shined
dark ruby, then toasted me with it. "To nocturnal mucus envelopes,"
she said. We walked back downstairs to the great model of the squid
and the sperm whale, not the famous big blue whale hanging from the
ceiling, but rather the squid and the sperm whale, no jokes now, the
sperm whale which, I'm trying to detox here, deVince, the sperm whale
which is the largest of the toothed whales, the sperm whale is, stop it I
said (*She's trouble, I tell you, abort, abort*), considers the squid a major
source of food, can remain submerged for more than an hour, can go
very deep (*very deep*), physeter catodon, and probably, one would
think, has one of the largest cocks—Stop it now!—is one of the largest
mammals and I think one of the most graceful.

The sperm whale is the largest of the toothed whales, a predator of
the squid, and one of the most graceful mammals in the world.

There.

We walked back past the totem poles and tribal masks and the green
and blue and clear gems. Somehow we made it back to the theater,
though it wasn't thanks to me because a good ninety percent of my
energy was being spent on keeping Vince the Maniac from taking over.
He was in an especially foul, lascivious mood this drizzly Saturday;
maybe it was the weather, maybe he was getting his period. Most likely
it was the smell of something threatening and real, an authentic whiff of
in-synch loveliness. I took a big breath as the lights in the theater
dimmed. I highly recommend the award-winning *Beavers* for kids and
adults both, if it's playing in an IMAX theater near you. It's about the

dam-building, mating, and migratory habits of the wondrous beaver, engineer of the animal world. How they get cameras up inside those little stick houses is pretty amazing. Sasha and I loved it. We decided to walk all the way down to the Village for dinner, if it wasn't raining anymore.

It wasn't raining anymore.

On the way out of the museum she said she guessed she was still in love with the man she'd broken up with.

Off and on it rained, but lightly, and it was warmish for a late April afternoon. Sasha said she adored walking, and she tied her black jacket around her waist. She had few enough freckles that you could still count them, but many more would be forthcoming with the prodding of a little spring sun. A squirrel beside the park struggled mightily to unroll a cigarette into a sort of welcome mat, something only a New York squirrel would think to do; I love this fucking city, I thought. Sasha and I walked past or near so many of the provocative landmarks Julie and I had once considered prime love safari real estate (the Dakota, Tavern on the Green), walked down Broadway, through Times Square, Sasha made a face when we passed the Winter Garden and *Cats,* we walked among all the city gems and city shit, which seemed now somehow under glass. Sasha undressed a stick of gum, offered me one, then set it like a wafer on her tongue. We were in the heart of New York filth when we passed a newsstand. Sasha stopped to scan the covers and headlines while I watched her jaw folding the gum over muscularly. She spotted ————r and said she'd heard from our mutual friend Lily that sometimes I wrote for them and I said, yes, well, in fact, um, you know, I'm Vince.

Sasha was not impressed.

"Wait," she said, blowing a bubble, "did you write that article last year where you talk about how you like to drool on women?"

Thank God, no. For once, no. Bless your perverted heart, whoever wrote that. "Wasn't me," I told Sasha.

Instead of asking questions about my Vincehood—ha!—Sasha said she'd heard they were looking for a new Juliet.

"A new Juliet?"

"In Verona," she said, "they hire someone to answer all the mail Juliet gets from around the world—like Santa, like the Tooth Fairy." Like Vince, I might have added. "Romeo gets nothing. Wouldn't it be wild," she wondered, "to be Juliet for a while?"

I don't know about that. You might not like it as much as you think you would, Sasha.

"I'm sure you'd make a great Juliet," I said, and I bet she would. "Apply. It's interesting. You feel like *Ueber*person and no person."

"Being half-Jewish and half-WASP in New York, I already feel like that," she said. "I belong to the club, I don't belong to the club, I'm chosen, I'm not chosen . . ."

Oh, don't do this to yourself . . .

JEWISH AND NON-JEWISH STUDS, SEX MANIACS, AND SIMILAR DEVIANTS

Onan: coitus interruptus
Noah: fathered three sons at age 905
*Lot: incest**
Shechem, countless others: rape
The Nephilim, countless others: bigamy
All of them: adultery
Abraham: kinkiness (circumcised at age 99)
Vince, current incarnation:

(*excusable because daughters got him drunk, wife pillar of salt)*

We hit the Flatiron in full stride and talked about how much we loved New York, black-and-white photographs of New York, not just Steichen's and Stieglitz's; how much we loved New York's subterranean, prenuclear holocaust charm. I asked about her job at MOMA, where she helped put together catalogs on special exhibitions. I asked her if the eccentricities of the New York art scene—mostly learned through my friend Lincoln—were as petty and inscrutable as they appeared and Sasha said, You're being kind. As we passed the Barnes & Noble on Eighteenth Street, I wondered, Where do I turn in my Vince badge? Did my contract have an out clause? *Excuse me*, Vince wondered, *but your finances and career are in such wonderful condition that you can afford to back out of the most prestigious professional situation you have—have ever had, might ever have?* Sasha and I talked books, Salinger, Nabokov, foods we hated.

"How can anyone hate cilantro?" she wondered.

"It tastes like soap," I said.

"It does not taste like *soap*," she said.

She touched my arm easily, companion-like. Must call Lily to thank her. At a crowded corner, waiting for the light to change, I noticed in the reflection of the mirrored building across from us a tallish young man with a hunted, panicked look in his eyes. In my curiosity I was aching to turn and pick him out among those jostling for street-crossing position. I wanted to elbow Sasha conspiratorially (*Don't turn around—Don't, I said!—but check out the guy next to you when you can*). The light turned green, the crowd began to cross, and I realized I was walking toward me.

It's a powerful and disorienting sensation, to no longer recognize yourself on contact.

At Anglers and Writers, I ordered but didn't eat. *#17: Don't not eat,* I'd advised in the blind date Vince. *Eat something. At least pick at a roll to give the appearance that you're having fun.* But I am having fun. I'm having more than fun. I just can't eat.

Pick at a roll, any roll. Take your own advice, for crying out loud.

Shh, shhh. We've heard quite enough of you, Vince.

Fuck you, hypocrite.

Hey, no name-calling, you ageless, faceless, pseudonymous Miss Lonelyhearts.

Pathetic manipulator of the cachet I provide you.
Fiction.
Nonfiction.
Asshole.
Schizo.
"Do you feel all right?" Sasha asked.
"Yes, I feel fine," replied one of us—Andrew, I think. "I'm just not very hungry."
"Would you like some of mine?" She pushed forward her plate of succulent chicken breast and veggies.
"No, thanks," I said.

VINCE: A MAN'S VIEW

First of all, you really do feel something happening in your heart.

Ooh, that's deep. Watch out, Keats. Heads up, Byron.

Things were going too well for me to ask more about the guy she'd broken up with—the guy Lily had *assured* me Sasha had broken up with—and to press Sasha on why the hell she was sitting here with me on a blind date if she was in love with another man. After dinner we walked in the warm rain to yet another movie, this time a regular, non-four-story-high-screen movie in Chelsea. The next showing had already begun, so we bought tickets for the midnight and picked up the Sunday *Times* and sat in a garishly lit coffee shop and did the crossword puzzle. Sasha fell asleep in the theater but did not rest her head on my shoulder.

Nothing is sexier than decorum. Maybe it's the way she folds her hands in her lap, in sleep. Or the way she ignores Vince altogether.

Sitting in the dark theater, I concocted a theory, a Lincolnesque theory, about sex: The arousal is a pulse simmering, welling, bubbling; the climb is the sensation of a second pulse now racing to meet the boiling first pulse, racing as if to catch it and even stamp it out; the climax, the end of the chase, is when the second pulse coalesces with the first, punctures it, two rivers coming together, a confluence.

That's sex. But love?

Walking Sasha back to her apartment I said, Will I—Can I see you again?

She's in love with someone else, big boy. The best you can hope for is to be on the business end of a garden-variety rebound.

"I'm away most of next week," said Sasha. "But why don't you give me a call after that?"

Can't you see she's letting you down easy?

Yeah? Then how come we just spent twelve hours together? On a blind date? Two in the afternoon to two in the morning on a goddamn blind date?

"Great," I said. "I'll do that."

Don't hold your breath. #24.

Shut up. You're just pissed because she's not weak-in-the-knees impressed with Vince. Should I kiss her?

Do what you want. It's your funeral.

At her door we shook hands. "I'll call you then," I said. "I had a wonderful time."

"I had a wonderful time, too," she said, smiled, no kiss, turned, went inside. I had my next Vince.

Don't be an idiot.

Shut up and walk. You can dump the real-estate section and the classifieds in this trash can if that'll make our walk home any easier. Would you like to hear my lead or not?

Do I have a choice?

No.

Then let's hear it.

First: Do you wish me well?

I don't know. What's the lead?

I may have to kill you.

What's the lead?

I may have to kill you off. It may just require my castrating you. I may have to dynamite the devil-may-care devil you've been for three-and-a-half decades—

What's the lead already? It's two-ten in the morning.

That's right, pal, two-ten, she and I just spent twelve whole hours together, saw three movies, had a great dinner—

—though you couldn't eat a bite, probably because she loves another guy, tough titties—

No, this time, Vee, the joke's on you, pal. I'm sure of my lead. I like it even better than my "At this very moment, I do not have an erection" blue plate special.

That was a good one, wasn't it.

Oh, don't get chummy. You're so transparent it's beyond pathetic, Mr. Vince, Mr. Vincent Gordon, born 1956, the most genial, worldly bachelor anyone ever knew. It won't work because Andrew's got his lead, even if he—even if *I* have to put it under your name.

VINCE: A MAN'S VIEW

I think I'm falling in love.

Everyone: I'm saying it once more, just in case he tries to undermine me:

I think I'm falling in love.

7/The Will to Self-Destruction

I STOOD on the Fourteenth Street #2/#3 subway platform at six-fifteen on a May morning wondering, Do the handful of earlybird commuters around me realize they are in the presence of a television personality-to-be? A *reluctant* television personality-to-be? "5 Ways Men Have Changed," in the June issue, had just hit the newsstand, my first article for ———*r* under my own name. I'd said a few things ("Change #1: We're less masculine"; "Change #3: We expect women to make money") that the TV morning news show thought it could make hay out of and, as Brell had warned, they called me to appear. I would watch a taped "round table" discussion in which women and men talked about how men had changed (*if* men had changed) over the last five years, ten years, a generation. I would then comment on their comments. I felt strangely calm waiting for the train, downright peaceful that I had nothing important to say. Odds were even decent, Brell would be happy to know, that I would not blurt out on live television that I was Vince.

Rolling uptown I read the galleys of a future column, my man-as-woman rumination (*"Inside every man is another man fantasizing what it's like to be a woman"*). At the TV studio I signed in. It was seven oh-four and I was supposed to be on live at seven thirty-five. I began to feel a little sick. An intern came to the lobby and led me to a cozy conference room. There are coffee and crullers, if you'd like, she said. Thank you, I would not like, I said, and please pronounce it correctly, I thought. I might be interested in a toilet to barf in, I did not say. A cheery makeup woman opened her tool kit and got to work on me—not too much, just a little pancake for the forehead shine. Seven-eleven.

Sally, the host of my segment, introduced herself and sat down at the conference table. She was tall, snappily dressed, and bubbling with morning energy; human Alka-Seltzer. She looked a lot like she did on TV, a touch less real maybe. For the record, no wedding band. Seven-sixteen.

"Andrew, why don't we just go over a few points in the article," Sally said.

You're fine, you'll be okay, I told myself. As long as she doesn't ask you on live TV when was the last time you made love, who are you going out with, what gives you the right, how have *you* changed? Sally rifled through her notes while the makeup lady combed my eyebrows.

5 IDEAL PENIS SIZES, ACCORDING TO JULIE
(in descending order of preference)

7 inches
6 inches
8 inches
9 inches
5 inches

That had better not happen on the air. No, no; maybe it's good. Maybe I'm just getting it all out of my system now. Maybe this is healthy. Seven twenty-four.

7 GROUPS THE WORLD HATES IRRATIONALLY

Women who are either attractive or unattractive
Women who don't marry or who don't have children
Women who don't betray paralyzing weakness
Meter Maids
Umpires
Snakes
Mimes

Ed Koch walked into the conference room, having just finished his weekly segment on the show. Sally hopped to attention. Even through her TV makeup you could see she was blushing. "Hello, Mayor Koch," she said. "Andrew, I'd like you to meet the mayor."

Not anymore he ain't. "Mr. Koch," I said, reaching up to shake his hand. He really was as tall as they always said. Seven twenty-eight.

"Mayor Koch," Sally said, "Andrew's a writer who'll be talking about how men have changed. Mayor, how do *you* think men have changed?"

Koch picked up a napkin from the makeup woman's pile and began wiping pancake from his face. "We've grown kinder and gentler," Hizz ex-oner said.

Sally laughed. I smiled. Such a tired, not to mention Republican, quip, Big Ed. And to think that once I'd voted for you, to think we all had. Would I too grow into this kind of lassitude after reaching a certain age, or height?

The intern walked in. "You're on after the next commercial," she said to Sally and me. Seven-thirty. *Yikes.*

I followed Sally into the studio, trying hard not to think about what might happen if during the live interview I unintentionally, autonomically blurted that I was Vince or, worse, something nonsensical, obscene, misogynistic, patronizing. ("You know, Sally, the Sensitive New Age Man of the nineties really respects girls—I mean *women,* I meant *women,* Sally, I meant *women!*") In my deep focus I managed to put myself in something of a trance, as a technician dreamily fit a microphone around me and swiveled my chair closer to the desk.

I sort of remember being introduced to the anchorman and watching a nasal decongestant commercial playing on the dozen monitors around the set. Loosen up, man, it's cool. You're naturally sensitive and feminized, no way your basest instincts can ruin you. That's your appeal, remember? You *have* no base instincts. Only your buddies do. Tim, a management consultant. Danny, a children's book illustrator. Frank, a science teacher. Ed, a former big-city mayor. Lincoln, an art broker and aspiring child molester.

But most of those are you, remember?

After the commercial I sort of recall a traffic report about an overturned tractor-trailer on the Major Deegan causing major problems. Maybe they should just change the name to Major Problems, I thought.

Concentrate, asshole. And whatever you do, don't use the word *asshole.*

Is this TV studio hot or is it just me?

5 REASONS SHE'D BE AN IDIOT NOT TO PURSUE ME

We had a great time.
We laughed constantly.
We like the same things.
We're both New York kids.
I can't stop thinking about her.

I sort of remember hearing Sally begin. "We're here with the author of a new article on . . ."

But quickly it all began to fade. I started swiveling in my chair and tapping my finger on the desk. I was looking down on myself as if from an overhead perch, one of those Zeus-like buckets at the end of a dollying camera with the torsion of a dinosaur neck, positioning myself for some innovative tracking shot from the fifties, when television was youthful and exciting and *live* and I could not stop swiveling in the chair.

Should I panic? I had no history of panicking. I *did* have a history of fainting. You know, Vince, you know, Andrew, if you really think about it, this is actually one of the half-dozen most crucial two-minute intervals of your life.

Stop it.

You could be suffering the early stages of heat prostration. I could tell my face started flushing. Flushing New York? That sounds like a good idea.

Stop it.

"Tell us . . ." Sally was saying to me.

Fortunately, St. Vincent was concealed to all outward appearances. Unfortunately, he had started burrowing deeper inward.

Before I knew it, the taped "round table" segment was over and the interview was coming to a close. Marvelous. But what had I said? Had I stuck my foot in my mouth? My head up my ass? Or had I perhaps gotten off a winning remark or two? Must get videotape.

"So, Andrew," Sally was saying, "you say men may once again be chivalrous with a certain kind of impunity, yet you no longer feel shackled by your masculinity."

Did I *really*? How about that.

"Andrew," Sally asked, "would you say men have changed for better or worse?"

Ah, general wrap-up thoughts on change. Bread and butter.

"Butter," I answered Sally, "much, much butter." Briefly I caught a shot of myself in profile on one of the dozen TV monitors. I curled my lower lip down and watched it curl down a dozen times. Somewhere in Sheepshead Bay, a cute Italian girl in her white cotton Calvin Kleins is stopping before the kitchen table TV to listen and learn. Say her name is Gina-Marie. Reads Vince religiously, *naturellement*. Say she eats a carrot muffin and pops some multivitamins and puts water on to boil. Still lives at home with the folks, works at the family card shop, dates a nice guy, not great, a glazier. What's a glazier, you ask? It's someone who replaces car windshields for a living. The square of kitchen where Gina-Marie stands—perfect posture, lovely neon-white buns—is an ecstasy of morning sunlight. Gina-Marie talcs her small, wonderful breasts that would just fill wineglasses. She thinks the little curling lip the swiveling guy on TV makes is cute. Big fucking deal.

"And, uh, would you care to elaborate on that conclusion?" Sally pressed on, pulling teeth. Remy Kleinwort. In the chair. Couldn't get it up with the dentist. That was the laughing gas talking, not me. Still, failure with the D.D.S. is failure with the D.D.S. Q.E.D. F.Y.I. U.S.A. P.M.S. *Stop it.* Gina-Marie also awaits my conclusion.

"Because men are becoming better at speaking the language that women speak," I answered Sally, "and that women would *like* men to speak. Maybe it's part gimmick on our part, but at least it gives us a better foundation for communicating, a sort of Esperanto for the post–sexual revolution."

"Thank you, Andrew," Sally said.

A sort of Esperanto for the post–sexual revolution?

I nodded my head weakly and the anchorman started gurgling about the weather up next. I saw his face now on the several monitors in the studio. I removed the microphone from around my neck, let my head fall back, rubbed my eyes.

"You were fine," Sally was saying to me back in the Green Room, "just fine. We'll probably have you back on in the future, for other relationship articles I'm sure you'll be writing for ———*r.*" Sally shook my hand warmly. "What are the odds you'd want to do TV again? Fifty-fifty? Seventy-thirty, ninety-ten?"

Got anything in the zero-hundred range?

Monica called mid-morning. "You were terrific," she said. "A natural. You should have your own show."

"Really?" I said.

"Absolutely," she said. "Absolutely. The only one tiny little thing I'd say is, don't swivel so much. You were kind of moving back and forth in your chair. Other than that, you were fabulous." Monica said there was a small problem with my latest Vince column, about what to do when men don't call after we promise we'll call. "They want to change the phrase 'blow off' to 'brush off,' " Monica told me.

" 'Brush off'?" I said. "That's Eisenhower-era."

"I know. But they don't like the other connotation. Blow off. Blow." She sounded a little fed up herself.

I hesitated, to show I was at least considering playing the prima donna. "Okay," I said, "but promise me you'll tell people it was *their* minds in the gutter, not mine."

"Deal," Monica said. "Now we also need a bio from you for 'Five Reasons Why Men Lie.' Obviously the Vince credential won't do."

"When do you need it?" I said.

"Right away," Monica said. "Yesterday."

I thought for a moment, humming into the phone. "Okay, how about, 'The author, from New York, is currently working on his first novel.' "

"Fine," said Monica. "What's the novel about?"

"Guy thinks he can keep his integrity if he only sticks to the small compromises, like changing 'blow off' to 'brush off,' but then discovers that's how moral decay always begins, with the small compromises. Then he goes on a wild killing spree in a post office."

Monica snapped her gum half a borough to the northeast. "Try higher sunblock," she said.

My phone rang throughout the morning, people who'd seen me on TV. My parents said I did a great job, though at one point they got scared that I was swiveling in the chair so much I might fly off the screen. Another caller, whose voice I didn't recognize, asked if my name was what it was and I confirmed. "And are you Vince?" she said.

"Who wants to know?" I asked.

"I'm with *Cosmopolitan*," she said. "We heard you were Vince and we were wondering if your contract was up soon."

"As a matter of fact," I said, smiling at the idea of leveraging ———r, "it is. Wudjahavinmind?"

The ultimate New York assignation: lunch.

✿   ✿   ✿

Plans to get together with Sasha didn't work out the following week, or the week after—so okay, *her* plans didn't work out. Twice she blew me off. Vince hoped I would just drop it and move on—*New York's full of fabulous women, yes?* was the gist of his screed—but I wasn't about to let go so easily. For starters, in our phone conversations she'd used the words *Latinate* and *bifurcated,* and once again we got into a pronunciation argument, this time over the Tappan Zee Bridge. She was insisting Tappan *Zee* was the proper Dutch stress when she got beeped. After ten seconds she returned. "I think I should take this call," she said. Ten bucks says it's the ex.

Just tell her to call you back. No sweat.

Oh, no. I know that trick, smart guy. If I tell her to call back, then she's got the option not to. You think I'm waiting around all night, checking every five minutes for a dial tone?

"How about the River Café for dinner next Friday?" I asked. "We'll walk there and back." Her kindness an Achilles—and a lover waiting impatiently on the other line—Sasha gave in.

Drastic measures were necessary.

The morning of my *Cosmopolitan* lunch I realized that the novel I'd been working on for the past year, *The Heartcomber,* was in fact a piece of shit. Consequently, I did something I never thought I would do: I opened the butter bin of my refrigerator, uncrinkled the twist of silver foil my friend Brian had left as a temptation during our last poker game, and took out three twisted ropes of hallucinogenic mushroom, veined like blue cheese, dry and cracked as parchment.

I know what you're thinking: But our hero isn't a drug person, never was. Why in the world would he eat mushrooms?

Why? Because I'd been told the mushrooms would give me new perspective on things, help artistically. Brian said that when mushrooms are taken in moderation, the effect lasts about two hours. It was nine in the morning as I stood in my tiny Greenwich Village kitchen chugging from the plastic container of apple cider to wash away the salty, loamy, repulsive flavor the mushrooms left in the back of my throat. My *Cosmo* lunch was at twelve-thirty. According to my math, that gave me a cool ninety minutes to wind down.

Excitedly, I sat at my desk to work. So let's see, I thought, how useful *fungus psilocybensis* is in helping me figure out what my novel is really about.

Not useful at all, it would appear. The mushrooms left an aftertaste like excrement, even after I'd thoroughly chewed and swallowed them. This was supposed to open the world to me? Turn my mind into some sort of limitless beachfront? I swigged apple cider and sat there at my rolltop desk, looking out at the Bleecker Playground kids and moms, at the splash of color provided by the fruit and flower bins of the Korean market catty-corner from me. In the window across the street, Candy Woman took a handful of what I guessed were chocolate turtles, then departed. I could make a good cop on stakeout.

5 PROOFS SHE CAN'T BE INTERESTED

She canceled twice.
She constantly mentions how much work she has.
She alludes to moving someplace far away.
She's on the rebound.
She's not on the rebound but in fact in love with someone else.

To do right by the drug, I put Pink Floyd's *The Wall* on the stereo, put on the headphones so I could crank it up, closed my eyes. Nothing. Good. I am in total control. I am impervious to the ills that befall the rest of the world, as a Vince should be. I am to some extent inVinceable.

TV perhaps? I hit a logjam of commercials, starting with Colt 45. In his next life, why doesn't Billy Dee Williams just become a pimp and cut out the middleman? I flipped. A cooking show. If I ever went gay, I'd need a boyfriend who could cook like this guy. He'll cook, I'll be in charge of buying beautiful strainers and copper utensils at Williams-

Sonoma or Dean & Deluca downtown. Channel 13's having another fund drive, its sixty-two millionth. My equilibrium is obviously intact. Congrats to Cher: The operation to make her look like she comes from another solar system has succeeded. On MTV, Alice Cooper. There's an attractive man.

Well, maybe mushrooms would be helpful for work on my next Vince; perhaps now was the time to try and tackle that touchy, precedent-busting, personality-transforming column about what makes men fall in love. But nothing seemed to be happening except for a vague massaging at the base of my skull. I listened to the second disc of *The Wall.* A colony of sperm swam across the page. It moved with the movement of my eyes every time I tried to track it down. It was pieces of sun that had broken off thousands of years ago and danced like amoebae. It was the schmutz in my eyes is what it was. It was the solipsism of drugs is what it was.

You know, I don't think I should have taken mushrooms before a business lunch, I mused, I really don't. What was I thinking? I was no druggie, I told you, never had been. Among my friends my intolerance for chemicals and alcohol was legendary. Two Amstel Lights turn me puffy-headed, three and I'm goonie. My concentration fritzes. I start hearing everyone, including myself, talking in dropped pronouns and sentence fragments.

My two hours of self-induced inspiration should have been up an hour ago, I noticed as I consulted my watch, and I'd so far scribbled into my notebook a whopping half-page of nonsense, and now I had to leave. For my lunch. Not only were the mushrooms refusing to subside, it felt as if they'd plugged themselves into a hole somewhere near the base of my brain. Oh, boy. I could call and cancel. Could, should. Tummyache, Grandma died, dog ate homework. Why chance it? On other hand, what's to lose? Sentence fragmentation was beginning. In earnest. Don't want to write for *Cosmo* anyway, not really. Fuck, starting to sound like Bush. But one ride on IRT will kill any whimsy, chemically induced or no. Yes?

I remember walking down the red-carpeted foyer of the Japanese restaurant and Camille, the *Cosmopolitan* editor, waving me down. No turning back now. Hands are being shaken now, sitting is occurring, smiling on both mouths, there is mutual sipping going on. The Japanese aren't kidding. This tea really is green.

Camille the Editor didn't mince words.

"We want you," she said. "To write. For us."

And I to write, I thought. For you. Been thinking of breaking away myself. But wasn't exactly thinking of rival women's magazines, no, ma'am. On other hand, man's-eye-view stuff is only thing I'm known to be good at so far, that and food captions, so maybe I need to break away gradually, creamily, dollopy. Start with something mainstream maybe, to work my way back into civilian culture. A *Reader's Digest* piece maybe. *I Am Joe's Scrotum.* I could do that. *I Am Joe's Sundried Tomato. I Am a Tomato Drying on Joe's Sunny Scrotum.*

I felt it entirely possible I was swiveling in my chair the way I had on TV.

"Well," I said, simulating tentativeness, "my contract comes up. Soon. I don't know if I'll stay with ———r. It says somewhere in my contract. That I'm not allowed to write. For *Cosmo.* Among others. *Mademoiselle.* And *Vogue,* I think. *Elle,* I think. Can you and Helen wait a few weeks? I'll see what happens. I'm very intrigued. By your. Offer."

"We don't pay a lot," Camille said. "And we don't plan on getting. Into a bidding. War with. Your employer."

"Why? Not?" I said, or thought I did. I mean, we're having lunch together. Aren't we? Won't you let me leverage you? Helen? If you really stop and think about it, eating sushi is the single most intense thing you can ever do in your life.

I could barely focus on my food or my lunch partner. I just had a magnificent epiphany. I just figured out why they call it a walnut: because of that sort of wall that divides the shell into a kind of two-bedroom natural garage. Maybe now you'll see why sometimes I seriously wonder whether I have the mind to be a novelist.

"But if we can steal you away for a few sex stories," the nice *Cosmo* editor whose name I suddenly forgot was saying, "we. Will." I want to sleep surrounded by white rice, with a panel of pink fish on my head.

You really should listen to Pink Floyd, I meant to tell the nice *Cosmo* editor whose name I could totally not remember because right now, I must tell you, *you are only coming through in waves.* This restaurant better have air bags.

"Until then," the nice *Cosmo* editor said, French name, like with an *L* or I don't know, Lisette? Claudine? "Call me," she said. "If you're ever feeling. In a particularly pseudonymous mood."

That's one mood I don't need to work up a lather for. (Claudine? No.) When *don't* I feel that way, is more the question you want to be asking. Me.

"Good. Bye. And. Rew," the *Cosmo* editor said. Maybe it's Claudine. What the hell. *Your lips move but I can't hear what you're saying.*

Idiot! I thought as I was hurled out into the big day, now why would a control freak like you ever think to do something as reckless as taking drugs before such an event, forget the inaccurate "it only lasts two hours" advice you got from your "friend"? (And who was this "friend," anyway? Adam, a gypsy cabbie? Trace, a quantum mechanic? Leander, a newspaper ombudsman?) Unless I ate more than I was supposed to. Ass. Hole.

On mushrooms, New York seemed an endless Hawaii. Say you're a guy walking down Manhattan Island for no apparent reason, maybe just to walk off the dog of your drug state. Say downtown seemed so far away—some Oz, Disneyland, Shangri-La

WONDERLANDS

Oz
Disneyland
Shangri-La
Downtown
Eden

Nirvana
the Ice Cream Float in Candyland
the ———r Reception Area
wherever Sasha happens to be

Just had a magnificent epiphany. I just realized I may not be as profound as I always thought I was.

Mom, Dad: I can't for sure promise I will never do mushrooms again.

In front of a stationery store, a little Indian girl, her shining black
hair whipped up tight in an onion-shaped bun, wildly rode a Jetsons
spaceship, jarring her insides. Don't, honey, I thought; you'll scram-
ble your uterus that way, I knew only too well from my days writing
medical shorts at ———'s. Approaching New York's downtown art
ghetto, my head felt increasingly fatigued. The sky had warped to
gray; the sun was covered by a large floating cloud mass, also on drugs.
The playground across the street was almost empty. A janitor swept
dust. A teenaged girl was perched on the top rail of a bench and talking with great animation to a man seated below her. She was pitched
forward and rocking from left to right, her hands gripping the rail. As
I watched her through the black iron bars cordoning the playground,
which gave the effect of seeing the scene through one of those nickel
arcade films, *thup thup thup thup,* her head bobbed from side to side
so that her straight, dark apricot–colored hair lapped back and forth
like a sleepy wave. The man put one hand on his chin, the other at the
back of his neck.

I stopped. Here came the sun.

He cracked it, first one way, then the other.

Why, you devil, you. Why, you fucking devil.

Ladies and gentlemen, my illustrious pal Lincoln Crye. Lincoln, a
Soho art dealer. Lincoln, a benchwarmer. Lincoln, a baby-sitter. Lincoln, a man in over his head and out of his fucking mind.

I could have hidden behind a parked car but I just stood at the fence,
watching. Lincoln was turned three-quarters toward me but couldn't

see me unless he was to turn his head farther. He was making no attempt to camouflage whatever it was he was doing. Anyone could guess what it was he was doing.

Very rapidly, I seemed to be emerging from the drug's domain. Blood spilled back to where it belonged, faculties reconvened after their five-hour sabbaticals. I was left unshielded now and feeling quite alone spying on my best, most troubled friend in the heart of Soho . . . I got it. Everybody: With the help of mushrooms, I just figured out John F. Kennedy. Holy shit.

Why was the administration that oversexed Jack reigned over called Camelot? Give up?

Came a lot.

Bad sign. For the third time over dinner at the River Café, Sasha referred to how busy she'd been, how busy she'd be. *Let's cut our losses,* Vince advised me. *Forget her, who needs her, call for the check, I'll buy you a drink at a sports bar.* No one knew better than Vince that when the second date feels significantly less magical than the first, it is always the *first* date that you must re-evaluate (*see our "Was I Dreaming?" column,* he reminded me), it is inevitably the first date where you weren't quite seeing straight. Looking out the window at the East River and downtown New York beyond, I tried not to let Vince fixate on the city's obvious phallocentricity, and concentrated instead on its vigor, its yellow light, the water's trembling reflections. "Vonnegut calls it 'Skyscraper National Park,' " I said.

"Where exactly did you grow up again?" she asked.

I turned and with my hand made a somewhat Napoleonic swipe behind us, as if Queens were all the rest of the world.

"A B and T," I said. "I guess once you make it in Manhattan, you never have to use a bridge or tunnel again."

"Have you made it?" Sasha asked.

"I don't know. But if you're born a B and T, you can never *not* be a B and T, despite what any of those who've turned their backs on the outer boroughs may say in later life. You grow old a B and T, you die a B and T. I shall not hang my head."

At some point around dessert, the conversation turned—go fig-ure—to Vince. "I don't know how you do it," Sasha said. "I don't mean to sound like I disrespect it. I just can't imagine exposing myself to the world like that."

"It *is* a pseudonym," I pointed out.

She didn't go for the bait, my medley of mock-humble and faux-indignant. "But everyone who knows you knows it's you. Your family, your friends," she said. "They know."

"They do," I confessed.

"I know," she said.

I nodded.

"Have you ever exploited being Vince?" she asked. "Did you ever let it slip out that you were Vince to get a woman to sleep with you?"

"Yes and no," I answered.

If only I could steal a moment alone with Sasha—just me and her, without the interference of Vince—perhaps I could slip her a message, tell her, Listen: Can *I* see you again—I, me? All I needed was for Sasha to give me a sign that she was more than a tiny bit interested, to slip me the psycho-romantico-emotional equivalent of the nail file in the choc-olate bundt.

"Okay," I said. "So what's the deal with this other guy? I always thought people who were in love liked to be together."

"It isn't so much what's going on with him as what's going on with me," she began.

We haven't heard that one before.

"I don't love him anymore," she continued. "Start again. I love him—I'll always love him—but I'm not *in* love with him anymore, and he wasn't right for me at all. That I'm sure of. I'm glad I have my work to sort of get lost in . . ."

Yes, we know.

". . . and I love the idea of having all this newfound freedom . . ."

If you don't signal for the check, I will.

"... not thinking about making something work, or how he's going to feel about me, or am I happy or not, or did I offend him in some small way, or what emotional state I'll be in a month from now. Adam's a great guy, attractive as hell, and totally, absolutely the wrong person for me. We talk a lot, but I told him it's probably best if he didn't call for—"

"A while," I finished.

She smiled and broke my heart. "That's right," she said. "I'm very content to be a single woman in New York for now. I'm very content to be having dinner with a new friend at the River Café."

I was not raised to deal with mixed messages. No fair.

"I don't know why I'm telling you this, Sasha," I said, having no idea where to go from here, "but I hate being Vince. You know I'm not here to collect material or write about you."

"I never thought you were," she said. "And you can write about me."

"I don't *want* to write about you," I said.

"Thanks a lot," Sasha said.

"No, I just mean—my private life is no one else's business but mine ... or, I mean, in this case, I guess, mine and yours. This is not another column here. It's just life."

Hey, weasel? Brell has candidates galore who'd give their right testicle to be me.

Out in the cobblestoned rotary, I bumped into a college acquaintance (tasteful rock on the marriage finger) and her presumed fiancé. Janice turned her face sideways to let me peck at it, and gave me the quick bio: recently ashore after several years abroad, advanced degrees at Oxford, mulling teaching offers from all over, no date yet on marriage to her very own Englishman, Philip (loving gaze). "We met and fell in love at university," said Janice.

I bet she says "zed," too, I thought, as Sasha's arm brushed mine in co-delight. I bet these days Janice crosses her sevens and zeds and spells it cofffeee shopppeee.

"That's terrific, Janice," I said. "I always knew you'd do something

Anglo. You were the only one in class who ever actually read Samuel Richardson."

"You'll permit a change of subject?" Janice asked. "Because I want to congratulate the fellow who penned the absolutely lovely 'Five Ways Men Have Changed.' "

"Thank you," I said.

". . . and?" said Janice.

"And?" I said.

"And . . . you're Vince," she said.

"How did you know?" I asked.

"Grapevine," she said. "Some party, I think. Really, I just can't remember. I could not be happier for you. For a while there you were writing the first chapter of a very great book."

"I was?" I said.

"I mean, in a manner of speaking," Janice said. "In school you were always talking about writing . . ."

"Oh, yeah," I said. "Yeah."

"Are you writing a book?" a clearly panicked Philip asked in a chichi accent.

"Yeah," I said.

"About what, may I ask?" he said.

You most certainly may, haughty gentleman from across the pond. "It's sort of a modern-day Oedipus tale set in Queens," I said.

Phil nodded, relieved. "That's brilliant," he said, the British meaning of *brilliant*, I'm afraid, not the American. What did he know? Probably he's related to Andrew Lloyd Webber. Probably he wears dresses.

"Now, how do you two go together?" Janice asked, her finger doing an eeny-meeny between me and Sasha.

"Friends," said Sasha.

"Oh?" said Janice. "And will we be reading about you in upcoming columns?"

"Apparently not," Sasha said.

"Do you realize that this man here," Janice warned Sasha, "probably influences more people than just about anyone from our graduating class?"

"Certainly he gives more instructions," said Sasha.

"I really must thank you for your lovely breakup column of some time ago," Janice said to me. "Margie—you remember Margie?—has been clipping copies and mailing them to me ever since we found out our classmate was this absolutely lovely pop icon in American women's magazines. Andrew, that column really helped me deal with a rather nasty situation." She and Philip shared another gooey gaze.

"I'm glad," I said. Man in New York writes column. Three months later, pretentious expatriate in England starts feeling better about self. Coincidence or supernatural occurrence?

"Yes, right after that," Janice said, "I went on holiday with Philip and, well, the rest is history . . ."

I felt a tingling at the edge of my mouth.

Did I mention that I get cold sores when I'm really stressed? That is, when I'm not fainting or swiveling? And here I thought if things went really well tonight I might even try kissing Sasha.

". . . and then I was briefly in hospital with a bout of the . . ."

I felt the tingling at the edge of my mouth spreading.

"Janice?" I said, touching Sasha's elbow. "We're actually late for a show. But it's just awesome seeing you and Phil."

The tingling kept spreading. In a half-hour, my face is going to be covered with a grotesque herpes.

I went to hail a cab.

"Weren't we going to walk back across?" Sasha asked.

"What?" I said. "Oh, yeah. Right."

"We don't have to," she said.

"No, that's fine," I said, putting my hand to the right side of my face, as if I had to scratch an itch. "I want to. I'd love to."

As we walked across the bridge, I made sure to walk on Sasha's right side so that I might contain the damage which would mean, best-case scenario, that in another ten minutes the right edge of my mouth would be covered by a pulsating cold sore the size of New Hampshire. Half-way across the bridge, Sasha stopped and moved to the rail to look out.

Kiss her. This is what you wanted, isn't it?

"It's something," she said, and I nodded, fingering my mouth as if deep in thought. A breeze now carried some lovely small perfume of Sasha's to me—her own or store-bought, who knew.

Tell her it's just a little thing, you get cold sores when you're nervous. It's what New Age Man would do. She'll understand.

Why did this have to happen now? "Yep," I said.

She does have great tits and an incredible ass, that's for damn sure.

I'm not going to dignify that remark.

By the time we got to her brownstone in Chelsea, Vince and I were in complete agreement that we dearly wanted to kiss Sasha, something I knew was clearly out of the question, given what—though a mirror would probably tell me otherwise—felt like an industrial-sized fungus. Yet another reference to what a chock-full-of-work week lay ahead for Sasha, as if I hadn't caught the first nine mentions.

Did I say before my cold sore was the size of New Hampshire? I meant Montana.

"I really want to kiss you."

No! Don't say that!

Sasha held onto the tip of my finger. I realized it was warm milk she smelled like.

"I don't know what's going on with me right now," she said as I continued to rub at my mouth, hiding my grotesqueness. "I just got out of a long ordeal and I love my freedom. I can't tell you how much I love it. I don't want to give up that freedom, I don't even want to think about where I'll be in six months or—"

"Sasha? I said I want to kiss you, not I want to take out a small business loan with you," I said.

Sasha let my hand slip from hers, and crossed her arms in front of her, as if she were about to settle something. "I hoped something like this wouldn't happen," she said. A neighbor walked outside, greeted

Sasha, nodded to me, and lit a cigarette. Sasha looked into the bay window of her brownstone. A light came from inside.

"My roommate's up," she said in a half-whisper. "Maybe I'll talk to you this week."

"Yeah," I said. "I know you've got a ton of work."

"What? Oh, right," she said. Time passed. "Was that a question or a statement?" she said.

"Was what?" I asked.

" 'I really want to kiss you,' " she said.

"Oh," I said. "Both."

She closed her eyes.

One regular writer or writers—a group calling itself Saints for Germ-Free Sex—sent me a finger-wagging yet strangely obsequious letter every time I wrote a column in which I described intercourse without explicitly stating that a condom was being worn.

> ... *Vince, as we pointed out in our last letter about your March column, in which you failed to mention that Justin, a vintner, was using protection from STDs, once again in April there was mention of a coupling—this between Marcia, a dolphin trainer, and Quincy, an ichthyologist—without specific reference to condom use. Perhaps you overlooked this? In the era of AIDS, and within the pages of a magazine that young people read, we cannot stress this enough.*
> *All best, S.G.F.S.*

She wants me, she doesn't want me. She wants me but in about four years, she doesn't want me. She wants me but not exclusively, she doesn't want me. She wants me but at some point we'll break up and I'll feel horrible (much worse than I do now), she doesn't want me. She wants me but as a friend (no touchie), she doesn't want me.

For those of you scoring at home, that's ten possibilities, just one of which is a plain, unadorned, She wants me.

❈   ❈   ❈

Year One as Vince was over. My initial pitch for Year Two as Vince was fifteen hundred dollars per column, a five-hundred-dollar-per-column raise. ———r said they weren't negotiating. Instead of trying to leverage them by telling them how hot Helen Gurley Brown was to snatch away the current Vince, namely *moi*, I humbly offered to take thirteen hundred per. ———r said they weren't negotiating. I offered to take twelve hundred per and said I wasn't happy about it. ———r said they weren't negotiating.

The ———r reader survey—the report on which stories in the previous year worked and which didn't—came out. Monica, lovely, tanned Monica, confirmed it for me: "What Men Don't Tell Women About Sex but Want To, by Vince" was ranked not only the most widely read article in the past year, but the most popular article in the magazine's entire history. At this very moment (I wanted to tell the entire staff of ———r), I most certainly *do* have an erection.

They came back with fifteen hundred per column.

Sold.

8/Spiro Agnew = Grow a Penis

IF ONCE I was a good Vince (certainly it seems unlikely I remained so, given that I was driven to blow the cover off of this glamorous, pseudonymous job, ruining it for all future Vinces, besmirching it for all past Vinces), then what was it that made me a good Vince?

Our hero is nine years old, the family's heading to the Hamptons for the summer, Dad's behind the wheel. Next to them on the Long Island Expressway is a station wagon just like their own: wood-paneled, luggage in the wayback, a Dad driving, a Mom next to him. True, in this car there are two little boys and a little girl, while the other car goes with the simpler two-little-girls configuration, one of whom presses her nose against the window.

Windows closed, air-conditioning. Amazing. Same deal in our hero's car.

The girl with the squished nose is roughly our hero's age. She's a little Incan princess who must have been kidnapped when she was a baby and raised by people from Queens. Perhaps this explains her sad expression.

Our hero blows her a kiss, but she turns her head away just as he does so, and her station wagon pulls ahead.

"Andy?" the father calls, looking at his son in the rearview mirror. "What are you doing?"

"Come on, Dad," he says. "I'll never see this girl again."

"You don't know who these people are," says Mom. "Stop it."

"Dad, please pull up to them again," our hero says, a pathetic, pleading look in his eyes. The hero's older brother, who astonishingly enough never gets carsick, is reading. The hero's kid sister has got Barbie down to just her white cotton briefs, the very same women's undie design Calvin Klein will one day market, for the express purpose of making our hero weak in the knees.

"Just this one time," our hero pleads.

The hero's father again pulls up alongside the companion station wagon. After what seems an excruciatingly long time, the Incan princess looks over once more. She sets her look on our hero and he blows her another kiss. She stares back, unblinking, and after a moment her small, beautiful fist, with its yellow polished thumbnail, barely but perceptibly opens, dreamy as a clam's mouth, to catch the kiss.

The princess's father now seems to be talking to her, reaches his arm around to the back to turn her around, smacks her. He pulls the car into the lane farthest from our hero's.

Or maybe that's not it at all. Maybe the crucial sculpting of our hero's nature happened much earlier.

"Who knows?" my father said to me more than a year into my reign as Vince. "Maybe you used the word *penis* when you were two years old and you got a good response."

Why are sex movies rated X, violent movies R? Column idea.

The wisdom and efficacy of jerking off before making any big life decision. Column idea.

Should I come out in one column?

How can two people not in love ever really "make love"? (Sum Greater Than Parts?)

Column idea, column idea, column idea.

My sex stories and "relationship pieces" under my own name ("The Condom Conundrum," "Men and Commitment: At 20, 30, 40," "5 Men, 5 Breakups, 5 Reconciliations") were being reprinted in magazines all over the world, each ludicrously adorned by photos of model slash actresses-actors overemoting. Dutch *Cosmopolitan* bought my stuff, South African *Cosmo* (I won't go into how I rationalized that one), women's magazines in Australia, New Zealand, Brazil, Great Britain. It was found money—two-fifty here, three hundred there—perhaps enough to start putting one of my credit card balances to rest, perhaps just enough to keep me living in the style befitting an active-sensitive tomcatter, a Pseudoman in New York.

Joan Rivers' people called, wanting me to chat about "5 Ways Women Are Wrong About Men," written under my own name. Somehow, on live national television, instead of talking about the five ways in which women are wrong about men, I managed to tell the story of how I fainted at my cousin's circumcision. I think it was my perverse, not altogether reckless way of pre-empting my ever-growing need to reveal my identity as Vince which—if done this publicly—would at once free me personally and ruin me professionally.

For my column three months hence, I proclaimed my feelings for Sasha. I called her "S.," but I included enough verbatim dialogue and factual description—swimming-pool blue eyes, tiny ears, the curious way she pronounced "barette" (*bar*-ette)—that she'd get it, if she read it, which was by no means a lock. I thought of calling our mutual friend Lily to see if a column in which Vince declares his love for S. was as fetching a gesture as I thought it was. But I decided not to. If you're in love, then you have an innate sense of what's the right or wrong thing to do. Plus, surprises are nice.

Letters to Vince kept tumbling in. They came equally and abundantly from all over—the Northeast Corridor, the Pacific Rim, the Emphysema Triangle, the Bread Basket, the Bible Belt, the Rust Belt, the Milk Belt, the Seat Belt, the Panhandles, the Rockies, both runoffs of the Continental Divide, up and down the great and muddy Mississip; they came from L. L. Bean Duck Country and from Fort Apache, the Bronx. After the appearance of my column on how to sign off a letter to a woman I was interested in ("Mandy" I called her, a telethon coordinator; a complete fabrication), I received a sackful of suggestions about how to write her back, many of my readers nakedly rooting me on to win her ("Just be yourself. Relax. Sign it, 'Thinking of you, Vince.' And I think Mandy will see just what a neat guy she's got on her hands"). They wrote me, Dani and Lisabeth and Bobbi and Kara-Ann did, in the impeccably bloated script of protracted girlhood, with its obeisance to line and margin, its rotund hand full of balls and hoops, ringlets and teardrops. You wanted to cry.

8:53.

8:54.

8:55.

Bet you can't guess what comes next.

Still 8:55.

8:56.

Dial tone working. Might as well untangle the cord while I've got the phone out of the cradle. She may be trying to call right this minute, wouldn't that be nice. I would call 8:56 "evening," wouldn't you?

8:57.

Dial tone still working.

8:58.

Knuckle wrinkles are some kind of cosmic joke. Why should we have knuckle wrinkles? Why should newborn babies have knuckle wrinkles? They're zero days old, for God's sake! Wrinkles are for aging! Are knuckle wrinkles God's curse for eating the apple? Candy Woman across the street has entered her kitchen three times for the sole purpose of pigging out on what I am guessing are milk chocolates. Just one per trip, bless her soul. It's really coming down in buckets.

9:00.

Sasha said she was "having a drink" with some "guy" who's "just a pal." After this "drink," Sasha would then be home, if I may quote, "all evening" and would "give me a call" as a "welcome break" from all her "work." Apparently, "evening" does not begin for Sasha until some-time after 8:35, 8:41, 8:53 (in shower for twelve minutes), 8:57, 8:59, and 9:02. Her machine picked up each time.

9:03.

What if she's screening? Then she knows I've been calling every five minutes and hanging up. She thinks I don't trust her to call in her own good time. Ergo, any infinitesimal chance I had with her an hour ago is now officially gone.

Oh, pardon me: Sasha doesn't want to be "exclusive." How progressive. That means I'm not the only guy who's calling her like an insane fucking person now that she really thinks she's *finito* with the old boyfriend if she's still out drinking with that fucking guy I'll—

I dial her number. Does she realize that her phone number gives her a straight to the eight in seven-card stud?

Her phone rings once. Twice.

Click. "Hi, you know who it is—"

Fucking machine.

Where the hell is she? She must be "in bed" with her "friend." Probably her "friend" is in fact her "new boyfriend." Right at this moment she is probably "falling in love" with Mr. Friday Evening Drink(s).

See, this is what happens when you go mushy in the head, Vince offered me. *You act like a sick schmuck. Control yourself.*

I have an idea. I dial my friend Brian, a budding screenwriter. His phone rings.

"Hello?" says Brian.

"Hey," I say.

" 'tsup?" he says.

"Would you call me?" I say. "Something's wrong with my phone."

"You got it," he says and hangs up.

Nothing.

Nothing.

He's obviously trying to call me right now and I'm not hearing anything. Those AT&T monsters—

Ring.

You know: That *could* be her. I mean, I know it's *probably* Brian calling me back. But it *could* be her.

Ring.

"Hello?" I say.

"Working okay?" Brian asks.

"Yeah," I say. "Great. Thanks. So . . . you using the binoculars tonight?"

"Very funny," says Brian. "Anyway, her blinds are drawn. I might go to a wrap party later. A film my friend directed. You wanna come?"

"I'd love to but I'm busy," I say.

"The cute one who works at MOMA?" he asks.

"Yep," I say. "Thanks for the call. Have fun at the party." I hang up.

Okay, this time I'm going to leave a message. She was delayed. Flooding in the subway from the torrent outside. I'm going to leave a message because I don't think it speaks well that I, the Great Vince, should be home when she calls on a Friday night, though I gruntingly suggested I *would* be home, furiously working on my great novel, *The Heartcomber,* that maybe I'd someday let Her Highness read. Sorry, Sash, something better just came up than waiting for your phone call, which I'm sure is coming any second, so just called to say hi. Here we go.

I dial. Her phone rings once, twice.

Click.

"Hi, you know who it is, you know what to say—after the beep, please." Smart girl, not to give her name.

Beep.

". . ."

Let me try that again.

My voice felt croaky and I didn't want to sound too eager. Here we go. I dial.

Her phone rings.

On the other hand, I don't want to sound completely blasé, either.

It rings a second time.

Come on, there's no risk she'll think you're blasé—after all, you're the one who's leaving the message, putz—

Click.

How about a message that asks for some info? An *excuse* message?

"Hi, you know who it is . . ."

Yeah, I like that idea. Like, Did you see that piece today in the *Times?*—

". . . after the beep, please."

I'm clearing my throat. Right now she's playing footsie with him under the table. Her foot is moving up to his—

Beep.

". . ."

9:22.

I can't take this. I can't believe I wrote a column telling the world how great she was.

I won't dwell. That's what Mom would tell me, that's what my friends and readers would tell me. That's what Oprah and this afternoon's guest, the author of *Sick Fucks and the Sick Fucks Who Love Them,* would tell me.

I'll run. In the torrential rain.

I stripped. I stretched. I scratched myself. Friday night, a pseudonymous national celebrity with hot balls and ever-diminishing faith in the promise of true love, and he's scratching himself. *Wunderbar. Weltanschauung.* I put on "Helter Skelter," cranked the stereo loud, so that maybe the neighbors would complain. Hey, it's not so bad, really: Some stages of your single life you're hot, other stages you convince yourself you really learned something valuable re-reading the *TV*

Guide cover story. Some weekends there's sex o' plenty, other weekends there's Cup o' Noodles. Slipping on my shorts, my T-shirt, my
running shoes, my windbreaker, I looked out at the rain boiling the
street and saw Chocolate Woman in her kitchen now polishing off the
box—two, four, seven, all gone. I heard the aching lament of pleasure
from my neighbor's washing machine. Dial tone still working. Must get
out of here. A watched pot.

I ran west to the river, down along the highway, inhaling those two
packs' worth I didn't bother with during the day. Through Battery Park
I ran, aroma of cut grass, how I don't know, fragrance of dog shit; the
Lady in the Harbor, is she single, in choppy marital waters, divorced?
Has she been made to feel neurotic that her breasts are not firm
enough, her pubococcygeal muscles are not well-toned enough, her
skin is not clear enough? I turned inland, felt a searing hunger. At a
Korean grocery, the fruit stacked in tiers like an audience, I grabbed an
apple and stuffed it in my mouth, rooting it there, doing the roast suck-
ling pig number for the small, bell-shaped girl behind the counter.
Coming in from the cold, I sensed steam rising from my head. The
counter girl, with hard, unerupted craters beneath her cheeks and chin,
raised her small almond eyes to me, the first time in generations, first
time in three dynasties. No, stupid: *Korean,* not Chinese. Or do the
Koreans also have dynasties? Sorry No Change, it warned over the cigarettes. Well, good; I didn't need change anyway—like, to use a pay
phone, you mean? 9:38. The counter girl took my dollar bill, smiled at
the steam curling up from my shoulders, my head; she swallowed a
laugh. Sorry, no punctuation or change. Also, declared a sign over the
fruit bran bars, We Are "Open Sundays," as if it were some hip new
slang. We apologize but we cannot Cash Checks. So, in conclusion,
"Sorry" we cannot "cash" checks or "make change." The silver slipped
from her hand onto the counter. I scooped it up and spirited out of the
store just as a car bounced in a pothole, found water, drenched me
more. There was a corner phone I shot past, proud of myself. 9:41.
That's almost fifteen minutes in which she may have called me. I bet it's

a sweet message she left. I bet it will turn my entire life around when I hear it. I bet by next week we will be shopping on Forty-seventh Street, Diamond Way, for a one carat–plus rock, solitaire-cut. Sasha ain't a pear-cut girl. Might she like baguettes on the sides? Column idea.

My temples pulsed, city buses fumed, in my head hounds bayed and swells gathered. The air hissed and spat with the sibilance of tire on wet road, the *squish-squawk* of wiper rubber on wet glass. With my palm I cleared my face of sweat and rain. I raced, my body taut and angled halfway between ground and heaven. *The Five Ways Men Make Change, or Cash Checks.* Somewhere in the middle of the Indian Ocean right now a seabird hops from whitecap to whitecap as if through hoops, glinting fish slice through the water like a set of new kitchen blades. Somewhere someone gives free dancing lessons, somewhere someone gives head.

The buildings of New York had turned gold in the night, and blue, with cherries on top, all around the sound of thunder, rolling thunder, the rolling sound of thunder. The city was about to explode. The cars start and the grates steam, the vendors appear and the lights go off, and the lights go on, and people are having drinks, or maybe they've relocated back to his place for the main course, and they are now both entirely naked and playing that game where you see how long you can go naked without touching and of course they are both failing miserably at it, and the trains roll below and perhaps she's even asked him if he wouldn't mind drooling on her. Doesn't appear as if there are major mass-transit delays. Almost ten. What if she's dead?

Skating the cold, shiny streets of lower Manhattan, dodging, darting Chinatown. How do those Chinese restaurants *do* that? All making the same dishes, the same sesame chicken, honoring the same General Tso, Happy Families (Chef's Suggestion) are all alike, crafting the same delicate bird's arbor of hard crispy noodles, handing out the same menus . . . Is there one accredited school everyone goes to? Are they all in this together? Is it fair to call it a monopoly? Are we looking at Sherman Antitrust violations here? Szechuan Mandarin Hunan Empire Balcony

Terrace Garden. We cannot "cash checks." Do you have "two tens" for a "five"? Do you believe in "magic"? If men "change," then in how many ways do they "change"?

It rained as if the skin of the universe had been turned inside out, and water on the inside was on the outside now, no longer dammed. The office buildings looked anorexic. Perhaps they just threw up. Perhaps they used to be hippier, with a little cottage cheese around the lobby area, and they just a moment ago excused themselves to go to the bathroom, where they stuck their finger down their throat, because men are pigs and this is a national problem. The rainy street glistened.

Why doesn't someone tell the Chinese that Chinatown needn't be laid out like Hong Kong? Why doesn't someone tell the Black Muslims to go easy on the incense?

At a phone—I couldn't help myself—I dialed her number.

It rings once.

Come on, Sash, pick up. Please, my darling.

It rings again.

That's fine, usually people pick up after the secon—

Click. "Hi, you know—"

Fuck!

Uptown, faster, more stands of oranges, apples, grapes. In front of Madison Square Garden two people kissed languorously . . . and I was jolted. Had I forgotten completely what it looked like? East Side, east. Fifth Avenue, my wife and my whore. Running past Lord & Taylor's I wondered, Do I look like Vince? What does a Vince look like?

The glamour of writing for the magazine was definitely wearing off. Let's put the *amour* back in *glamour.* I passed the New York Public Library, resented the vague stone sneer on the lion's face. What? Oh, just don't. I know you know.

The streets choked on buses and cars. From a second-floor dance studio came the pounding of a Madonna song. Ten leotarded, maybe a dozen, sprang and stretched, opened their arms wide, like popes before throngs. Madonna pumped. With my hand I unsmeared my face.

Why doesn't Madonna just admit it—that her one lasting regret in life is that she will never be able to blow Jesus?

You have to choose. You cannot have it both ways.

The idea of two gods is much older than the idea of one. Mom and Dad, Good and Evil, Art and Science, City and Country, National League and American, Nike and Reebok, Coke and Pepsi, coffee and tea, regular and decaf.

Up the avenue, traffic lights turned yellow and red in unison, like Rockettes. I wore ten pounds of rain. Red or green. I cannot have it both ways. No or yes. New or York. You have to choose. Well, I *have* chosen, damn it. I'm choosing Sasha.

She just hasn't chosen me.

I slowed, I'd run miles, the rain was now a light wash. It was a great, beefy Friday night in Times Square. *Don't fock with me,* New York City say. *As long as you out to have a good time,* New York she say, *okay then. All right. But start fockeen with me, mon . . .* I bobbed down Forty-second like a caught fish bouncing on the lake surface. I slowed to a walk, feeling as naked in public as I'd ever felt. Times Square is Candyland after the nuclear snow, nerve center of the nerve-damaged. The pigment in the dirty movie theater posters had died, pinks surrendering to gray, enervated yellows, a washy, recurring sepia-like shade, flesh now bone, a faint lavender that was once probably a rich, royal purple. Black strips like kidnapper's tape coyly covered pinups' headlights and beavers, and the girls' eyelids drooped from pills and exhaustion.

In a window a holograph of a penis that, as you pass it, goes from surly indifference to military attention, Times Square's blinky Jesus. T-shirts, natch. WHY A PICKLE IS BETTER THAN A MAN. WHY A COLD BEER IS BETTER THAN A WOMAN. I'M NOT GAY BUT MY BOYFRIEND IS.

Is it just me? I really wondered. This night had hair, it had barbed wire.

"Excuse me, do you have the time?" I asked.

"It's almost eleven, brother," the preacher answered.

In the subway, the graffiti on a movie poster read "Sexist, Racist, Gay-Bashing Pabulum." In response to this, someone had scrawled underneath, "You dumb intellectual fuck, you probably haven't even seen the film." An arrow pointing to the response read, "I agree with him. You."

On the train home I got the jaunty, "Step lively now!" conductor. After taking my usual pop quiz from the various interrogations of subway ticker tape ("Have you been mugged?" "Anal fissures? Warts?"), I noticed a woman reading ———r, reading the Vince column—*my* column! ("Is He Ready to Talk About the Future?") I felt dangerous, near to asphyxiating on my own excitement. I was reminded of my favorite scene in American literature, the one where Tom and Huck stand at the back of the church at their funeral, listening to their own eulogies.

The woman pored over Vince's exegesis on how women can tell when a man is ready to talk Commitment. She looked up at me, my bare legs, my soaking chest and head, I smiled, she glowered and returned to my brilliant commentary. As unrecognizable celebrities go, I'm right up there with the San Diego Chicken, Marni Nixon, the President's speechwriter.

As I approached home, I slowed to a walk. I breathed in the New York night air, which had unclenched after the rain. Why are you letting her get to you like this? Once, you thought girls were icky. Once, girls had cooties. 12345678910, I got my cootie shot. In a coffee shop window a group of gay men sat around a big round table, laughing. Which one has it? Which just infected, which the full-blown? Who gave it to whom, and how can a union bear the freight of that? How many days ago was the last funeral?

I hit Bank Street, found lobby, found elevator button, found key, found lock, found second lock, no blinking message, 11:27, no fucking blinking message, the dial tone is still working, 11:27 is most definitely "evening," for your information, Sasha. 11:28. I noticed my apartment was absolutely spotless, neat as a pin.

I forgot that I'd spent the entire afternoon and early evening dusting and polishing and scrubbing and cleaning every square inch while I waited for the call.

The upside of unrequited love.

Scrambling for ideas to make Vince a more significant force in American letters, to improve his standing in Sasha's eyes. A Lamaze class? A meditation on how probably ninety percent of women dislike what their boyfriends/husbands do when fondling their breasts—the aggressiveness (aggression?), the persistence, the massive ignorance, the lack of put-yourself-in-my-shoes-ness? The fact that we're even "fondling"? Something on date rape? No, no, no. My columns grew flatulent and Uncle Vincey (*"Don't, dear readers, go to bed with us the first three dates"*). Brell and Jacqueline, ———*r*'s editor-in-chief, turned them around and sent me back to the drawing board. Your job, I was reminded, is to give women some *new* insight about men that will help them. Okay, how about this: Socrates is a man, all men are pigs, therefore Socrates is a pig.

In the scuff marks on the floor of office buildings I started seeing post-nuclear-sized pricks, extra-Y-chromosome hieroglyphs. Any structure longer than it was wide set me off. Cab doors fly open at red light? Legs spreading. Construction worker tunes blowtorch? Breathy climax. Spiro Agnew? An anagram for Grow a Penis. This time it was I who phoned late at night.

"It's getting ridiculous," I said. "I see women yawn on the subway, I think, Blow job."

"You thought that before you were Vince," Lincoln said, sweetly commiserating.

"No, not like this," I said. "I was healthy then. I was a goddamn normal man then."

"I'd like to tell you it's just a stage you're going through," Lincoln said, "but I just think you're a late bloomer. Welcome to my life."

I tried to sleep but beneath my lids I saw ten thousand bras being unhooked for twenty thousand eyes, hundreds of stiff tri-state area cocks quivering to dock inside hundreds of tri-state area cunts, thigh flesh spreading, asses rolling, sweaty Niles of vaginal juice and semen spilling up First Avenue, down Tenth, across Forty-second, through the Upper West Side and Tribeca and Murray Hill, sloshing out into Nassau, Suffolk, Westchester, and Rockland counties, the city, the state, the lower 48, the squirming and heaving and twisting on Castros that open out, on Monsantoed floors, bodies in hard curvature like balloon animals, lashes closing, tongues poised like primeval spoons, lips parting, gums working, sphincters winking in Nautilus awakening, Munch's *Scream*, abdomens tightening, vulvas clenching, fetishists and dentists, adulterers and accountants, model/actresses and writer/directors and chairman/CEOs. I got out of bed, snapped on the bathroom light. I pushed toothpaste up the tube, but what I saw instead was a stiffening penis with COLGATE (with Dentifrice) branded up its shaft. Outside was no better: The heads of street lamps on Bank and Hudson streets bent to perform obscene acts. I turned on my desk lamp to work on my aimless novel, *The Heartcomber.* I procrastinated. I picked up the phone. I didn't know Sasha well enough to try a middle-of-the-night Lincoln on her. I flogged the dolphin. I read my mail.

Dear Mr. Postman:

By now you understand and appreciate the many benefits of Gold Card membership—the freedom and financial flexibility it brings you to fuck anyone you want . . .

I splashed cold water on my face, with my fingertips tapped icy water against my eyelids. Really, now, I thought. This has got to stop.

My great-uncle Irv, the closet pervert, passed on, rest his soul. I liked him, I did; he had a twinkle in his dirty old man's eye. When he was still ambulatory and a sizable family contingent could be rounded up to go out to the diner, he was the only person who ever found the menu word *bagelry* as funny as I did. Perhaps it wasn't much to build a relationship on.

It was an open-casket funeral, on the North Shore of Long Island. For the last time, I looked on my great-uncle Irving: the withdrawn Slavic cheekbones, the broad pink nose sloping in stages (suggesting about him, falsely, a long-ago colorful stint as prizefighter), and the wide-set eyes that, taken all together, gave him the look of some haunted Trofimov, some once-dashing Russian count with a passion for philosophy, cards, and countesses. His eyeglasses had been left on, a touch I wasn't expecting. Then again, I'd seen him without glasses only once, at Jones Beach when I was five, so probably it made sense to leave them on. That's how people knew him, I thought, as I filed past the coffin.

After the service, relatives and friends stood around telling Uncle Irv stories. Everyone was saying Irving was a gentle man, and that was true. They said he was a regular templegoer, that he was devoted to his brother and sister, and I'd heard that too over the years. But Uncle Irv was also unbelievably cheap. When his sister, my great-aunt Lotte, started to talk about how giving and generous Irving had been, I slipped out of the chapel.

My aunt Mildred, who *was* generous, unconscionably so, sending us all checks to commemorate the most dubious occasions (the day of Hitler's death, Brooklyn-Queens Day, her *own* birthday), caught my hand on her way back from the ladies' room. "Do you realize you can live a long life and never see a child-sized coffin? But now I seen one. Go look. It's back there. It's horrible."

"I think I will," I said.

"Not so fast," Aunt Mildred said, touching her short silver curls in her signature way to make sure they were still where they'd been for only the past eight decades. "Andrew, you're going with a girl?"

"I went out with someone interesting," I said. "I'll probably see her again."

"If you like her, marry her," Aunt Mildred said. "These days it don't pay to hang around loose. It's important to find a good mate and start being married. Jewish?"

"Half," I said.

"Good enough," Aunt Mildred said. "Good family?"

"I think so. I don't know her that well, Aunt Mildred."

"Well, start to. Do they talk about getting to first base and second base anymore?"

"I don't really think so," I said. She kissed my forehead and patted me along.

Before I could get to the back of the parlor it was my grandmother's turn to intercept me. She unpinned her lace doily and with a handkerchief wiped her brow. "Does some nice girl have your eye?" she asked.

"Not at the moment, Grandma. I'm sure someday, though."

"Don't be in a hurry," my grandmother said. "I'll say it again: Don't be in a hurry. Don't listen to what everyone's saying. If your aunt Mildred knew what the hell she was talking about, she wouldn't have three ex-husbands. You can break a few more hearts before you settle down."

Okay. I'd like to break, let's see, four more hearts, and then I'll be good and ready.

"You're good to me, Andrew," my grandmother said. "You call me every now and then to say hello, Grandma, how ya doin', Grandma. Others I can understand, your brother with his work and the baby, Tommy's a doctor, Amy's got the business, Renee's designing clothes, Janey's a lawyer *and* a professor, bless her heart, they're always so busy, everyone's busy, they don't have time to call and see how their grandmother's doing, God forbid. But you're not with anyone, you don't have to go to work in the morning. That's why you're one of my favorites."

When the regal and classy actor Charles Boyer killed himself after his beloved wife of many years died, it was from a broken heart. On the other hand, when the regal and classy actor George Sanders killed *himself*, his note explained simply that he was bored. These are true. I have no idea what they mean exactly or whether this is the time and place for them, but they're true. Consider it a public service.

My grandmother kissed my forehead.

People began filing out of the hot, stuffy chapel. Cousins I hadn't seen in years milled about sheepishly but not particularly somberly. I wondered how many of them knew that Uncle Irv was, in theory anyway, a pervert. I wondered how many of them contemplated the meaning of Irving's aggressive program of ass-pinching the youngest members of the family, girls and boys alike; or knew that his basement strongbox contained not only a well-thumbed copy of the somewhat defensible Kamasutra, but also several graphic, digest-sized S&M magazines, the literary quality of which I could not fully judge because they were all in Spanish; or accepted at face value Uncle Irv's explanation that keeping his hands down his pants, in full company, was necessitated by poor circulation and ice-cold hands.

PLAYING THE FIELD WITH SASHA:
HOW FAR VARIOUS MEN MAY HAVE GOTTEN WITH HER
THIS FISCAL YEAR

First Base—guy from work she always lunches with
Second Base—guy she runs Central Park reservoir
with Mondays, Wednesdays, Fridays (Paul?)
Shortstop—Mel Gibson
Third Base—ex-boyfriend (Adam)
Home—guy she won't dare mention to me because
she's so smitten with him she doesn't want to jinx it

Across the room I spotted my cousin Stanley, the once-truant, Yankee Stadium cousin who'd let Julie and me into the plaque garden in left-centerfield, site of our virgin love safari. He'd always suspected something but couldn't prove it. He was working on an atrocious goatee. I avoided eye contact.

"Christ was Jewish," I overheard my deeply browned Uncle Ralph, the extremely successful bond salesman, say to Uncle Irving's long-ago retired accountant. "Einstein," Uncle Ralph persisted. "Schweitzer, I think. Freud. All of them. Marx."

"He was a Communist," the accountant said.

"They were all Jewish," said Uncle Ralph.

"Leopold and Loeb," the accountant struck back, then grabbed me. "You're the kid who does the letters in the girl's magazine, correct? He's the kid, right? The Dear Abby thing? Who does someone your age let's say tend to go out these days anyway with?"

What a gift, speech. "What—you mean, like, women?" I said.

"Answer him," extremely successful Uncle Ralph said. His tan was the color of tea on the first bag, concentrated Lauderdale. "I want to hear this, too. Let's hear. What. Go."

"I see a few people," I said, "kind of off and on—"

"Listen, funny guy," Uncle Ralph said, "all these articles I read say you're no longer sleeping with just one person. You're sleeping with every one they've slept with for the past seven years—"

"—and everyone *those* people have slept with," added the accountant.

"That's right," said Uncle Ralph. "Be careful. Wear *two* condoms." He took off his tinted aviator glasses and dabbed his forehead. "When I was your age we didn't have to worry about any of this crap."

"When you were my age, Tommy was in kindergarten and Renee was two," I said.

He used the ceiling to calculate. "You know, he's right?" extremely successful Uncle Ralph said to the accountant.

I moved on. It was strange, but good, to see so many younger relatives, people I'd known since I was little, all got up in black dresses or dark suits. Actually, we made a surprisingly well-scrubbed tableau, I thought, and felt slightly giddy over it. Someday, I pondered, milling about the funeral parlor, stopping now and then for small talk, someday I hope to have a lovely wife whose name may or may not start with the letter S, a family of healthy boys with iron chests and healthy penises and tight balls and long, muscular asses, a family of healthy girls with healthy, wide-circumferenced breasts and thighs like steel and well-toned pubococcygeals. Maybe we'll have a dog, a nice-smelling one. We won't give it a precious name. Growing up in an apartment I'd always envied people with stairs: So maybe we'll have a sunken living room, I thought, and a fireplace, too, and pokers. I'd like to have to go turn on sprinklers. Someday I'd like to forget that I'd turned the sprinklers on and then go out at dusk only to find I'd just drenched our lime-velvet lawn. I'd put my hands on my hips and shake my head with an I-can't-believe-how-gosh-darn-forgetful-I-can-be-sometimes shake. My wife, my lovely wife—full of empathy and all kinds of love, and with a ferocious appetite, too—will come up from behind, touch me, I will jump, we will laugh over my jumpiness, my possibly-starts-with-an-S-named wife will hold me firmly from behind, make it all better. In the failing autumn light, pumpkin moon rising, we will cheat out there under a willow—just a kiss, I mean, just a touch, just an elliptical movement of our faces around each other's, no petting, no oral-genital contact, no tongue even, mostly fingertips and soft dry lips and fluent eyes—stealing tenderness in a place where, and at a time of life when, none is supposed to be found.

Was that anti-Semitic, what I just fantasized? Cheever overwhelming Malamud? Greenwich fucking Great Neck up the ass? I don't think so. I love what I did not choose to be, I don't love what I chose to be. I like what I am, I wasn't so crazy about who I was becoming. Andrew was okay, Vince could be a problem. Isn't that what this is all about?

My cousin Stanley nabbed me before I could slip outside. Quickly we caught up on basic family stuff—what year of grad school various siblings were in, what month of pregnancy his younger sister was suffering through, how often she was blowing chow. Stanley stroked his chin, showing off his new goatee. "You like?"

"Very much," I lied. "I've never been able to grow anything to speak of."

"A little too Federal Witness Relocation maybe," Stanley said.

"So what's going on with the front office?" I asked. "The Yanks desperately need starting pitching. For God's sake, Stanley, do something. Talk to George."

"I have nothing to do with on-field operations," Stanley replied with all the charm of a press release. "I couldn't care if they went zero and one hundred sixty-two. It has zero effect on what I do."

"Uh-huh," I said. "And you still like your job?"

"Thrice-promoted," Stanley said. "That's what you would say, 'thrice,' you and your friends, right?"

"I never use the word *thrice*," I said.

"Well, I've been thrice-promoted," Stanley said. "I practically run the place. So how's your friend—Julie? Was that her name?"

"Yes," I said. "We're not together anymore."

"Always liked her," Stanley said, which was stupid since he'd only met her that one time, and briefly and frostily at that. "Real big baseball fan, wasn't she?"

I raced through my dictionary of good comebacks. "Your mother wears army boots" didn't quite strike the desired note, especially since his mother also happened to be my relative, whom I liked and who stood about two yards away, pinned in a conversational half-nelson by Aunt Lotte.

"I hear you have quite a social life now," Stanley said to me. "Some famous people you've met. Television."

"I don't know where you're getting this stuff, Stanley. I just play piano and write. I can't even finish a chapter of my novel."

"Damn, I admire you," Stanley said. "To go on one of those shows and say all men are pigs, that was incredible."

"What? Did I say that?"

"You're telling me you didn't say that?" Stanley said.

"I can't remember," I said. "Did I say that?"

"Sure you did," said Stanley. "The funny thing is, these shows would never tolerate it if someone said all women are pigs, or all Jews, or blacks—and they shouldn't—but it's okay for them to say men are pigs."

Jesus.

"Stanley," I said, moving to the funeral parlor door, "it was really great seeing you."

"The question is," my cousin asked, a tad pugilistically, "with that job of yours—Lance, is it?"

"Vince," I said.

"That's right," Stanley said. "Question is, Vince, with that new job of yours . . . are you getting any?"

I snorted. "I ain't livin' the life of a monk," I said, abruptly turning away from my cousin and pushing open the heavy funeral parlor door and waving goodbye.

And technically, what I told Stanley was *not* a lie, so long as there are a few monks out there—and odds have it there must be—who are getting a little on the side.

I was awakened—ten, eleven, I had no idea—by the bullhorn. "Why is it do you think, Vincenzo, you've gone this long without sleeping with anyone?" Lincoln's voice from the Talking Car rolled up the side of the building to my second-floor window on a bright Saturday morning.

I leaned my head out. "Turn it off," I called down. The sky was an infinite blue vault.

"So this Sasha chick isn't taking the bait," Lincoln boomed up, ignoring my request. He had the microphone in one hand, a grape lollipop in the other. "Forget her. You really just need to get laid."

"That's funny," I said, rubbing my eyes and giving the thumbs-up to an old woman who'd stopped pushing her shopping cart to stare up at me and observe our exchange. "My mother says I just need to find a good woman."

"She's right, too," Lincoln's voice boomed.

"The Eagles say I better let somebody love me before it's too late."

"You're no desperado," Lincoln called up to me. "Don't flatter yourself."

"My grandmother says I need to break a few more hearts. My high-school basketball coach said I needed to use my left hand more. Shut up or park."

Once again past my deadline, I sat down to tackle my next column. I wrote the usual heading at the top of the page.

VINCE: A MAN'S VIEW

I crumpled the paper and threw it in the garbage.

VINCE: A MAN'S VIEW

I took out my novel, *The Heartcomber,* and

I sat
I buzzed Lincoln up
I just decided

laundry
cash machine!
student loan—call
work on abs, pecs
call Dad re car insur.
drop short card to S.?

I just opened all my windows and sat down to begin my account of what it has been like so far to be Vince, of "Vince: A Man's View," the famous pseudonymous men's column in ———r. I'm excited. I'm sitting in my high-ceilinged Greenwich Village apartment, at the vertex of Bank, Hudson, and Bleecker Streets. It's July. I'm wearing red basketball shorts and a New York Knicks cap, and within easy reach is a half-gallon container of Tropicana orange juice, Home Style ("with juicy bits of orange"). I am going this route, for anyone who cares, because Vince is getting on my nerves. Everyman is beginning to chafe. Vince has been the perfect guy to hide behind, even if it was *I* who told everyone he was I and I was he.

Hey! My friend Lincoln Crye has just walked in. He has just picked up my Voit basketball and is currently spinning it on his middle finger.

"What's this?" Lincoln is asking me, bending to read, sifting his left hand vainly through his dark blond curls. "The column or . . . ?"

"A new novel," I say. "Maybe not even a novel."

"You always write in pencil?" Lincoln asks.

"Most of the time."

"Boy, aren't you a dinosaur."

"Don't dribble against the wall," I say. "My neighbor's a real crank."

"What's this one about?" Lincoln wishes to know. "Are you going high-brow or low-brow?"

"I'm not sure," I say.

Lincoln reads. "Is it some kind of kiss-and-tell?" he asks.

"I wouldn't call it that." I wouldn't.

"Well, is there a lot of sex in it?"

"Yes and no. It depends how you define sex."

"I presume I'm the major character," Lincoln says.

"A major," I say.

"Then there's a lot of sex," says Lincoln, pounding the basketball now against the other wall. "Why is Lamaze circled in the phone book?"

I slam the New York White Pages closed. Easily distracted, Lincoln pursues this no further and boings on the TV, standing inches from it. In the video, a barefoot farm girl in a thin cotton dress washes her car in the backyard until a strange man grabs the hose and washes her down. It's been in the Top Ten over two months now. "Why don't you somehow make it easier for people to get to your book's sex scenes if they actually have a life, which you obviously at this point don't," my friend Lincoln says, turning up the volume. "What's with this new girl? Is Sasha interested or not? Fish or cut bait. You're sitting on a fucking gold mine, pal. Now, just one question: What could possibly be so wonderful about this Sasha character that she's making you act so stupid?"

For the drive to our basketball game, Lincoln kept the bullhorn out and broadcast comments to the traffic ("Friends, my passenger is a very powerful force in pseudonymous magazine journalism today, thanks to yours truly"; "It's hazy out there today, people, let's look alive, look alive . . ."). I replayed for him Sasha's whole I'm-still-getting-over-someone-else-I-just-may-move-to-Paris-or-trek-in-the-Himalayas-and-the-last-thing-I-need-right-now-is-a-serious-involvement number, to get his analysis. Lincoln nodded with more than his usual empathy, which wasn't much of a stretch.

"So give her space," he said. "That's what Vince would advise. If she had zero interest in you, she wouldn't bother calling at all."

"Yeah, but always calling back a day after she says she will is a sign, too," I said.

"Yeah, it's a sign she's spacey," said Lincoln.

"No, it's a sign she's not really interested in me," I said.

"You are such a woman, sometimes I can't believe it," Lincoln said. The bumper sticker on the car ahead of us read, SO MANY PEDESTRIANS, SO LITTLE TIME.

"She's so New York," I said. "She knew what Dylan Thomas's last drink at the White Horse was."

"Cool," he said. "Sounds like you may have Bingo."

"My next column says I think I've fallen in love."

He didn't say anything.

"You think that was stupid?" I asked.

"I don't know," said Lincoln.

"Maybe it was dumb," I said. "It's too late to pull it. Shit."

"What fruit does she remind you of?" he asked.

"Damn. I can't believe how stupid that was."

"Stop worrying about things you can't control," Lincoln said, in a frightening moment of lucidity. "What fruit does she remind you of?" he asked.

"Don't talk about the woman I love like that," I said.

"Come on," he said. "What fruit?"

"No," I said.

"Fruit," he said.

"The ass, a small beautiful peach," I relented. "What about you, Mr. Crye? How's the gallery?" He looked at me blankly, unwilling to entertain a question as trivial as one about work. "How's life?" I asked.

"Well, actually," said Lincoln, considerably more pleased with this question; "actually," he repeated, taking the remnant of his clear purple lollipop from his mouth with great deliberation, "I sort of got arrested."

Horatio Alger liked little boys, Lewis Carroll little girls. Gandhi slept in between a couple of fourteen-year-olds. It happens.

Still, as Lincoln revealed to me more details of his near-offense—a thirteen-year-old named Pie *he* thought was seventeen; Pie's father first catching them "just talking" (possibly on that very day and on the very bench I'd seen them months before); the later confrontation between father and daughter in which Pie, as Lincoln put it, "cracked"—oily tears lapped at the holding tank just back of my eyes; my throat warmed and hurt. He was my friend.

The girl's father had called Lincoln to inform him that he was calling the police to charge him with statutory rape.

"It's a felony, you know," Lincoln said. As we sat at a red light he closed his eyes and cracked his neck. "New York State Penal Code, one-thirty point two-five, third-degree rape, E felony: 'A male is guilty of rape in the third degree when being twenty-one years old or more he engages in sexual intercourse with a female less than seventeen years old.' "

I felt repulsion.

I listened in a daze as Lincoln concluded his story, told me how the father was just bluffing, how the man had threatened Lincoln if he ever went near his daughter again, or if Lincoln didn't seek treatment for, in the father's words, "this disease of yours."

"So the storm has passed," Lincoln said. "For a while there I thought

I might have to plead insanity." The car behind us honked. "Maybe even go Twinkie defense," Lincoln smiled.

"What's wrong with you?" I asked. "Don't you understand what's going on?"

"And what's going on?" Lincoln said.

"You have a problem," I began and immediately sounded trite to myself. "When's your appointment to see someone?"

"I have a new theory I'm working on," Lincoln said. "Would you like to hear it?"

"Did you make an appointment to see a doctor?" I asked.

"Do you want to hear my theory or not?" he asked.

"Did you make an appointment to see a doctor?" I repeated.

"Do you want to hear my theory?" he asked.

I sighed.

"It makes perfect sense," Lincoln said, "that the same guy who gave us Mickey, the Magic Kingdom, and Futureland also wanted to be frozen. Perfect sense!"

"Have you made an appointment?" I asked again as a taxi zoomed up alongside us. The driver gave us the finger for going too slow, I guess, and we both gave him the finger back. "Have you even called anyone?" I asked Lincoln. "Why would you treat what this girl's father said so lightly? What would possess you to do that? You want a recommendation? I'll give you one. I know people who can recommend good therapists. My parents know people. I'm happy to call them. I'll call them today. I'll call them right now."

"Disney was more frightened of death than anyone who's ever lived," Lincoln continued. *"Ever."*

I shook my head. "And?" I said. "Come on, make your damn point."

"Every boy is a child," Lincoln said, "and every man is a child. And every man spends his adult life merely covering up the pathetic fact that he's growing into a more and more grotesque version of what he was, is—a child, filling out into an ever less successful version of what he is. Because even the most cheerful, willful adult can never, ever achieve the heights available to even a mediocre kid. Christ, look at the size of that cop. Have these people never heard the word *cholesterol*? The terror in getting old isn't that death is approaching but that childhood is receding. That's the point so many seem to miss."

"Lincoln," I said tiredly, "I have to confess I have no idea anymore why you say what you say."

Lincoln looked in the rearview mirror and flashed himself Nicholson's smile in *The Shining.* "He must have been miserable," Lincoln said, staring at himself. He squeezed a nonexistent blackhead, then sifted his fingers through the handsome dark blond mess on his head. "Deep down, Walt Disney must have lived a miserable life. I think that's pretty obvious."

"What's obvious is that you're in no mood to be helped," I said.

"Sure I am, Chief," he said. "Come up with a way to keep me young and I'm all ears. Maybe it's just more important to me to stay youthful than it is to the average person. Or you." He picked the microphone out of its holder on the dashboard, but simply massaged it nervously, without turning it on. "Look," he said, "don't patronize me. I'm not that far off. The only important experience I may have missed—*may have*—was a healthy, normal childhood. Other than that, I had everything."

"Lincoln," I asked quietly, "what is the problem?"

"There *is* no problem, and stop talking to me like I'm a two-year-old," he said, and held my stare for a long moment during which I briefly forgot where I was. "At certain points," he went on, placidly, clinically, "that part of my brain that governs ethical decisions just misses its synaptic turn-off. In freeway terms, it's an ornate cloverleaf system, and whenever the exit for restraint comes up, I just keep going past it. I get over to the right-hand lane when I see the sign coming, I always signal, and then, at the last second, I, like . . . 'Cerebral arrhythmia,' that's my name for it. A condition in which the brain seems to skip a beat every defining moment of character or so."

"I really don't know what you want from me, then," I said. "You really are tragically glib. All this . . . garbage about Disney is not what I would call asking for help."

"Oh, but it is, Chief," Lincoln said with grave finality.

I shook my head and must have smiled thinly.

"What?" he asked.

"You remind me of the guy," I said, "caught in a van with a naked skinhead teenage girl, he's got a bong in one hand, needles sticking out of both arms, a cache of AK-47s and hand grenades and Nazi child porno literature, she's got his tool in her mouth, and when the SWAT team flings open the van doors, he says, 'It's not what you think . . .' "

Lincoln raised his eyebrows. "Where'd *that* image come from?" he asked.

"I don't know. It just came to me."

"You ought to think about being a writer someday, Chief," he said, knowing just how to play me.

"And you ought to think about getting some real help," I said.

Lincoln darted into a parking space. "Oh, Vincent?" he said, rubbing his eyes. "Fucking eat me."

At the basketball court on Columbus, we met Jeremy and Brian and Brian's younger brother Alec. The five of us stayed on for quite a while, thanks mostly to Alec Marchand, a great shooter and ball-handler who'd played varsity for Princeton. I rebounded well and Lincoln actually played under control. We repeatedly beat a team of ambulatory Calvin Klein ads, a bunch of male models with no jumpshots who'd just returned from L.A. boasting of their nonspeaking roles in the latest Schwarzenegger vehicle. When we finally lost and Lincoln and Jeremy and Alec went to buy drinks, Brian and I sat against the fence. A runner jogged through the playground, sweat bathing her cider-colored legs. Every ballplayer there stopped to watch. "They're all over the lot," Brian said.

"They hold secret meetings someplace," I said. Two more women walked by. A group of three carrying bats and gloves, all with their baseball caps on backward. A Roller Blader. I apologize whenever this story deteriorates into a beer commercial, I really do.

"I don't think she exists in nature," Brian said, dribbling a ball between his long, well-muscled legs. A woman wheeled by on her ten-speed and Brian shook his head. "You think just because you can imagine her, trait by trait, situation response by situation response, body part by body part, that she could exist. But just because she can be extrapolated from all the other ones you've met so far in your life doesn't mean she's *possible*. There's just so much to choose from, nothing seems exactly right."

"Bri, life is not a menu at a Greek diner," I said.

"Wouldn't it be great if it was, though?" he said, and poked me to look at the next trio of softball players crossing the yard. "The one with the haircut," he said. "She makes a lot of noise."

"You can never tell who's going to make noise, I really don't think."

"Is that what the next column is about?" Brian asked. From his backpack, he pulled out his binoculars and scanned the area. "Because I have much to say on the subject. Title: 'Some Come Loudly.' Get it?"

"Cute," I said.

Brian stood and moved to the foul line. I stood, lazily, to rebound. "This week Big Dave's talking about moving to Hollywood," Brian said, swishing shot after shot. "He asked me to set up some meetings. He thinks he's cut out to run a studio."

"At least he's not writing a screenplay," I said.

"Things," Brian said deliberately, cocking his elbow and aiming to shoot, "must be getting pretty hairy with The Wife. That's fourteen in a row."

"Fifteen," I said, bouncing the ball back to him.

"Talk to him," said Brian. "He respects your views on this relationship business."

"I really can't help," I said as he finally missed a shot.

In the kiln of the constant sun, two huge, hungry Dobermans across the street pawed and boxed and humped each other, all sweaty balls and darting, muscular tongues. I walked to Ninety-second Street to use the bathroom in the corner pub. Lincoln was leaning against a building, wincing and holding his knee, while the runner with the apple cider–colored legs stood over him. She was nineteen, tops.

Let me guess: a feigned basketball injury.

"Excuse me," I asked the runner, dying to confirm what I suspected. "But what's his problem?"

She looked to Lincoln to see if my question constituted some breach of privacy. He shrugged his shoulders.

"It's his knee," she said. "He may have ruptured his patella tendon again playing basketball."

"But then how could he get all the way over here?" I said.

Lincoln half-opened one eye at me, a look that said either *Give me a break, I'm winging it here* or *Chief, if you mess this up I'll kill you.*

When men smell the smell, fraternity goes out the window. Column idea. Fuck column ideas.

"I mean," I said to the woman, "if it's a ruptured patella, he'd be writhing on the ground back on the basketball court, I'd imagine."

The runner leaned closer to Lincoln and now put her hand on his shoulder. "Vince?" she said. "Can you stand?"

"Oh, that's pathetic," I said. She turned on me, her look utterly reproachful. "It's just so pathetic that he didn't wear his knee brace," I said.

"You're friends?" she asked me.

"We've played ball together," I said. "I've seen him around. I'd be happy to help—Vince is it?—Vince home."

The runner nodded, then told Lincoln—who with an exaggerated limp attempted a few baby steps, and closed his eyes to simulate suffering—her last name and her street and the fact that she was listed. "You're sure you'll be all right?" she asked with a smile. "And you'll mail me some of your articles?" Lincoln winced once more, a little icing, and nodded. "Okay, then," she said, and got her apple cider–colored legs and Air Huarached feet moving again as she headed up the street. "Bye, Vince," she called out to Lincoln. "Bye, Vince's friend."

On one occasion I found myself riding an elevator alone and I said aloud, as if it were a reflex or a spasm, "I love you."

FOR: BRELL MACLAINE
FROM: VINCE
OF PAGES INCLUDING COVER PAGE: 4

VINCE: A MAN'S VIEW
The Limits of Empathy

As a man, I am able to understand only so much about women. This is true no matter how hard I try to overcome certain facts of my sex—and believe me, I try. Yesterday I had a nightmare that I was a woman running through the streets, after dark.

. . . I passed men running who were smaller than me, smaller than many women. And yet I felt more fear than I knew they did because I knew I could be targeted at least as much for my sex as for my size. Which is why I mind when people insist that rape is not an act of sex but one of violence. For such sticklers for semantics, they seem sloppy to me. Rape is, by my understanding, an act of both sex *and* violence; it is an act of sexual violence. If not, then why wouldn't small men who can't defend themselves be attacked as frequently and brutally as women?

. . . if men are ordained with a sense of power—and we are—then each man, consciously or not, chooses at some point to harness that power and live gently and compassionately, or to unbridle it and live violently. Even though I and the majority of men live gently, it frightened me—in the worst moments, it sickened me—to think that for members of my sex, living violently is the other option.

. . . My nightmare made me realize the boundaries of my own empathy, a man's empathy, no matter how hard I may try to overstep them. I don't feel entitled—if I ever tacitly did—to consider my feelings of empathy and pain about sexual violence commensurate with any woman's, much as the burden of mortality felt by a soldier at the front should, in its way, be sanctified before those of a comrade who toils well behind the lines. Context is everything.

It's sunny outside now, the day after my nightmare. I'm still thinking about it. Tonight, in my sleep, I may once again become that runner. If you're a woman, you don't have to imagine.

Jacqueline, the editor-in-chief, liked it, though she said it rambled in parts. Monica liked it a lot. Brell did, too, but pointed out that it was spotty, overwrought, and—she was absolutely right here—its conclusion emerged somewhat inorganically from its premise. Everyone said Bravo, but that it fell short and would I please rework it? I told Brell thanks but forget it, I'd tried. I was just grateful that she and ———r would seriously let me tinker with the delicate formula that had made Vince such a popular, happy-go-lucky columnist for more than a third of a century now.

I wrote about how men feel about women's makeup. Stop the fucking presses.

I dropped by the Museum of Modern Art at lunch to show Sasha my and Vince's "I think I may be falling in love" column, which I'd just gotten in the mail. Sasha wore a blue-and-white striped shirt, khaki Bermuda shorts, and sandals. She looked happy to see me and gave me her standard chaste kiss on the cheek, though her hug was firm enough that I got to feel softness and muscle both.

"Whatcha reading?" I asked. She turned the paperback over. "Good?" I asked.

She let her head bounce left and right, like one of those disturbing jiggling dashboard creatures. "I guess," she said without enthusiasm. "You pretty much know what you're getting. One of those countless Latin American surrealist glassblowers."

"I won't keep you," I said, my voice shaking a bit, "but I know you probably don't read trashy women's magazines." Sasha smiled broadly. It's a cliché to talk about how pretty someone's eyes are, so I won't. I took a big swallow. "And I wanted to show you this," I said.

I handed Sasha the tear sheet of my confessional and watched her.

After about two paragraphs, her face turned pale and her shoulders slumped as if she'd just learned of some great loss, a death even.

"Oh, God," I said.

"I was hoping something like this wouldn't happen," she said.

"Fuck," I muttered.

She looked down again at the page but I could see she was now skimming.

"Shit," I said. "*Damn* it."

She let out a big breath. "I'm—" She gathered her strength. "I'm—"

"Don't say anything," I said, and I put my hand out for the page. "Just don't say anything."

"I'm flattered," she said, "but I'm also . . . very troubled by this. First of all, you're not in love with me. You don't know me. I really, truly don't want anyone to be in love with me right now. I don't know where I'll be six months from now, I could be in Paris for all I know—" Suddenly she stopped, like a runner hitting the wall.

"I really blew it—"

"You didn't blow anything," she said.

"Just forget it," I said.

"How can I forget it? I wish you'd said whatever you wanted to say to me in private," she said. "What am I supposed to say to a love letter delivered in front of ten million people?" Her face was now almost all pink. "I was really hoping something like this wouldn't happen," she said, shaking her head.

"I'm not feeling too wonderful myself," I said.

She handed me back the column without reading the rest and smiled tightly. "I mean, it's very flattering—"

"I just thought, you're seeing all those people . . ." I said.

"What people am I seeing?" she said. "I meet people, I do stuff with them."

". . . and I thought, Well, what can I do to set myself apart from the rest? And I thought of this. Writing under this pseudonym about how, you know, how terrific you are."

"Vince is not you," she said.

"In a way, he is," I said. "Some part of him is me."

"No," she said. "He's not you." I felt like throwing up. "Listen, I have to get back," she said and picked at some invisible lint on my sweater, one of the greatest passive-aggressive gestures I have ever witnessed. "Thanks and . . . thanks." She turned and walked away briskly, as if half-racing to catch an elevator, except there was no elevator to catch.

We're all dying, says Lincoln. We're just dying at different rates.

9/Well, How Did I Get Here?

I WROTE Sasha apologizing for declaring my amorous feelings for "S." in a national magazine with a circulation of millions. On a Saturday afternoon, I walked to her Chelsea brownstone, hoping to hand-deliver my note and make amends. I framed a sepia-toned print of a shot of the Brooklyn Bridge under construction, and bought a small bag of New York State apples. How come Sasha got to me so? I have no idea; how come "A man, a plan, a canal—Panama" actually works? Sasha liked the idea of having expensive taste more than actually having it. Her smell was nothing at all like the scent strip in the women's magazines. The summer had left her with over one hundred freckles—best guess—the majority of which could be found within shouting distance of the upper bridge of her nose. As I walked up her street, hoping her roommate wasn't home, rehearsing in my head what I would say before I gave her the photograph and the apples and the note—which would likely render the note redundant—I wasn't prepared to see Sasha right

there in her second-floor bay window, reading. So you fall for a voracious reader after all, I thought. A lamp with a green-glass shade stood
guard over her. She wore gray sweatpants and a purple T-shirt. Her
legs were bent, her left arm was wrapped around her lower legs, and
her chin rested sleepily on her knees. Her hair must have been wet
because it looked darker than I remembered. She reminded me of a
cat, especially when her shoulders briefly crowded her neck in a feline
manner, as if her back suddenly pained her. She bit her thumbnail. She
lifted a cup of coffee and sipped without ever taking her eyes off the
page. I couldn't make out the book. Perhaps one of those countless
Latin American surrealist glassblowers.

I do not love you, Julie—*love you* love you, that is.

Remy Kleinwort, D.D.S., I do not love you, though I would like to
make an appointment for a cleaning.

Sonee, Sonie, Psony, what can I say? I do not love you and I cannot
spell your name.

Cheryl, I admire your tolerance for alcohol, the phenomenal night
vision of your hands, your pointy shoe-boots, but I do not love you.

Sasha, I wish it weren't on the newsstands and in the supermarkets
and in the beauty parlors, but it's written on my heart: I do not think I
may be in love with you. I love you.

Sasha turned her head away from the window at some sound that
must have come from deep in the room. A man with just a towel
wrapped around his waist now stood over her. In profile, I could see
Sasha's face light up, the seed of a laugh, a big laugh.

She put down the book she'd been reading so intently, took her coffee cup, and they disappeared into the house.

My Saturday wedding at the Marchand compound in New Jersey
promised to be a festive occasion, though the previous day on Wall
Street the Dow had dipped quite a bit and the hosts and guests at this
party were just the type to get cranky over such an event. I'd been invited because Brian and I had been friends since college, and because

I knew all the Marchands: parents, bride-to-be Blaine, Alison, Alec. The invitation didn't surprise me, considering there would be four hundred nearest and dearest.

Heading down Seventh Avenue to the Holland Tunnel in my dark green suit, my shiny wedding gift for Blaine and Walt (wicker picnic basket from Jenny B. Goode's) enjoying its own seat beside me, I thought (*I* thought), Your problem is simple: Men of your generation are not more evolved than ever but, in fact, more retarded, because you were under the apprehension, from pre-K on, that women and men were the same, and that to believe otherwise was Neanderthal. Consequently, it has taken you boys longer to realize not only that women and men are different, but just *how* different. And while we're on the subject of serious misapprehensions, what gave you the idea that sex and love weren't often at cross-purposes? Or *were?* What makes your friends think being inside someone could give them any significant clue as to what makes that someone tick? Or makes *them* tick? What makes you think looking at someone could give you any significant clue as to what they're like? Your Honor, would you please instruct the witness to answer the questions? The bumper sticker on the car in front: HIT ME, I COULD USE THE INSURANCE.

Immersed in my thoughts, I guess I'd maybe weaved from the left lane to the middle, just as he was moving from the right to the middle. I never looked. It was definitely my fault. We pulled to the side.

"Shit," I said.

"You never even *looked*," whined the blond businessman, rushing out of his car and circling it.

"And you did, I suppose," I said. My dilapidated '79 VW Bug convertible had a thick scrape across the passenger door. I'd barely scratched the driver's side of his BMW, 735i series.

"Damn right I did," the blond businessman said as several people gathered to watch. "I looked at *least* the recommended amount—one Mississippi, two Mississippi. I signaled. You didn't even signal! You were going fifteen miles over the speed limit!" My front right fender hung maybe an inch off the ground. Together we examined the tiny scrape on his spectacular blue machine. "It's a small scratch," I said thoughtfully.

"It's a BMW," the man said. "There's no such *thing* as a small scratch." The look on his face was miserable. The space shuttle disaster didn't compare. He ran his finger along the scrape.

"Well, you've got insurance," I said.

"Oh, beautiful!" the businessman yelled, aiming his rage—for civility's sake—just over my head. I felt the tide among the onlookers turn in my favor. A lovely woman emerged from the BMW. Don't confuse matters, I thought.

"Can you spray paint it?" she asked him. Was *this* the woman I'd marry? I avoided her eyes and instead looked into the sun to catch its light, to bring out the pale amber in my eyes for her. "Honey, might that work?" she said to the blond businessman.

The woman had a slight gap between her two front teeth. In *The Canterbury Tales*, the Wife of Bath has a space between her teeth. In Chaucer's time this was considered very appealing sexually. Also in my time.

"I don't believe it will," the blond businessman said, his face red with fury.

The blond man and I exchanged insurance numbers, license plate numbers, phone numbers. He was Gregory, she was Rachel. Greg took out a Polaroid camera he kept under the seat for just such emergencies and began taking pictures of everything—his car, my car—he ran back up Seventh Avenue in search of signs I may have ignored.

Rachel's fingers, all ten of them, were ringless.

"I'm really sorry about your car," I said to her. "It was all my fault."

"Oh, don't worry about us," she said. "This car's fine. But yours looks like it's seen better days."

"I should get rid of this wreck," I said, and there is a tingling one gets at the base of the neck that must be the warning sign that one is slowly, gradually experiencing a complete character breakdown, "seeing as how I really don't need a car in my line of work."

"Yes?" Rachel said distractedly. *That gap between the teeth is driving me nuts. If she pulls out a Milky Way bar and starts squeezing gooey creme through the space like Play-Doh, I'm marrying her, word of honor.* "What do you do?" she asked.

"Oh, I'm a writer," I said.

"Minuscule world," said Rachel. "Book publishing." I asked where and she named an Exceptionally Classy House. "What do you write?" she asked, mostly to be polite.

We'll show her.

"Well, actually," I said, ever-so-slightly lowering the volume, "I write a column under a pseudonym. For ———*r*. It's called 'Vince: A Man's—' "

" '—A Man's View,' sure!"

There we go.

Her boyfriend Greg—her *presumed* boyfriend Greg—looked up briefly from his photo session, then returned to the work at hand. He was now snapping away at incontestably damning sections of curb.

"You're Vince?" Rachel said, considerably more animated now.

"That I am," I said a tad regally, a tad assholey.

"The New Man, how interesting," Rachel said. "All talking and feeling."

"You got it," I said. "Backrub City."

"That's marvelous," Rachel said. "I've actually read your column for many years and it's remarkable how energetic it's been lately. I can't quite believe how . . . *active* you and your friends are. For a while there, you know, he was in real danger of becoming sort of pathetic. But no more."

"Oh, I don't know," I blushed. "You'll give me a fat head." *Do not blame Rachel for the fat head.*

"I've always wanted to know," said Rachel. "Is Vince happily involved?"

"Am *I*, you mean?" I said.

"Who else?" she said.

"I'm bound by law never to answer that question," I said. "Especially not to someone in the media world. Are you?"

"Am I what?" Rachel said.

"Happily involved?" I said. "With Ansel Adams over there."

Rachel smiled in spite of herself.

"Look, Rachel," I said, "we've been in an accident together. We know we can handle the bad times."

"I happen to be happily involved," she said, fighting to suppress a grin or a smirk, I couldn't tell. "We've been going out for two years. Why am I even telling you this?"

"Still fireworks?" I asked.

"I've never had such a ridiculous conversation." Now Rachel looked a little angry. "What we have is really none of your business," she said. When the relationship's in trouble, they rarely mention the guy's name. It's always "we." Poor Greg. Column idea.

Greg closed the trunk and came around with his Polaroid, and shoved some more film into its mouth. "Just want to get the left rear," he said. By now he'd calmed down considerably and even seemed content, a pig in shit.

Right there on Seventh Avenue, Rachel Luck the Book Editor from the Extremely Classy Publishing House handed me her card and asked if perhaps I wouldn't maybe possibly be interested in writing a book explaining men to women (*"you* to *us,"* as she put it), a nonfiction, self-helpy, entertaining, and very personal book explaining what American men really like, love, hate, talk about, worry about, fear? Sex, love, work, money, family, marriage, kids, penises and death, secrets and secretions, mortgages and prostates, the gestalt, the gumbo, the entire jambalaya? Naturally, her Extremely Classy House would want to play up the Vince angle, which was utterly taboo according to my ———r contract.

Her boyfriend Greg's a putz, Vince thought. *Ask her out.*

"Wow," I said. "That's very flattering, but I don't know that legally I'm allowed to. Anyway, I'm busy writing a novel."

"Oh, yes? Marvelous," she said. "What's your novel about?"

Should I tell her the plot? Rachel was someone to be open with. Rachel was well-positioned. Rachel, whom I really only knew enough to like (How can you love someone after one small fender-bender? You can't, that's how), might even be able to advise you on how to keep your novel from turning into *Swallowing in America*, into *Pinocchio Groin*, into *The Shame of Flushing*. "Can we keep it between ourselves what it's about?" I asked Rachel.

"Of course," she said.

"It's about Vince," I said. "About what it's like being the pseudony-mous man's representative to two million women—"

"Is that ———*r*'s circulation?" Rachel asked. "I thought it was more."

"Yes, two point two," I said. "Ten million in pass-along."

"Go on, go on," Rachel said.

"The running joke in the book is, I don't always know what I'm talk-ing about, yet I'm supposed to be such an authority." For her benefit I brayed at the very notion—me, an expert. Harumph. "Me, an expert," I pshawed. "I'm as confused as everyone else. At *least* as confused."

"You will absolutely send it to me the second you're finished," she said.

She smells like fucking cinnamon, Vince pointed out. I no longer knew whom my allegiance was to—me or him, Sasha or not-Sasha. My heart cracked.

Greg finished with his photos and kindly asked if I wanted to get a few myself for insurance purposes. I held the camera and took a picture of the two of them; then, when Greg briefly turned away, one of just Rachel.

"Now just you in front of the Beemer, Greg," I said. Greg stood there with his arms stubbornly crossed in front of him. "Good. Work with me, Greg."

"Hey, come on," he said. The eye I'd closed to help frame the shot I now opened. Rachel was smiling.

"And now how about just you without the car, Greg," I said. "Give me presidential."

"Game over," Greg said. "This isn't for the album." I came out of my crouch and handed him the Polaroid. He waved to me and headed to his car. I waved back. Now Rachel waved.

"It was very interesting to meet you, Vince," Rachel called back as she got into the car.

"You, too," I said as she and Greg sailed off in their barely scratched BMW, "Rachel."

Driving through the Jersey burg where the Marchand compound was located, you could actually see one income bracket give way to the one above it—brick grew a gradually but inexorably darker pitch of red, front lawns became longer, houses were set back farther, the landscaping was finer and subtler, streets and avenues gave way to crescents. Duck motifs appeared increasingly on mailboxes. Garages that several roads back had housed just two cars—though by and large German and English ones—now could handle three and four and finally six: I'd entered carriage-house garage country. This is not the Jersey Springsteen has in mind.

I hadn't been out here since college. I parked my wreck with the falling-off fender at the end of the road. A tuxedoed supervisor wearing sunglasses and an unbuttoned trenchcoat stood at the mouth of the huge, pebble-covered circle and waved out a gray limo. I peered in the car, hoping for a glimpse, but the tinted windows were closed. Kissinger? Cronkite? Hepburn? As I walked to the front door, a choir of insane country birds serenaded me from their perch in a tangle of branches high above. It never ceases to astonish me what you can get the world to do for you—even make seem random for you—when you are worth eight or more figures, as the Marchands were. I heard little crackles: the crispy deaths of small populations of mosquitoes somewhere so we wouldn't have to be exposed to them. At the door my overcoat was taken by one tuxedoed helper, my package by another ("Presents are nice," he winked at me. "Big presents are nicer"). So far everyone had been wearing a tuxedo, even the valet goons outside; everyone, that is, but me. I retreated to the back of the rotunda and took out my invitation. No; no mention of black tie. I put away the invitation, feeling no easier.

Before diving into the fray I simply watched the crowd, listened to the knit and purl of grown-up conversation. My eye was drawn not to the ladies (in colorful, multifolded, breathtaking gowns) or gentlemen (tuxedo, tuxedo, tuxedo) but rather to the drinks that people were holding and (tuxedoed) waiters were serving—cool green, cherry red, peacock blue; some had a lid of color more intense than the liquid below, some steaming heads of cream sprinkled with nutmeg, some ice cubes bobbing like clear jewels, some slices of fruit. One tray held dozens of slender glasses of pink wine, champagne perhaps. The room staggered me anew; it was a Currier and Ives interior. Each guest reeked of world travel, fully-paid-for tuxedos, a more-than-passing familiarity with the *arrondissements* of Paris . . . here were your Americans who first saw Broadway shows when they opened on the West End, here were your people who summered in Mallorca. Fuck summered; these people *wintered.* They sprang, they fell—

"Vince! Here's my Vince."

Brian's kid sister Alison blindsided me with an expensively ruby kiss just shy of my mouth. A slice of kiwi floated like a lily pad in her beautiful lime drink. I made more meaningful eye contact with Alison than I was inclined to because in her red satin floor-length deal she was sporting some serious cleavage. "Alison, you . . . animal. You're stunning," I said. "I think I saw that dress on the Oscars."

"Well, thank you," she said. "You look pretty handsome yourself."

Edging toward her, I got clobbered by a French whiff that, if they charged for inhaling, would have cleaned out my wallet. "Listen, Alison," I mumbled while stealing a snapshot look down her dress, "how come every man but me is wearing a tuxedo? I'm afraid to ask, but it makes no mention on the invite."

"Didn't you talk to Bri?" Alison asked.

"Men never talk clothes," I said stupidly.

Alison shook her head. "I *knew* this would happen," she said. "It's all Blaine's fault. At least ten times I told her it should say it *explicitly* on the invitation. She said everyone in the world knows Saturday-night wedding means black tie."

"Well, I feel like an idiot," I said.

"Don't," said Alison.

"I should have asked," I lamented.

Alison's infatuation with me, which Brian periodically updated me on, created no sexual tension on my part because (a) I always thought of her as Brian's baby sister; (b) it was Vince, not Andrew, with whom she was infatuated; and (c) you can toss (a) and (b) because I simply wasn't interested. Alison took my hand, steered me to a table where I picked up a drink just like hers (vodka, Midori liqueur, a splash of vermouth, my own thick, succulent kiwi patty), and right away insinuated us into a huddle of silver-haired industrialists, L. L. Bean charter shoppers, duck hunters, a regular G.O.P. circle jerk. It was best I meet people six and eight a pop because I felt obliged to apologize to everyone there for my non-tuxedo. "I didn't know Saturday-night wedding automatically means tuxedo," I said for the fourth time, this time to a trio of sisters— Sexy, Less Sexy, and Voracious Reader.

"All *right* already," Alison said. "Would you guys tell him he looks fine?"

"You look fine," the three sisters said in something resembling unison.

"I want to tell you guys who Andrew is," Alison said, as if she were about to turn over all the cards on "What's My Line?" "You guys read ———*r*?"

"Sure," said Sexy.

"When I was younger," said Less Sexy. "Not so much anymore."

"I never read those magazines," sniffed Voracious Reader.

Alison, bless her heart, was undaunted by the mixed reception. "This, my friends," she said, "is Vince."

"Oh, right," Sexy said vaguely, reorienting to face me. "Alison was telling me about that. You're like this celebrity without being a celebrity? What's a day in the life of Vince like?"

"Well, it's pretty . . . interesting," I said. God, you should be a writer.

"Yeah, yeah," Sexy continued, "oh, *now* I remember. You wrote that thing about how men would like to inform women . . . or what they *don't* want women . . . ."

I put up my hand in a placating It-was-I-who-cut-down-the-cherry-tree gesture. " 'What Men Don't Tell Women About Sex but Want To,' " I said.

"That's it. Oh, that was *funny,*" Sexy said. "I remember that thing you said about Toyota was really funny. Do you remember?" She leered at me.

"What did he say?" Less Sexy asked her sister. "What did you say?" she asked me.

"Alison doesn't stop telling me about you," Sexy said.

"All untrue, I'm sure," I said.

"Now, wait—the *article,*" asked Less Sexy. "What did you say in the article?"

Voracious Reader, clearly bored, craned her neck, scouting the room for another group she might cast a pall over.

"What'd you say about Toyota?" Less Sexy pursued.

"I think I said something like 'Year in, year out, oral sex is the carnal Honda of consumer satisfaction.' Something along those lines," I said.

"Excuse me," said Voracious, finally spotting a splinter group of uniformly sullen rich people.

"Don't mind her," Sexy said.

One drink in me and I started feeling less self-conscious about my green suit. I soon found myself talking to Nina, an ex-deb from somewhere deep in the Connecticut steppes. "Are you the one who's Vince?" Nina asked, engagement-ringlessly, wedding-bandlessly.

"Guilty," I said.

"Blaine told me," said Nina. "Now I want to hear everything about your job, the scrapes you've gotten into . . . your *qualifications.* Your *research.* And don't you dare skimp on details. Now I forgot your real name again?"

I told her.

"Do you always ring twice?" Nina laughed at herself. "Do people just say that to you all the time?"

"No. Actually, they don't. That's very, very clever."

Fortunately, Nina was a little drunk, too, and any hint she had that I was mocking her dissolved with a couple more sips of criminally expensive pink champagne. "Tell me, Vince," Nina said, "if a man and I hit it off well at a party and he asks for my number and then doesn't call, can I call him? Or is that suicide? Will he recoil in horror? Who is the 'New Man'? More importantly, *where* is the New Man? So, this gentleman. What do you think? I'm tired of waiting for my boyfriend to decide if he loves me or not. I have this creeping feeling he's playing around behind my back but it's virtually impossible to prove anything and don't suggest hitting Redial, *please.*" Familiar faces—from Wall Street? former Marchand shindigs? the society pages?—floated by me.

"Just how well did you and this new gentleman at the party get along?" I asked as a waiter swooped in to arm me with a fresh drink.

"Fabulous," Nina said. "Couldn't have gone better had I written the script."

"How long has it been since the party?" I asked.

"A week," said Nina.

"Give him four more days," I said with great certainty and took a heavy gulp of my drink. "If he doesn't call by Wednesday, then call him in the next three to seven days after that. But don't wait any longer than that three-to-seven-day window or you enter the self-esteem danger zone."

Nina nodded gravely. "Four more, then three to seven," she recited. "Four, three to seven. Got it."

Nina's mother, a Mrs. Fletcher from Old Greenwich, swooped in. Mrs. Fletcher was a frail half-woman, half-bird whose hair was whipped

into a nest so delicate that it appeared that the slightest movement—
the uncouth slamming of a Bentley door, say—would collapse it. I could
tell it had been done recently, that very afternoon most likely; one thing
Vince believes every man must know if he ever hopes to understand
women is just how close to the actual festivity—hours, minutes even—
women have their hair done. Next up: my theories on atomic fission.
"Your hair looks lovely," I told Mrs. Fletcher.

My comment made her utterly sad and just as utterly grateful, and I
could tell how badly she wanted to touch her head to make sure the
bouffant was still structurally sound. "It doesn't, I'm sure, but thank
you anyway," Mrs. Fletcher said. "Isn't he adorable, Nina?"

"Mother, we were talking," Nina said. From across the room, a wedding guest about my age stared at me. College?

"I'm sorry, darling," Mrs. Fletcher said to her daughter. "What does
the young man do?"

"He writes an advice column for ———r, Mother," Nina said.

"Oh, yes?" She put her white-gloved hand on my sleeve, flirtatiously.
"Tell me, then: Why can't men just stay put with a good woman who
treats them nicely?"

As Eddie Murphy says, Mrs. Fletcher: It's a dick thing. "That's the
Riddle of the Sphinx," I non-answered. "That's the $64,000 Question."

"Do you have anything in the works now, dear?" Mrs. Fletcher asked
me.

"Just the column," I said. "And I'm writing a novel."

"Oh, my," Mrs. Fletcher said. "Can I be the love interest?"

Let's not get carried away, dear.

I felt loose enough by now to reach two fingers into my drink and fish
out the juicy kiwi slice, and lay it wetly on my outstretched tongue.

The guy staring at me from across the room now approached. Bob
Slocum from varsity lacrosse?

"Are you the great Vince?" he asked. Once I'd thought I would actually love the brazen anonymity I would possess, the bizarrely public
anonymity. That seemed the distant past now.

"At your service," I said.

"The name is Richard ———son," he said hotly, not extending a hand. "We met once. Julie," he said.

Watermelon Man!

He was corrupt with health—tall, black-haired, the wide shoulders tapering down, the classic V-cut build. His slightly too-snug tuxedo— probably bought at Barneys for more than retail—made his vigor almost ostentatious. It was hard to imagine him talking baby talk to Julie. "Hello, Richard," I said. "I didn't know you knew the Marchands."

"Give me a break," Watermelon Guy said disgustedly. "Jerry and I have invested together for years. What the hell are you doing here?"

"Well," I said, unnerved by his hostility, "I've known the Marchands since Brian and I roomed togeth—"

"Yeah, listen," he said bitterly, "I've been meaning to tell you if I ran into you again that I honestly don't understand what Julie ever saw in you."

"She always mentioned something about a phenomenal erection," I said. I really shouldn't drink so much. "How about yourself?"

Watermelon Nazi snorted. "You think I don't know about your little shit at Yankee Stadium and the Bronx Zoo? What, you think that makes you and her, like—" He was sputtering.

"Richard, I have nothing to say. Good luck with your seedless process."

"We drive past the Cloisters," he said bitterly, "Julie *has* to say something, since we have this full-disclosure pact. I know about the library lion."

"I have no comment," I said. "Give Julie my regards. I'm glad we finally touched base."

He leaned in. "How—?" he began. "I mean, what were you guys, were you guys trying to break some record? I mean—I mean—did you—and the U.N.? I mean—did she—does she—did she ever bother to tell you how much she hated your little stunts—"

"Richard, listen, Richard, *Richard,*" I said, curdling his name thickly in my mouth, "I have nothing to say about this. She loves you. You're a very lucky man, don't ever forget that. Julie is terrific. F.Y.I., I'm sorry."

"Why don't you write a column about all the places you screwed around?" Watermelon Man said. "How come? You know so much about women."

"It's not something I want to write about," I said, scratching my nose with my middle finger, juvenile that I am. "Richard, maybe you just need a vacation."

"We can't," he said. "We're too busy these days. We're way too leveraged professionally right now."

"You or Julie?" I asked.

"Me or Julie?" Richard contemplated.

"Nice ego boundaries," I said.

"You really don't know shit," he said.

You got that right, Richie, babe.

As I walked away, Mr. Marchand, who was much further along than I, clenched me to his bosom for the first time in our history, then slung his arm over my shoulder. Get ready for some major speechifying from the father of the bride.

"Boy," Mr. Marchand said, gulping champagne, "we really took a bath on the Street yesterday, didn't we, Andrew?"

"Cleaned me out, Mr. M," I said. "Had all my money tied up in hog bellies, can you believe it."

"I'm telling you, Andrew," Mr. Marchand said, and drew me even closer, "the meaning of life should deepen as we get older, yet for so many of them out there it's just the other way around. They burst into the world with a divinity, poor and rich, black and white, Jew and Christian, Democran and Republicat, girl and boy, exit mother with an explosion, the very spirit of life in their lungs, and the slow ones the doctor even has a good swift spank on the rear for them, to get it started. Verve! Nutrition! Colors! Furniture! Lights! Camera! Action!"

Mr. Marchand pumped his fist in the air and snapped at an hors d'oeuvres–laden waiter whose back was to us, as if the help might be armed with three-hundred-sixty-degree radar. Even being worth eight figures and having millions socked away in Swiss accounts and Bahamian tax shelters couldn't get the oblivious waiter to turn around.

"And what slowly begins to happen?" Mr. Marchand continued, the conversational equivalent of vacation slides, carousel #2. "Everything starts getting stepped on, sucked out, dried up. The interoffice memo is killing us, just *killing* us. Now, I ask you this question, Andrew, because of the respect I hold for you, as a writer, as the man we Marchands all love and adore as Vince, and for what he would think about all this. And so my question to you: If a man's dream shatters and no one is there to hear it—maybe he doesn't even hear it himself—does it make a noise? Or must he have canine hearing?" As I readied my answer, Mr. Marchand reached out over another retreating waiter's shoulder to snatch a mushroom quiche the size of a postage stamp.

"You *bet* it makes a noise," Mr. Marchand went on, flakes of quiche crust springing off his lower lip as he spoke. "And it *changes* him, it starts to die him off, the worm turns. It's been a difficult millennium and an especially difficult century, hasn't it, Andrew? As a culture we have much collective grief work before us, and not until we do that will we feel we've earned the right to look forward with high hope to the twenty-first century. So, in the meantime, I'm here to give us all some hope." He dug his fingers into my neck muscles and started kneading. I knew from Brian all about Señor Marchand's midlife crisis: experiments with Outward Bound, Eastern philosophy, deep-tissue massage, increasingly younger secretarial quim. A nasty divorce was the other shoe waiting to drop. "What's better today than yesterday?" Mr. Marchand queried me. "Penicillin. Athletes are more spectacular. This Shaq kid is something, isn't he? Large-print books, that's good. My mother-in-law feels like a new woman with those, she can read again. Most states now have seat belt laws, which seems to have saved a few lives. And dual air bags. We can preserve food longer, though more people than ever go without. We can send back great satellite photos. Our special effects are incredible."

"What about love?" I said.

Mr. Marchand looked at me dumbly. "What about it? Ah, Alec. The next of my strapping brood to marry."

Alec, the bride's younger brother, abandoned his fiancée, a Smith graduate who actually goes by the name of Boo-boo, and moved in to save me.

"That's not what life should be," Mr. Marchand continued, like a car, though a slow-moving one, out of control. "We get sick, we can no longer take the stairs two at a time, a good bowel movement becomes more important than good sex—okay, that's all manageable. Our essence should broaden. You chose not to wear a tuxedo. I respect that. What time does for a river, why can't it do that for a man?"

"What time does for wine and cheese," said Alec, "why can't it do for a man?"

"Shut up, Alec," said Mr. Marchand, and I thought I actually saw one of the minor veins in his left nostril explode and a fine blueberry-colored estuary begin winding its way up his soft pink nose. "The problem with Alec here is that he's heard my speech—"

"—a thousand times," Alec said. "Try ten thousand."

"And yet Alec has yet to *listen* to what I'm saying," Mr. Marchand said.

"Alec *looks* but he does not *see*," Alec said, bolting for the refuge of third-person narration, as the drama of a lifelong Oedipal tussle between the two men, Princeton '59 and Princeton '93, began to rear its inebriated head. "What other people see as a wall," Alec said, "Alec here sees as a ceiling that has fallen ninety degrees from grace. Alec *eats* but he does not *taste*. Alec *inhales* but he does not *smell*."

Intriguing as it was to confront all these brittle WASP dynamics one after another, I badly needed a bathroom.

SOME PREPPIE GIRLS IN COLLEGE
I HAD ABSOLUTELY NO CHANCE OF SLEEPING WITH

Binky (Andover)
Muffy (Miss Porter's)
Buffy (Choate)
Scruffie (St. Paul's)
Bootie (Exeter)
Tootie (National Cathedral)
Doodie (Hotchkiss)

When I emerged from the toilet, I went searching for Brian through this Britishly civilized Eden, among the singing glasses and round foamy drinks and frothy cleavage and Picasso prints and duck paraphernalia (duck-headed fire pokers, duck-decorated china, goose liver pâté). Percent of American men who say they enjoy sex more than money: 47. Percent of American women who say this: 26. Roper Gallup Times CBS. I settled next to an orphaned silver tray of gravlax and chervil (*chervil,* for Christ's sake) until chimes sounded to inform us we were to move to the ballroom, which had been converted into a chapel. I finally found Brian, who planted a big kiss on my cheek, before he moved on, working the room. Sexy and Less Sexy swooped in and insisted I sit with them.

Someone poked me from behind.

"Dear, would you do this for me?" asked Mrs. Fletcher as she handed me her video camera. "I've never been able to understand the instructions. Those awful Japanese. Thank you, dear."

A harpsichordist began to play Vivaldi. She was competent on her arpeggios, less so on her circles of fifths. She should keep a tip snifter out just in case, I thought. Percent of American women in 1970 who say men are quote basically kind gentle and thoughtful unquote: 67. Percent who say that today: 51. With a genteel rustle of the finest European fabric plus whatever my green suit was made of, all of us in the ballroom-chapel turned to enjoy the erect pageantry of the wedding procession, to smile and *aaah* and chuckle genteelly over the flower girl and the ring-bearer, two petite xanthochroids who in their outrageous getups—intricate pearl-encrusted gown for her, morning coat and top hat for him—looked more like child actors than children. I hate child actors. So maybe I was more than tipsy. Finally, the bride, Blaine Marchand, floated in, trailed by a lacy white train the size of a small oil spill, a diamond tiara atop her head. I imagined escorting Sasha to the premiere of the film version of my novel at Mann's Chinese, she in a blue gown and diamond tiara, me in a snazzy, unrented, greenless tuxedo. So maybe I was more than a little tipsy. Did I say that already? "Thank you," I said, beginning my Academy Award acceptance speech.

"What?" Sexy was talk-whispering at me.

"What?" I said.

"You just said thank you," she said.

"Oh. Sorry."

She shrugged her shoulders. I stood to videotape the bride. Straining to frame her in the lens of Mrs. Fletcher's camera—why was Blaine moving down the aisle so damn fast?—I noticed the first snow of the season, certainly the first one indoors. So maybe the story ends here and I just don't get the girl. Very possible. Don't Shakespeare's romantic comedies always end with a wedding? Chance a man is with a woman when he shops for clothes: 2 in 3. There was applause for Blaine— something I'd never heard this early in a wedding ceremony—like the sound of crashing surf, the rushing of trains, the falling of snow. Percent of American men who deal with depression by trying to sort out problems: 23. Percent who deal with depression by watching tv: 35.

The bride looked at me through the lens through her veil and she was definitely not smiling.

Hours passed, perhaps decades.

I may have married, fathered children, or maybe the marriage had already ended, and acrimoniously at that. Julie was there, somewhere, and my mother, and I think the young Joey Heatherton. The double-dimpled girl in the Cayuga Squaws at day camp who always wore white moccasins was there, as was Ms. Cangelosi, my favorite teller at the Flushing branch of Citibank, and Diane Delepopolopoulos, my junior-high-school crush, or Colopopolopolous, something that went on an opolopol longer than you thought it should, and the little Incan princess in the station wagon on the Long Island Expressway and the Double Mint Twins and girls in lipstick years ahead of me in elementary school, bad girls from the third-grade classroom all the way down the hall with the broken fluorescent light and the smell of cabbage, stringy-haired girls indifferent to the dried chocolate ice cream on their hands and chins, women I'd seen on Broadway and on Lex and in the subway and never said hello to, debutantes in the Sunday *New York Times* fashion sketches who didn't exist, they were all there when the smell of NH$_3$ hit the bottom of my stomach and I felt a series of smacks on my cheeks and the back of my neck.

"Unhitch his belt," someone was saying. A chaos of faces, hands. "Good, now his tie. Another button."

Above me was an oversized animal's face. Not Sasha. Why the hell not?

"Oppa," I attempted. My teeth hurt like eating snow.

"Are you okay?"

"Annh," I said. It was as if a movie reel had broken, and reality was returning, inevitable but offhand. "Hoppa?" I asked.

"He sounds like a boxer. You passed out, champ. Just lie there for a second."

I fought a brief thought about hanged men: the predicament of lost bowel control. Stop thinking about it. I sniffed hard. I realized the only strong odor was still tincture of ammonia, thank God. I had no idea where I was.

"Whassa wer?" I said. Slowly, the rest of the world began coming back.

"What's he saying?" two women said in unison.

Women at weddings adopt same menstrual cycle? Column idea. My strength was returning.

I was helped from the chapel by Brian and Alec. Everyone must have stared, I thought once I was in the other room. The bed was hard, the linen clean and lemony. A black maid in white entered and laid a wet rag across my forehead, then left me alone. My mouth was not cut, as I'd thought. Wedding march music started again down the long hall- way, followed by a spooky silence; I strained without success to hear the minister mumble the age-old admonitions at them. Finally there was a cheer; some real applause. A little later I heard a combo strike up Gersh- win's "He Loves and She Loves," Blaine and Walt's wedding song. Fine choice.

VINCE: A MAN'S VIEW

Men Are Pigs

No, really, we are, you're absolutely right. Anyone who pos- tulates that a man's motives are not completely (if often in- directly) groin-driven is either (a) a naive woman; (b) a repressed man; (c) a man who thinks such a formulation will ultimately improve his chance of getting some action; (d) a eunuch.

My friend Brian? Carries field glasses at all times to look in promising windows, ogle unsuspecting women from a dis- tance. Hangs out at the 92nd Street Y, to catch spillover from academic/feminist/literary lectures. The crowd is intriguing, prefiltered liberal, birth-controlled. His scam line? His film production company's casting a new movie (true) and hunt- ing nationwide for the next Jean Seberg (false).

My pal Big Dave? Gets psychotically jealous at The Wife if she isn't home exactly when she says she'll be home, but there isn't a city he travels to that he doesn't go out looking for some.

My friend Lincoln Crye? Are you kidding me? How old are you? Are you toilet-trained? Did you have awotuv homewuk today?

Me? Well, which one of us are you talking about, exactly?

10/We're Killing Each Other

EVER SINCE Vince, bitter Vince, had fought me over my misguided column/love letter to Sasha, he'd weakened considerably. You wouldn't have recognized him anymore. That the column had proved a disaster with Sasha was almost irrelevant; the simple fact that I (Andrew) had professed my heart to S. in Vince's name was enough to precipitate his deterioration. Vince was bedridden now—vomiting, fever, chills. He pleaded with me to bring him ginger ale, Pepto-Bismol, dry toast, but I refused, or at least took my sweet time about it. On those rare occasions he was able to sleep, swaddled in three and four blankets, I'd sneak into the room, throw open the window and let in a huge front of cold, late-autumn air. Vince woke groggily, shivering, his teeth chattering, and I'd slam the window shut. "Sorry," I'd whisper and tiptoe out before he knew what had happened. I moved my writing chair to just outside the bedroom and wrote my exposé-as-novel from there, so that when Vince would burst from the room, doubled over, frantic for the bathroom, I'd just happen to have my legs out and watch him fall on his face. I think it was after the sixth time I tripped him that he realized I fully meant to kill him.

The letters never ceased.

> *... admire your authority. You're one of those rare men still left who I bet knows how to treat women like "ladies." I imagine any woman you would set your sights on would be very lucky. I wish my oldest boy's confidence was half yours. His self-esteem is so low I worry constantly for him ...*

> *Vince, I spent $138.00 on a dress and do not have to worry about anybody being mad at me. For the first time I'm starting to like myself ...*

> *... every time a new magazine comes in the mail I turn straight to your column. One day I read one of them to my father and my father said that your opinion resembles one of a homosexual, and he asked me what is the author's name, and it is never shown, so I wonder, is it really a woman writing your column?*
> *Even so, I enjoy it very much.*

I remember exactly what my digital clock read when the phone call came: 3:23. Lincoln, I thought as I put down my pencil, obviously doesn't understand. Orange juice is my only fuel these days, running my only extracurricular, Pepperidge Farm cookie bags litter the floor surrounding my desk. I'm on such a roll, trying to finish my goddamn book and execute my pseudonymous alter ego, that I hardly even fondle my glass paperweight dome anymore, though I do check periodically to see if Candy Woman across the street is snarfing chocolates.

"Make it good," I said, picking up on the second ring.

"Oh—gosh," said a woman's voice. "Is this Andy?"

"Yes." My pulse shot out of the blocks.

"Uh, this is Uta, a friend of Lincoln's. I'm very sorry to call so late but Lincoln is hurt."

"What?" I said. "What do you mean?"

"He'll be okay, he will, he will," she said. "He will. Right now there's, like, a lot of blood? And he's a little dizzy?" Someone in the background—Lincoln—said something to her and then she covered the phone. "What?" was all I was sure I heard her say. "We're going to the emergency room now," she said to me when she returned. "And he asked me to let you know where we're going."

"Of course," I said and realized I was almost shouting. "How bad is he? What happened?"

I could hear him in the background, but couldn't make out what he was saying. I heard her say, okay, okay, *okay*. She came back to the phone.

"We'll, um, so then you'll meet us there?" she said and told me where as I jammed my feet into my running shoes. Just before I hung up I heard Uta call out to me. "Hello?" she said. "Are you there? Hello?"

"I'm here," I said.

"He did it to himself," she said.

In the waiting room, I found Uta's powers of description utterly compelling. She looked extremely young (surprise), with white-blond hair and a look at once virtuous and wanton, in a 1940s fan-magazine way. She told me how Lincoln and she had gotten into a huge fight. She said they fought almost every time they saw each other. I didn't know which surprised me more: that he often got into fights or that Uta was even in the picture. Uta said that suddenly, in the middle of their fight, Lincoln was holding up heavy scissors, and he opened them and put one of the steel blades to his right earlobe and pushed the point in until it punctured the skin and blood plumed out, and then he dragged the blade in and down to the start of his jawline and then turned it around and pulled it back around to the side of his neck and behind his ear, though at no point—she emphasized this—at no point did he ever stick the point in too deep. To help me visualize better, Uta folded and tugged at her own ear, and scraped her fingernail along the side of her face. I was shocked by the event but also hypnotized by the steady tone in which she reported it.

"I yelled 'Stop it!' at him," Uta said to me, taking a breath between sips of coffee in the waiting room. " 'Stop it! What are you doing?' But just as I got to him he snapped the blades together and, like, let them close down on each other. There was a . . . like a hiss, a soft sound, until the other blade sank into the, like, *pulp?* of his ear. He dropped the scissors. Blood was all over the side of his face . . . oh . . . uchh . . . it's making me sick . . ."

I put my hand on her neck. "Put your head between your knees," I said. I took the coffee cup from her and brought her water. After about three minutes she looked up.

"Feel a little better?" I said.

"Yes," she said, swallowing. "Sorry."

"There's nothing to be sorry about," I said.

Her color was returning. "Are you the one he calls in the middle of the night?" she said.

"Yes," I said.

"It was like red shampoo in his hair," she said quietly. "His earlobe dangled forward, not down. Like a swinging door almost. I think I was just so shocked I didn't do anything for maybe a minute? Could that be? It was more like something you'd see maybe in a really bad movie. And then?" Her smile was tinged by disgust. "Lincoln turns to the mirror to look at himself, almost proud."

Once Lincoln's head was bandaged, he was moved to the psychiatric wing, which I thought was excessive—or, correction, *wanted* to think was excessive. When finally I got in to see him, the right side of his head was wrapped all in white. Lincoln raised his eyebrows at me, as if to indicate he had no more clue than I did, as if it were just a very poor joke that no one got, not even him.

"I've thought about the van Gogh implications, so save your breath," he said in an unfrightened voice. "No, that was not the inspiration. Yes, I know who I am. No, I don't exactly know what happened. There's nothing to explain, so don't ask for one. No, I wasn't trying to off myself and I'm not in denial, so no jokes, please. No, I don't really want to talk more about it, now or tomorrow."

The bullying thought that is supposed to form in the minds of loved ones at this point—didn't you see this coming?—made its appearance on cue. But I truly and honestly could tell myself the answer was, No. I did not.

The next morning he called from his hospital room. Though I'd only gotten home a few hours before, I was up, wide awake, thinking about him. "My stepfather," Lincoln said, "was a prick."

"Okay," I said.

"That's all. I just wanted to say that."

"How was he a prick," I said.

"He was *reeaal* primitive," Lincoln said, stretching out the word in an earnest, melodramatic way completely unlike him. "And I mean that in a derogatory sense."

"How was he primitive?" I asked.

"I don't care," Lincoln said, fatigued. It really wasn't such a non sequitur, I thought, after hearing it echo for a few seconds in my mind's ear.

Lincoln didn't exactly withdraw, but he suggested I needn't visit so often. He wanted lots of books—anything, everything, it made no difference what. He was assigned an in-house shrink and seemed surprisingly agreeable to the idea. (I found out that he had no choice *but* to see one; that New York State law mandated that he couldn't leave until he saw one and was no longer deemed a threat to himself.) Uta—the only one of Lincoln's female friends who visited him, or at least the only one I ever saw there—dropped hints to me that Lincoln was more complicated than I'd imagined: He slept with his eyes partly opened; he wept in his sleep and had no memory of it on awakening; in bed he often flinched violently at her touch, and never—*never*—let her touch his neck; he almost never wanted to make love. The obvious guess was abuse, but it was also the convenient explanation. Anyway, she said she was in the dark about the details.

It unnerved me to see Lincoln so serious, so lacking in irony. At one point, when I said it might help him to talk things out, he said, "Of *course* there was a reason I did what I did besides mere fascination. For now, that's between me and . . . I don't know. My rabbi." I was left to wonder what exactly his stepfather had done, where his father was, what his mother was like. I asked once, then not again. If he wanted me to know, he'd tell me.

Men don't push. Hands off. A man's way of looking at the world. Column idea.

Lincoln's bloody act paralyzed me. He didn't phone, late at night or otherwise. I thought of ways I might be of help to him, but I realized there weren't any. I blackened in *Times* crossword puzzle squares I didn't get. I surfed past TV stations more aimlessly than usual. I grew weepy over commercials. Where does meat end, where do meat byproducts begin? Who wins the cash, who the cash prizes? What's the difference between our detergent and this leading brand? What the hell *are* factory-to-dealer incentives? On a talk show about celibacy, a sixty-year-old guy called himself a "born-again virgin" because he hadn't slept with anyone in twenty-five years. He spoke of "developing sensuality beyond sex." Right, Chief. Nothing a little "Hide the Salami" won't cure, you fucking asshole.

No previous Vince had ever resigned, claiming ignorance or self-loathing. No Vince runner-up had ever been called in the middle of the night to quick get dressed and hurry down to the ———r Madison Avenue offices to claim the relinquished title of Vince, the bejeweled crown of a writing gig for any single man in America. Anyway, overwrought as I was, with all the horrendous men out there, who knew how much worse my emergency successor might be? Did you know that over four thousand American women a year die at the hands of their husbands, lovers, and boyfriends? You want me to punch up the numbers on mutilation, rape, and your everyday, orbit-shattering roundhouse to the face? Believe me, ———r could have done much, much worse than me.

Lily, my yente, stopped by Scrabbles at happy hour. She wore a gas station attendant's shirt with the name *Manny!* chirping in red script over the breast pocket. I was at the piano making my way through Marcel's Body Parts medley. Lily took several miniature spring rolls and a napkin from the food cart, then sat beside me on my bench.

"I want an explanation why it didn't work out with Sasha," she said, then kissed me on the cheek.

"*You* want an explanation?" I said.

"That's right," she said. "You liked her, didn't you?"

"Yes, Lily," I smiled tightly. "I also fell in love with her. Also, Lily, you told me she was finished with Mr. Wrong."

"She *is* finished with him," Lily said.

"Not according to her," I said as I segued into "If I Only Had a Brain."

"You take things too literally," she said. "Women lie constantly. Sometimes it amazes me how little you know about women."

"That makes two of us," I said. I gestured for Diana to come take Lily's drink order.

"Do you know who's at fault for this not working out with Sasha?" Lily said.

"Let me guess," I said. "Uh . . . *you* are?"

"The two of you were *made* for each other," she said. "Does the phrase 'perfect for each other' mean anything? You're a complete goon. You two were meant to be together even before you were born."

"Since when did you become Shirley MacLaine?" I said.

"Hey, you do pretty well," Lily said as she sifted her fingers through the bills in my tip glass, which was rather verdant for so early on a weeknight. "I love the way you play this song."

"It's not my version," I snapped. "I stole it from Harry Connick. Hundreds of people play it better."

"So I blew it," said Lily. "Let she who is without sin. I'm here because I want another chance." Garth, the manager, came over with his fingers stuffed in his ears, his sign that I should soften the hammers. When I did he smiled and made his fingers into a gun and shot me. Then he turned and shot Diana, who was delivering a Heineken to Lily. Then Garth smiled at Lily and shot her.

"I don't think so, Lily," I told her. "I don't trust your scouting reports."

"Well, tough shit, because you don't have a choice. It's not a blind date. It's a movable party."

"I'm working hard these days, Lily," I said. "I want to be alone."

"Bullshit and bullshit," she said. "You can take one lousy evening off." She took a big swig from her beer. "This girl I want you to meet is terrific. She's got even more going for her than Sasha did."

"You mean, she's happily married?" I said.

"Ha, ha," said Lily.

"I appreciate your efforts, Lil, but I need some time to get over the hump." Oh, boy, Freud wouldn't even charge for that one.

"So I'm sending you the invitation," she said. "I'm having a Secret Santa thing after work at the Rockefeller Center tree. I'm sending everyone something special, and they have to bring it with them and see who they match up with. I'm totally manipulating it. Then we all go to a bar and drink hot toddies and get trashed." Guy walked by and smiled at us. "He's cute," Lily said after he passed. "I'd invite him to meet her if he wasn't gay."

"How do you know?" I asked.

She just looked at me. "Now, you must bring what I send you. Your dream girl will have the other half."

"Sounds too romantical for words, Lil," I said.

She beamed a lottery winner's smile. "I know how to pick girls—don't I?" she said.

"You know how to pick *up* girls," I said. I modulated into "Smoke Gets in Your Eyes."

Lily put one hand on each thigh and lifted herself from the bench unhurriedly, as if putting herself together piece by piece. She kissed me on the cheek.

"Hey," I called after her.

"Yes?" she turned.

"Sasha didn't happen to say anything about me—you know, in particular. Did she?"

Lily just shrugged.

Blood appeared in my stools. I called Lincoln at the hospital, hoping that by sharing misery, something women do so much better than men, some of his troubles might dissolve. "What do you think it could be?" I asked.

"Maybe you're getting your period," Lincoln said.

Bagelry: My Ideal Dozen

3 poppy
2 sesame
2 cinnamon raisin
1 pumpernickel
1 combo (ses + pop)
1 onion
1 garlic
1 egg

That should give you some idea just how fast I was falling. That's an entire day's work there, that bagel hit parade.

"Is there something wrong?" asked Monica, perpetually tanned

Monica, when I stopped by ————r to turn in my next Vince column, a lame-o thousand words trying to make the case for men's bathroom habits ("Let's Put Down the Seat, Not Each Other"). She stopped me at the eleventh-floor elevator bank. I was unaware just how awful I must have looked.

"I'm just a little tired, I guess," I said. Also, I have blood in my stools, I didn't add.

"We just got the next issue and tear sheets, if you want to come back with me for a sec," Monica said. "Did I ever tell you how much I loved your August column?"

"I can't remember which one that was," I said.

"You're in love," she said.

"Oh," I said. "Yeah."

"Are you?" she asked excitedly. "It's *so* sweet. I would love to have someone declare their love to me in front of the whole country," she said.

"Even if it's not signed?" I said.

"Even if it's not signed. 'S.' must be pretty thrilled right now—" Monica put her hand on my shoulder. "Hey," she said.

"Maybe I'll pick up my stuff another time," I said, looking down at the floor. "I have to go."

"Are you okay?" Monica asked. She placed three fingers under my chin to raise my head but I wouldn't let her. "Hey," she said.

"Yep," I said.

Lincoln was on antidepressants and seeing an in-house therapist and happy about neither. He said he'd grown tired of the shrink: Lincoln would say rude or nonsensical things to him, the shrink would ask what he meant by that, Lincoln would reply, "Why would anyone in their right mind really want to know what I mean by that?" And the shrink took it all down.

I organized cliques of buddies to visit. We all brought Lincoln books. A pal from his art gallery, a petite coworker who obviously knew nothing of Lincoln's weakness, gave him a copy of *Seventeen,* an unwittingly cruel, ironic error in judgment. Big Dave Navinsky brought nonfiction thrillers about white-collar crime. He wanted to stay longer because he hated going home; you could see in Big Dave's eyes how pained he was by his crumbling marriage. But staying at the hospital was worse. Big Dave couldn't handle hospitals. He paced the room, stopped to look over at Lincoln every few seconds, then emitted an otherworldly, baritone groan, as if he were about to throw up.

"Lincoln, I'm taking Big Dave home," Brian said. "He can't take it."

"Can't take what?" asked Lincoln, propped up in bed, flipping through *Seventeen* studiously and looking okay except for the white bandage—though a much daintier one now—that covered his right ear and ran down the side of his neck for inches. He looked up. "What can't Dave take?"

"Hospitals," Brian answered for him. Big Dave slumped against the window ledge, blocking out light.

"Then go, Navinsky," Lincoln said. "Get out of here, go home. Take off your clothes, slip into a hot bath."

"It's okay?" Big Dave asked, tilting his head up weakly, as if it were a sack of rocks. His face was a chalky lime color.

"How do I know?" Lincoln said. "I don't make the rules. There are no rules, Sizable Dave. I'll make the rules now. Go home. You look unwell."

Big Dave swayed as if any second he might drop. None of us relished the idea of helping the nurses clean up after a guy as big and potentially sour-smelling as Big Dave.

"Dave, go," I said. "It's fine. I'll stay."

"Me, too," said Lincoln's colleague from work.

"So long, Mr. Marchand, Mr. Navinsky," Lincoln said. "Don't think I don't appreciate your patronage, because I don't." He cracked his neck, then gave them a genuine smile.

Now it was just me, Lincoln, and his diminutive office mate from the gallery. On TV, a PBS type in a lumberjack shirt was teaching painting—a pastoral scene, adding stones to the lake bank. You could add ten stones or a hundred, the painter said, it didn't matter. He demonstrated a dabbing motion, swishing the brush like a fish tail. "Light, dark, thin, thick," he said.

Lincoln watched enchanted, then returned to his magazine. "You're the guys I really wanted in here anyhow," he said. "O'Rourke, Vince," Lincoln said, by way of introduction. "Vince, O'Rourke. You know what my theory is? I want to live by the sword. That's it. The other part I don't need."

"You can't live by it and not die by it," I said. "You can't have it both ways. That's what Dr. Eustace Chesser says."

"Who's Dr. Eustace Chesser?" Lincoln asked.

"He wrote a dumb sex manual in the fifties called *Love Without Fear*. You can't have both hard and soft, fast and slow, he says. You have to choose. I'm thinking of using it as an epigraph for my book."

"Have they caught onto you yet? Have you broken the vow of the Franciscan order yet? Are you still Vince, Vince?"

"You'll be happy to know I've finally descended to premenstrual syndrome," I said. "This month: 'For Men, P.M.S. Is Also a Four-Letter Word.' I don't believe it one bit, but it's easier and funnier for Vince to agree than disagree. You know."

Lincoln nodded, then his colleague did, as if he knew what we were talking about.

"They have what we want, boys," Lincoln said to me and O'Rourke, nodding down at the issue of *Seventeen*. Not back to a celebration of the twelve-year-old, please; we'd been doing so well lately. "They have what *everyone* wants," Lincoln went on. "I mean youth, not beauty, though beauty helps, too. But really I mean youth. No hair yet in the pits, on the legs, around the groin, in the anus, over the lip, on the chest. Nubs, buds."

How fortunate it was that Lincoln's shrink was an old man. When Lincoln had gotten his strength back, he'd asked to be switched to a young woman; request denied. "Rest," I advised Lincoln now.

"Listen, O'Rourke," Lincoln said, "there's only ever one tragedy, only one: lost innocence. Right? Who made life this way, where you keep getting more and more infirm? Brilliant fucking concept. Start off helpless, end up helpless, terrific, it's symmetrical. It wouldn't be so bad if every boy wasn't a slut at heart." He shut his eyes briefly; the afternoon medication was kicking in. "And every boy's a slut at heart—wouldn't you agree, O'Rourke?" Lincoln said.

"I wouldn't know, Mr. Crye," O'Rourke said.

"Don't call me that," Lincoln said. "These days a man can't cut—*cut*, mind you, not cut *off*—his own ear—his *own*, mind you, nobody else's—in peace without the holy tribunal declaring him bunny feathers. What is it, O'Rourke? Sick?"

O'Rourke had faltered back into a chair and covered his stomach.

"I know what you mean," Lincoln said. "Hospitals make everyone queasy. Look at Navinsky. He's built like a downtown office building, he screws people by the minute uncovering legal loopholes, The Wife isn't enough for him, and look at him."

"I'm not O'Rourke, Mr. Crye," his office mate said. "I'm Benson. You always make this mistake. I think you do it intentionally. O'Rourke is the other gentleman we share our office with."

"Oh." Lincoln looked out the windows of his corner room. The nurse wouldn't let him forget how lucky he was to have two windows; you were blessed to have one. The views weren't much—a square of cloudless blue, a wall opposite the air shaft. But the golden sunlight of late afternoon slanted up the wall. It was one of those heart-melting, early-winter days when New York is telling San Francisco, Rome, even the Vermont countryside: Eat me.

"Listen, Benson," Lincoln said, "it was you, wasn't it, that had his eye on the laptop I have in my office? The Toshiba? It's yours."

"Don't say that," Benson said.

"Such a dummy, hey, Anj?" Lincoln thumbed at Benson. "I offer him my laptop, he totally waxes me. What do you got there, O'Rour—Benson?"

Benson opened a jumbo get-well card. The inside was covered by a naive drizzle of exclamation points and instructed Lincoln to just quit it, will ya, and get back to the office, what a slimeball way to squeeze a few extra weeks' vacation. Benson handed the card to Lincoln, and Lincoln stared at the cartoon on the front of a man wrapped in loose, noodlelike bandages. Lincoln handed the card back to Benson, who flipped from the front of the card to the inside and back again. He kept flipping and smiling to himself.

"You married, Benson?" Lincoln asked.

"Yes," he said.

"People get divorced over the cap not getting put on the toothpaste, I hear. Less."

"I guess I know that, sir," Benson said.

"Stop calling me *sir*," Lincoln said. "I'm barely older than you. You're the same generation as my pal Vince here and me. Kids?"

"We're five months pregnant," Benson said.

"Oh, yeah, I guess I knew that," Lincoln said. "I even congratulated you, didn't I?"

"Yes, thank you again," Benson said.

"Well," Lincoln said.

Benson watched Lincoln.

"I'm waiting, O'Rourke," Lincoln said.

"Waiting for what?" Benson asked.

"Read the card already!" Lincoln ordered. "I'd like to hear the names of all my wonderful colleagues before they release me from this shithole."

For the first time in weeks I smiled a real smile for Lincoln. He wanted to be released; he'd let it slip.

"Oh, sure," Benson said, nervously, finally opening the card. While he read the names aloud, the nurse entered with a tray, set down Lincoln's afternoon snack, and left.

"O'Rourke, you and your wife happy?" asked Lincoln.

"Very," Benson said. "Though she's a little stressed out right now, what with the pregnancy and all. It's Benson—"

"Just act like a *mensch*, Benson," Lincoln said, "don't panic, act like a *mensch*, and whenever things start getting real gnarly, walk a mile in her shoes. Most important point. Can't stress enough."

"In her *shoes*, Benson, not her underwear," I said. "We've heard about you."

"We saw you checking out that nurse, Benson," Lincoln said. "Nice Filipino body, yes?"

"Stop, you guys," Benson said. "I'm married."

"Sure you are," Lincoln said. "You think just because you take a vow it changes? You know, Benson, women are much more for the having than most men seem to think, except we're such complete morons going after it. And I mean all kinds of women. Fat ones, skinny ones, ones who climb on rocks."

"Sure," I jumped in, "tall ones, short ones, even girls with chicken pox."

"Black ones, green ones," Lincoln said, "ones with—"

"Black ones?" Benson asked. "Black women, too?"

"Sure," Lincoln said. "Women are women. You have a sex life these days, O'Rourke?"

"Not much," Benson said.

"*Did* you?" Lincoln asked. "Once upon a time?"

"Sure," Benson said. "Absolutely. It's *Benson.*"

"Tell Lincoln how it was, Benson," said Lincoln.

"It was really quite excellent," Benson said.

"You were satisfied with it, were you?"

"I—Yes," Benson said. "Yes, I was. We were." Benson looked down at his hands, stretched his fingers and scrutinized them in a decidedly effeminate manner. "But you know," he said, "as long as my wife enjoyed herself, if you know what I mean, I was happy."

"I see," Lincoln said. "Very, very interesting." He cracked his neck from side to side. "Anj, what do you make of that?"

"I agree with Benson," I said. "Long as his wife enjoys herself, I'm happy," and immediately I hated the way it sounded coming out of my mouth. I wished all my flippancy gone.

Benson smiled weakly and looked at the floor. "I didn't realize you'd hurt yourself," he said to Lincoln.

Lincoln looked at him, then me, then him again. "It was sort of an accident, Benson," Lincoln said. "You may find it hard to believe me but it was. Ask my friend Vincent."

Benson just nodded. When he looked up he was on the verge of tears.

"Go ahead, ask him," Lincoln instructed Benson.

"I don't want to," said Benson.

Lincoln looked up at the TV for a long moment, and his face grew flushed.

Benson and I looked at each other awkwardly.

"Was it an accident?" Benson asked me, heavy with reluctance. The final trace of sunlight was just a golden filament against the wall in the window. "Was it an accident?" he asked me.

"No," I said. "I think Lincoln wanted to hurt himself."

Lincoln turned to me. He appeared restless to get going.

" 'Wanted,' " I clarified, and smiled gently at him. " 'ted.' Past tense."

"Oh, go to hell, anyway," Lincoln said with a small smirk in return.

Walking through the growing dark and cold, happy my friend was doing better, for whatever reasons I didn't know, I saw a yellow sports car pull up at a red light. I was about to cross when the woman in the passenger seat bent toward the man behind the wheel. Her head bobbed up and down in his lap. The driver closed his eyes.

I really don't want to see this, people.

The light turned green but the car didn't move. Clearly they hadn't seen me. No one else was near.

Why now? Why here? Why couldn't they wait to get home, get undressed, keep their love a private act? Why—?

The woman sat up, smiled. Her cheeks high with color and effort, she held up a road map.

A road map.

Thank God. She was just picking up a road map fallen under the seat, that's all. The man looked at her, said something with a laugh, put the car in gear, flipped on his wipers to push a few snowflakes off the windshield, and the shiny yellow coupe turned south onto Second Avenue, floating downtown. License plate Pennsylvania. The Keystone State.

✲   ✲   ✲

Julie got engaged. Watermelon Guy gave her a 3.07-carat diamond ring, three times the size she said would make her happy. Not only did I know it was Julie calling, I knew *why* she was calling. Don't ask me to explain. Order the Time-Life series on the occult.

"Steinbeck," Julie said meaningfully, after we'd exchanged well-wishes, "I just wanted to tell you I'm getting married."

"I know. Congratulations," I said, furiously grinding out my Vince novel-exposé. My living-room floor was littered with crumpled Pepperidge Farm bags for cookies from all over Europe—Milano, Lido, Capri, Brussels.

"How did you know?" Julie asked.

"I could just tell," I said. "It was about time."

"No, really. How did you know? Who told you?" I could just see the creases around her mouth growing more distinct.

"No one told me, Jule. You're wonderful, brilliant, successful, and you can't seriously believe you're living one of the more shocking lives of our time."

"Oh," said Julie, taking it in. "Well, I guess I never thought of it that way."

"How many people at the wedding?" I asked.

"Small. Two thousand."

"*Two thousand?* Two thousand people? Are you out of—"

"It was a *joke*," Julie said.

"Oh," I said. "Well, you got me."

"Two hundred, about."

"That's a good number. Am I invited?"

"Let's take the wait-and-see," Julie said.

"Don't worry, I wouldn't attend," I said, pleased she was even considering it.

"Don't worry, I wouldn't invite you. Boy, Hemingway, you really are slow today," she said. "Richard was able to get the Rainbow Room in ten weeks. He's in a big rush."

I wondered if Watermelon Boy had mentioned to Julie our encounter at the Marchand wedding, the nature of our discussion, the fact that I'd fainted. Julie must really care for him, I thought. I was glad to know she would always eat well and have nice overpriced down comforters and seedless watermelon balls and a place in the Hamptons.

Who am I kidding? He was a prick. "Have you decided on a honeymoon spot?" I asked.

"Not yet," Julie said. "The South Pacific, maybe the Orient . . . So I read a recent column of yours at my gym the other day. Do you really think you might possibly be falling in love?"

"Oh, well, we'll have to just see about that," I said, and I heard Vince scamper from the bedroom to the bathroom just in time to let out a particularly explosive, retching heave.

"That's wonderful," she said. "That's the best thing Vince could have done."

"Anyway, the best thing *I* could have done," I lied. I told her a bit about Sasha. I didn't mention that the feeling was not your dictionary definition of *reciprocal*.

"Seriously," Julie said, "if you'd like to come to the wedding, or if you'd like to bring your friend . . ."

Maybe another time, Jule, I thought. Anyway, I may well have a funeral to plan in the near future for a once-dear pseudonymous *Doppelgänger*. "I don't want to ruin your big day," I said, listening to the sweet chorus of Vince's groaning and retching. "Or Richard's."

"Well, that's sweet," Julie said. "I heard through some people that your friend Lincoln was having some problems. I meant to call but I've just been so busy lately. I heard he was having a tough time."

"Yeah, he was," I said. "But he's doing better now. Last week I got one of his four-in-the-morning phone calls waking me up, so I take that as a good sign."

"Good, good," said Julie. "That's good to hear. He always sounded a little wild but nice."

"Yup," I said. "I still say he may have been raised by wolves."

A moment later the phone call was over. Good for Julie.

❖   ❖   ❖

I showed up for the Secret Santa bash at Rockefeller Center with my assigned jigsaw piece—the second page of the sheet music for Gershwin's "He Loves and She Loves." I was touched Lily remembered that it was my nightly finale at Scrabbles. I didn't recognize anyone waiting by the uptown edge of the Christmas tree, our meeting place, so I bought a dry hot pretzel with three packets of mustard and watched the huddled masses inch around the ice-skating rink. The temperature seemed to be dropping a degree every few minutes. As great as Lily's fix-up sounded—my friend had proven good taste, I had to admit—I knew it was unwise either to hold my breath (*Vince Blind Date Directive #24*) or, in fairness, to give up hope (#25). I'd make some new acquaintances and drink hot chocolate with whipped cream while everyone else got plowed.

In the middle of the rink, a storybook picture of romance came to life: An older couple, partners on ice and probably off for who knows how long, spun neatly in synchronized, opposite-turning corkscrews. When they were finished, and her girlish, pleated white skater's skirt finally settled back down against her legs, the New Yorkers and out-of-towners lining the promenade cheered, demanding more. Her mittened hand found his gloved hand and they bowed campily, setting off more cheering. Perhaps the most useful I can be, I thought, is to tour New York–area schools and talk to the boys, make sure they don't get on the wrong track, tell them: If she likes you, if you like her, if you each think the other's the least bit cute and funny and bright, if neither of you throws up at the idea of sitting across the table from the other, just the two of you, at some café five years from now, ten years—do it. Ask her. Learn from the shattered rubble of my own—

A tap on my shoulder.

"Hey, there," she said.

In my big winter coat I turned slowly and found myself staring into two small swimming pools masquerading as eyes.

"Hey," I said. "Small town."

Sasha pressed her warm mouth against my cold cheek. "Aren't they great?" she said, shivering and nodding at the couple in the rink. The older woman was now hamming it up, circling lazily while leaning back from the waist and making wavy motions with her arms.

"It makes you want to take up skating," I said. Sasha looked lovely in a long tweed overcoat, jeans, Doc Martens, and a pathetically thin, decorative scarf. She carried a roughed-up burgundy knapsack on her back. "You learn the name of that move during the Olympics, then you forget it for another four years," I said.

"Layback," said Sasha.

"That's it," I said. "You're walking home from work in this weather?"

"I *was*," she said, hugging herself, her teeth chattering. "Wasn't it balmy this morning? Are you here to skate? Look at the tree?"

"You must think writers have all the time in the world," I said.

"Well, they *do*," she said. "That's why they become writers, isn't it? But now it's after normal work hours, so you're entitled to be here, just like the rest of us."

We watched for a few moments, a foot or so apart, and I became more aware of the jaunty skating music blaring from the rink speakers. "I'm just meeting some people," I said. "And looking at the tree." We craned our necks to look at the star on top. "The inside dope," I said as I angled my mouth closer to her ear, "is that this one's some kind of spruce from Canada. A ringer."

"Doesn't it renew your faith?" she said.

"Not exactly for a Jewish kid from Queens," I said. "Yes, it does."

"Every day since it's been up I walk out of my way just to see it," said Sasha. "How are you?" she asked, still looking up at the star.

"Pretty good," I said. "I'm all right. You?"

"Well," and she took a deep breath, "the big news is I'm moving to Paris."

"That's terrific. That's . . . a dream come true."

"It is," she said. "Young aimless American woman living in Paris studio in spring is one of those clichés I'm perfectly willing to accept."

I wondered if the guy in the towel I'd seen in her window thought of the *girl-goes-abroad-to-find-fame-fortune-and-a-French-director-named-Jean-Christophe* as a cliché he too was willing to accept. "Wow," I said. "Good for you."

She nodded yes. "Now I just need to save enough money so I don't have to get a job *right* when I land, and I can just be a slacker for a while. I'm giving up my place, which I could never afford anyway, and moving back in with my parents for a few months. I should be overseas by May." She shuddered again, and her head retreated into her coat.

I looked at my watch. Lily, notoriously tardy, was now twenty minutes late. I didn't see any lost-looking Secret Santas loitering by the tree.

"It looks like Vince got stood up," she said.

"I'm sure it's just a subway thing," I said. "Big shopping day."

"If I stand out here much longer, I think frostbite may set in," she said.

"Yeah," I said. "Yep." I realized that very moment how atrocious I was at thinking on my feet, how atrocious I'd always been.

"Would you want to get something warm and quick?" Sasha asked. "Or could we at least stand in the lobby over there? You can watch for your friends."

"Sure," I said.

As we crossed the street to 30 Rockefeller Plaza, Sasha asked what I had in the manila envelope.

"It's a silly game for, like, a Secret Santa thing," I said.

"God, I haven't played that since I was eight or nine," she said.

"We were all supposed to bring something that matches someone else's," I said. "Very festive, very corny." I held the door for her.

"And what's yours?" she asked. Once indoors, she stuck out her tongue in gratitude for the warmth.

"It's stupid," I said. "It's nothing."

She undid the top two buttons of her coat, let her arms slip out of the loops of the knapsack, and placed it on the floor between her feet. She rubbed her rosy cheeks warm. I looked back out at the tree. If Crayola included only the five colors of the Rockefeller Center Christmas tree lights, they'd get no objections from me.

"Are you sure you got the meeting place right?" asked Sasha.

"Yes," I said.

"The time?" she asked.

"Yes," I said.

"They're not coming," she said.

"Maybe not," I said, watching one Mediterranean driver after another pull black sedans up to the door, letting people out, picking people up.

"I think this is what you're looking for," she said. She pulled a manila envelope from her knapsack. "Open it," she said.

I tweezered up the envelope clips, opened the flap, and pulled out the front page of the sheet music for "He Loves and She Loves." Sasha suddenly put her hand to her forehead, as if she had a bad headache.

"Please tell me you have the other page or I'm going to look like a total idiot," said Sasha. I handed her my envelope and she pulled out my page and we held the two together.

"I guess no one else is showing up," I said. "Lily, anyone."

"I'd say that's a good guess," said Sasha. "I only figured it out when I saw you standing there all by yourself in the cold and I thought, Wait, this is *too* strange. What did she tell you?"

"She wanted me to meet someone who was even better than you," I said.

"That should have tipped off it was a lie right there," said Sasha. "You knew that was impossible."

We stared at each other for what, logically, could not have been more than three or four seconds. To get her eyes, take Crayola cornflower blue, add a dab of moonlight, let simmer, then throw the whole thing out and try again. "You're seeing someone," I informed her.

"I am?" said Sasha. "What does he look like?"

"He wears towels. That's all I know."

"Towels?" she said.

"Forget it," I said. "I don't want to know. Fortunately I have a rather limited imagination," I lied.

"No, really," she said, "if I'm involved with someone, I'd at least like to know what he looks like, so when he crawls into my bed I don't scream."

"I saw a man in a towel in your brownstone," I said. "You were reading in the window. I don't know the book. I came to apologize for telling the world how I felt about 'S.' "

"Ahhh," she said, nodding slowly, and I could see now that what I feared was true. "Good eyesight," she said and chewed on her lip, then stopped, as if it were a habit she'd long ago trained herself out of and had just suffered a brief relapse. "This reminds me of a Thomas Hardy novel," Sasha said. "That was Adam."

I nodded.

"He came down from Boston to propose," she said.

I nodded.

"As soon as the words were out of his mouth," she said, "it became so clear to both of us that if we got married, we'd be divorced in three years. I'm glad you didn't see me the other ninety-two percent of the weekend. I was a wreck. I've never cried so much. Though a stalker outside my window would have been a welcome diversion."

"I'm sorry it didn't work out," I said. "Actually, I'm thrilled it didn't work out."

"Good," she said. She was suddenly a step closer to me, and I could see the tiniest sickle-shaped scar under her left eye. She wrapped her hand around my thumb. "Damn Lily," she said.

"Damn Lily," I said. "God damn her to hell." It dimly registered that people were walking in and out of the lobby, conducting business. "I have a feeling no one else is coming," I said. "I guess we're it."

Sasha nodded. "Two Jews waiting around to play Secret Santa," she said.

I dropped off my latest column ("Bash Me, Not All Men") and on the flimsiest pretext made my way to the archive room, where I checked out microfilm of old issues of ———*r.* The reel started with the very first column back in February 1956, when "Vince: A Man's View —Of Girls" (as it was known then) was born. (Some other features from that year: "The Gentle Girdle"; "What Makes You Marriageable?"; "Job Idea: Nurse's Aide"; "Your Slip Is Showing.") The inaugural Vince article was concerned with dates—"dinner dates, specifically. What does a man expect of his guest at a rather expensive form of entertainment? From here on, it's all Vince . . ." The subject of the column three months later was "When can a girl go to a man's apartment?" On the microfilm projector I spun through years of Vinces. Themes recurred (Is chivalry dead or not?; trust; commitment; what is sex appeal?), while typefaces changed to reflect the era. In the May 1966 column, a Q&A, one of the burning questions Vince answered was "Do men in the service mean what they say?" Another letter-writer asked him (me? us? let's just say Vince): "Why do you write a column for a women's magazine? Do you have a Miss Lonelyheart's [sic] complex? Are you trying to solve all of our problems?"

To this, the 1966 Vince answered, "No, I have enough problems of my own as it is . . ."

Touché, my predecessor.

No previous Vince, as far as I could see, had ever used the column to declare his love.

As I was skimming the January '76 column ("How Do You Tell the Secure Men from the Emotional Thumb-suckers?"), a groaning voice, the voice of Vinces Past, rumbled through my head.

She's not for you, reproached Vince, sounding wan but determined. *No way it works out. Remember that Vince column about rebound relationships? About how they were doomed to fail? Was that you or a previous me who wrote that?*

It was me, all right (I answered him), but I think she's rebounded from the rebound and, anyway, I've changed my mind. Love conquers all. I'll turn a deficit into an asset, make our life together utterly romantic.

PLACES SASHA AND I WILL SOMEDAY TRAVEL TOGETHER:
PEPPERIDGE FARM WORLD TOUR

Milano
Lido
Tahiti
Nassau
Bordeaux
Nantucket*
Capri
Brussels
Southport⁺
Geneva
Santa Fe*
Orleans

* big cookies   ⁺ assortment

She's moving to Paris. Wasn't it you who wrote about how long-distance relationships never work?

Would you mind? I'm trying to fact-check here.

Even though you've treated me horribly lately, even though you're trying to kill me, Dracula-like, by exposing me to the cruel light, even though you will destroy my mystery by outing me . . . I still have feelings for my caretakers. Especially you. Thanks to you, I've never been more popular.

Don't waste your breath. I'm impervious to flattery at this point.

Look, I know Sasha's smart and funny and lovely and tall, I can see why you'd go all mushy in the brain. But as your pseudonym, I can see things you can't. And what I see is a man heading for a fall. Your heart will be broken.

I can take care of myself, thank you.

Here are a few things I always tell myself to make it all better: It wasn't meant to be. There are more fish in the sea. These things hap—

"Excuse me, Vincent?"

Monica, naturally streaked dark blonde stud of the ———r Research Department, leaned over me from behind.

"Vincent, my sweet," she said, draping her arms across my chest, "I just want to know how much longer you think you might be using the machine."

"In fact, Monica, my sweet," I told her, reversing the microfilm advance button, choking my master's voice, and casually closing my notepad, which contained one of the very last chapters of my book exposing Vince, "I'm finished here."

11/The First Chapter

DO YOU know how a book is made? Physically, technically? Would you like to? I picked up a study of printmaking and bookbinding the other day at Shakespeare & Co. and I thought you might be interested to hear how it's done. A mixture of rags, esparto grass, eucalyptus fiber, wood pulp, china clay, chalk, starch, dyes, and water is boiled, beaten, drained, and pressed. The resultant substance is sorted and cut, and dust is removed after another boiling. The rag pulp is ground and bleached and coloring materials are added. Before delivery, the sheets are cut into narrower widths by revolving knives. (Some paper grades pass through a solution of animal glue and are then pressed and dried for glazing.) These in turn are cut to size, sorted, counted, and packed in wrappers. This high-grade paper then sits in a warehouse until, say, some classy publishing house sends in an order to have a book printed. Say the classy house has just won the much-coveted right to publish some hot, sexy new book.

It is spring. It is seventy-four degrees Fahrenheit and it is a Monday
in late May, 10:01 A.M. and 57 seconds, 58, 59, it is 10:02 A.M. At
the present moment I am sitting on the Circle Line ferry (upper
deck, bow), just south of the Manhattan tip, heading toward the
Statue of Liberty. The skyscrapers recede behind us and the air
smells of salt and a touch of gasoline and sulfur. I am writing this sentence in pencil, in longhand, a legible script by male standards, illeg-
ible by female (column idea?), writing on a white legal pad. As always,
orange juice (carton purchased just before boarding) is within easy
reach.

This is the last day of an incredible Memorial Day weekend with
Sasha. Sasha is as lovely to me here as she has been every day for the five
previous months we have been seeing each other, as she likes to say,
"quasi-semi-demi-hemi-exclusively"—meaning, we haven't seen anyone else. What am I saying? As I look at her now, sitting across from me,
doing the puzzle in yesterday's *New York Times Magazine*—she looks
up, smiles—she is even lovelier. I wish I could describe how pretty her
candied blue eyes are. You can kiss objectivity *au revoir*.

She moves to Paris in seventeen days, nine hours. Just this moment
she has leaned forward and for no apparent reason nuzzled my cheek.

"Most books begin their lives as flat printed sheets," says my study of
bookbinding. This flat printed sheet is subdivided by cutting and folding. Typically, a sixteen-page section is created, eight pages printed per
side. A "bone-folder" is used to make three successive pleats so the
section will fold tightly and not crease. The sections that make up the
text are then gathered and placed between pressing boards for consol-
idation. My friend Lincoln Crye left for Japan exactly two months ago,
to teach English and study Japanese art. After Lincoln left the hospital,
he took an open-ended sabbatical from the gallery and said he was
heading for points west. He said I needn't worry, he had no interest in
repeating what he'd done to himself and I believed him; more to the
point, I guess, is that his counselor at the hospital believed him. Lincoln
threw paints, brushes, and canvases into his Chevy Impala and took his

P.A. system so that on our great highways he could talk to his fellow Americans. When he returned, looking tanned and rested, he said the traveling bug had hit him big time and he headed straight for Japan. Since there, he has called me four times, on three of those occasions collect. Because of the time difference his calls almost never wake me, try as he might. He sounds upbeat. He's seeing a Canadian teacher who has, in his words, "a wonderful Jewish-Quebec body." Incredibly, she is actually beyond voting age; indeed, she is practically in her dotage at twenty-three. When he left, Lincoln still had a nasty gash behind his right ear. But according to the doctor it will fade in time to almost nothing. Lincoln should be back in New York (which I was happy to hear him refer to twice as "home") around Christmastime, though he insists it is Hanukkah he is returning for.

Richard, the Watermelon Consultant, took an embarrassing financial dive when finally, after a nasty, drawn-out power play, he tried to wrest control of the seedless watermelon company from its current management. I confess I wasn't unhappy to read in the *Journal* of his costly miscalculation. But then—wouldn't you know—weeks later he made a killing in some deal with a Taiwanese firm purportedly working on a fax machine that's something like the size of your fingernail, and his gains from that more than offset his melon losses. In celebration, Richard bought a custom Crayola-ruby Maserati convertible. About a month ago, while I was running my loop to Battery Park, Richard, in his new car, hailed me down. He did not curse me out for tainting New York for him because of my love safaris with Julie; now that he's married to her he thinks he has nothing to worry about. We talked, he took two calls on his car phone, and then he let me drive the Maserati up the West Side Highway. She handled like a dream.

Julie . . . is three months pregnant. I got the message before the weekend began but I've been in such a sweet fog that I haven't had the time (or inclination) to call her yet. Since she and Richard got married the end of February, they must have pulled the goalie sometime during the Bali honeymoon. She said on her message that she'll take an extended leave from the bank when the baby's born. The Great Lucite Sandwich Chase may have to wait.

About some of my friends who helped make Vince whatever he was: Brian Marchand, of the insanely wealthy New Jersey Marchands, has just finished writing his first screenplay. I can't talk about it except to say it's very funny and that there's a minor character in it, a single guy who writes a Miss Lonelyhearts–type advice column and eventually realizes he's gay. If that's some sort of payback, fine. I really do want my friends, especially my best friends, to succeed, I really do.

Big Dave Navinsky is separated and beyond miserable. Lizzie, The Wife, was miserable for their first month apart, much more than Big Dave was initially. He did not treat her well. But now she's started seeing one of Dave's law acquaintances, so she's much less miserable, while Big Dave has entered the realm of the virtually inconsolable. I told him to try therapy but he won't listen. Up until about two weeks ago, he called me maybe once every two nights to ask if I thought it was likely that The Wife and his law acquaintance—*former* law acquaintance, I should say—had slept together. I tell him I don't know. And, of course, I don't, for sure. All the poker boys ask me to call them when I have an issue of the heart or groin to write about.

Remy Kleinwort, D.D.S., and I are not in touch. I went to see Cheryl in an early Lanford Wilson play Off-Off-Broadway. I'm no theater critic but I thought she was excellent. We had a very sunny, pleasant drink afterward—no sexual quadruple entendres, no *Sturm und Drang*.

Somehow, by some process, the book is sewed and glued, I think, and someone slaps on a nice cover.

The crisp, handsome, finished books are loaded into boxes, the boxes onto trucks, and the trucks head out across the nation. We just this minute watched a flock of seagulls take off for Jersey City. The sky looks like it's been swabbed and buffed.

I play piano at Scrabbles maybe twice a month, when they need someone to sub for Marcel. I haven't paid off any of my credit card debts, and for my first trip to Paris (we've agreed I'll come visit around July fourth, after Sasha gets settled), I burrowed deeper into the well by getting suckered into another MasterCard, though why I'm being offered cards with my present balance (I know, they adore people like me) just goes to show the loopholes in our monetary system.

6 PLACES I WROTE THIS BOOK

#204, 99 Bank Street, Greenwich Village
IRT, especially the #2 and #3 lines
Flushing, Queens
Lobby, 11th-floor reception area, and elevator
(express and local), 350 Madison Avenue
Scrabbles, Upper East Side
Sculpture garden, Museum of Modern Art, while
waiting for Sasha to get off work

I was briefly, pointlessly obsessed by the idea of who in the world might replace me as Vince. But I got over it. *Cosmo* called a month ago. "There's a nasty rumor going around town," said Camille, one of Helen Gurley Brown's lieutenants (the editor who'd taken me to a Japanese lunch the year before, when hallucinogenic mushrooms had me hearing in sentence fragments), "that you're going to retire as Vince and be free to write for the competition." I told her I was flattered by her suggestion but would have to take a wait-and-see. Once again I could use them to leverage myself with ———*r*.

The next day the producer for a morning TV show called to ask me to come talk about "5 Ways Marriage Surprises Men," an article I wrote under my own name for the issue of ———*r* on the stands right now. In the pre-appearance phone interview, an intern for the show asked me, "So how does it feel to be married?" "I'm not married," I said. "Oh," she said, flustered. "Well, if you *were* married, how do you *think* you'd feel?" On every occasion before this one I'd said yes to TV, believing the exposure was good and that my collegial spirit would only help my

relationship with ———r and that each experience might provide
worthwhile material for any thinly veiled autobiographical novel I
might one day write. But I always hated doing these TV shows and in
fact they taught me almost nothing. I called the producer back and canceled, telling her that—though I'd written "5 Surprises"—I myself
wasn't married, never had been, maybe never would be, and thus felt
ill-equipped to discuss on TV what's surprising or not surprising about
the institution. I actually told the producer that "I'd be seriously com-
promising myself by going on." She should have told me to have the
pickle up my ass removed.

Then ———r called a few days later to say my contract was up. I
know, I said. We'd certainly like to renew it, Brell said. And she said
they wanted to give me a big hug in the form of another raise . . . and
now I'm Vince for one more year, which will be, I promise you here and
now, my absolute last. I did not inform Brell that I'd some time ago lost
my grip on the column and the Vince mentality and that I was now
going on automatic pilot, and that virtually everyone I knew, even pe-
ripherally, knew that I was Vince. Nor did I tell ———r that I was
doing it now solely for the money. But that's really none of ———r's
business, so long as I turn my columns in on time (I don't) and they're
reasonable, somewhat amusing, safe little offerings (I've given up for
good on the here's-why-other-men-fall-in-love idea; it's such an individual thing) which always include a couple of p.c. bromides about men
and women you can hang your hat on, and every now and then provide
the short, provocative little stroke that inspires a few canceled subscriptions or a mash note or three or four.

The truck drivers arrive with their exciting cargo at the various book
chains or major dealers or your local bookstore. I don't understand how
the distribution channels work. The unloading begins.

Things are totally jake with ———r. They're happy I may be in love.
They've expressed hope that I'll have enough interesting things happen
to me in love to write about. I don't really know what that means. It's

hard to imagine a less private place than a column, pseudonymous or otherwise, that's read by two point two million people, ten million in pass-along, for conducting a love affair. Love should be a private act. I guess I didn't have to tell so many people I was Vince; probably that's why ——— r has such a strict, if unwritten, policy about keeping Vince's identity secret. Then again, I believe that pretty much any young man who might have become Vince, with his uniquely nineties mandate (sensitive yet manly, tomcatting yet condom-wearing), would have blabbed the way I did. Who knows? If the young guy who was runner-up to me had beaten me out, maybe he would have called a national press conference his very first day on the job to announce it. I find the attempt by ——— r to maintain the secret of Vince's fountain-of-youth identity ultimately silly, yet I understand it. Brell's been a good editor. I hope she won't be too angry with me.

Though Sasha was upset with me for writing the column about her last summer, things are different now and she has no problem with my writing this book. In fact, it seems to tickle her quite a bit. She did ask me to change her name, and I've changed the color of her eyes, for my own personal reasons.

I have no pets to mention here. I wonder how Cat and Not-Cat are doing. My preferred Kamasutra position is Roman six: "When the heads of two lovers are bent toward each other, and when so bent, kissing takes place, it is called a 'bent kiss.' " I love my family, immediate and extended. I promise never again to faint at a wedding or a circumcision. I feel especially confident about the latter vow, mostly because I plan never again to attend a circumcision, even if I should someday father a son. If it's up to me, filming will be forbidden.

I read where Crayola—"for the first time in crayon history"—has "retired" eight of the original sixty-four colors, including lemon yellow, maize, and, yes, raw umber. These have been replaced by eight new shades, including tangerine, teal blue, and dandelion. I just had to go out and buy myself a box. The smell was incredible. The metals are still the hardest to sharpen.

Manhattan is breathtaking from here.

Through a family friend, Sasha has lined up a fabulous, sunny studio in the 7th *arrondissement*, just down the block from the Musée Rodin. She's got several strong job possibilities—museum work, but also leads for teaching and even (spit twice) doing production work on a major movie that's filming at least three months in Paris. She's collecting cookbooks so she can save money in France, but until then we've been eating our way from one end of New York to the other. For my birthday a couple of weeks ago, Sasha took me out to a romantic French dinner (I didn't even bother offering to kick in for the tip) that was so delicious that by the time her fig *crêpe* and my *crème brûlée* arrived (we shared both desserts, I love sharing food with women), we were near tears.

It's difficult for me to say, from the vantage of here and now, sitting on the ferry, which has just passed Ellis Island on our right, whether blowing the pseudonym, at least my tenure as the pseudonym, was the wise decision. *Ciao,* 1956. *Auf Wiedersehen,* world's most genial and worldly bachelor. *Au revoir,* Vince. Thanks, and I'll miss you. You always hurt the ones you love.

I'm halfway down page twelve of my twenty-third white legal pad and this Eberhard Faber Mongol #2 pencil, which cries out for sharpening, is the fourth-to-last one in the seventh box I used to write this book. I can smell the end. I am kissing the word *end* in that last sentence. Kissing my pad—that's how far gone I am, and how far I've come. I'd better wrap up soon before I rattle off too many more seesaw pseudo-profound sentiments.

WHAT I HAVE LEARNED FROM FORTUNE COOKIES

YOU ARE GOING TO HAVE SOME NEW CLOTHES.

PEACE IS HAPPINESS DIGESTING.

YOU WILL GO FARM [SIC], BUT BE SURE TO COME BACK.

THIS IS A NIGHT FOR LOVE AND AFFECTION.

IF YOU CANNOT BE GOOD, BE CAREFUL.

EVEN A BROKEN CLOCK IS RIGHT TWICE A DAY.
YOU MAY ATTEND A PARTY WHERE STRANGE CUSTOMS PREVAIL.
YOU HAVE YEARNING FOR PERFECTION.
HE WHO LAUGHS LAST DIDN'T GET THE JOKE AT FIRST.

Across the aisle an old man reads a spy novel, the teenager behind him a British or Australian women's magazine. Nosy me, I see she's on an article entitled "Faking Orgasm: Don't Do It Too Much!" So it *isn't* only me, or Americans.

I just squeezed Sasha's hand and she squeezed back, without our looking up at each other. The mid-morning New York light is lucky to caress her face. Words are truly beginning to fail me.

Finally, there is a palpable excitement, not to mention smell, in the air. Fresh new books have arrived at the bookstore. The crisp volumes are placed on the shelf. I lean forward and read Sasha's crossword puzzle upside-down. The book sits there on the shelf, waiting for someone to dig in. I told her I loved her one night in March, but she hasn't said it to me yet. She's said a lot of other really sweet things, though, which I prefer not to share here; these endearments are offset periodically by moments when she looks at me and shakes her head and says, "Why did this have to happen now?" I don't want to think too much about her moving to Paris. The odds of maintaining a long-distance relationship like this one, as Vince is more than happy to tell you, are not great. I follow the rise from her shoulder to wherever it takes me—her neck, for now. The book sits there, eager to share itself with someone.

So now you know everything.

Twenty-third pad, fifteenth page. I am restless and happy, looking at the magnificent approaching Lady in the Harbor, and I'm stroking Sasha's long, lovely leg quite vigorously now. I'm getting hungry, too. We should be docking in just a few minutes. "I'm starved," I say.

Sasha nods and takes my left hand in both of hers. A very serious look crosses her face.

"I have to tell you something," she says, pulling me close.

Shit.

Her mouth touches my ear. "I've been thinking," she whispers.

"Okay," I say. Cut to the chase, Sasha. I know A Talk when I hear one.

"It's been an incredible weekend," she says.

"Yes, it has," I agree.

"It's been an incredible spring so far," she says.

"Mmm," I say. *Shit.*

"Maybe," says Sasha, "there's a way to hang out in the crown after everyone leaves."

I lean back in my seat to stare at her.

"Or somehow sneak up to the torch," she says, staring back and blushing.

A man, a plan, a canal.

Sasha stands, stuffs the magazine into her knapsack, kicks the sack under the bench, and walks over to the rail. The wind frolics and gambols in her hair. She turns back to me, suppresses a silly smile, and looks back at the Lady.

Will there be life after Vince? You tell me.

The old man across the aisle also watches Sasha at the rail. His book is in his lap and now I can feel him looking at me. I try not to smile.

Our boat beats on, ripping through the harbor waves, gulls explode out of nowhere, a horn blast. I feel tears coming. Damn. I will never be able to write a book like this again.

About the Author

Andrew Postman was born and raised in New York, worked as an editor for *McCall's*, and played in piano bars. For four years he was the voice behind the pseudonym for a well-known "man's view" column in a glamorous women's magazine. This is his first novel.